PRAISE FOR THE  SERIES

'Wild, funny, lavishly illustrated
and filled with excitement'
Guardian

'A heart-stopping tale [that]
really lives up to the hype'
Sunday Post

'[A] gloriously imagined first novel'
Telegraph

'Littler is an expert at pushing
reluctant readers from
one chapter to the next'
The Times

Jamie Littler is an author-illustrator whose debut middle-grade novel, *Frostheart*, was a number-one bestseller which garnered rave reviews, as well as a shortlist nomination for the prestigious Branford Boase Award. He has also illustrated *Hamish and the WorldStoppers*, which was the bestselling children's debut of 2015, and *Wilf the Mighty Worrier*, which was shortlisted for the Laugh Out Loud Book Awards. His interests are pretty varied, though he does have a soft spot for wild animals and things which go bump in the night. He lives in Brighton.

Books by Jamie Littler

Frostheart

Frostheart 2: Escape from Aurora

Frostheart 3: Rise of the World Eater

Arkspire

JAMIE LITTLER

ARKSPIRE

PUFFIN

PUFFIN BOOKS

UK | USA | Canada | Ireland | Australia
India | New Zealand | South Africa

Puffin Books is part of the Penguin Random House group of companies
whose addresses can be found at global.penguinrandomhouse.com.

www.penguin.co.uk   www.puffin.co.uk   www.ladybird.co.uk

First published 2023
001

Text and illustrations copyright © Jamie Littler, 2023

Set in Baskerville MT Pro
Text design by Janene Spencer
Printed in Great Britain by Clays Ltd, Elcograf S.p.A.

The authorized representative in the EEA is Penguin Random House Ireland,
Morrison Chambers, 32 Nassau Street, Dublin D02 YH68

A CIP catalogue record for this book is available from the British Library

ISBN: 978–0–241–58614–3

All correspondence to:
Puffin Books
Penguin Random House Children's
One Embassy Gardens, 8 Viaduct Gardens, London SW11 7BW

For Lil, my partner in ~~crime~~ relic hunting,

without whom this book wouldn't exist.

PROSPERITY IN

THE ARCANE

THE ARCANISTS

What is it to be more than human? To be given unimaginable power? How would you choose to use it?

The five Arcanists of Arkspire are the only people in the world with the power to wield magic, and they choose to use it in the service of others.

When the glorious being known as The Visitor first shared its magic with humans all those centuries ago, it was only the five Arcanists who proved themselves worthy of keeping such a power.

The Arcanists were brave.

They were just.

They were blessed.

They saved us all from the terrible evil of the Betrayers.

Out of the ruins of a world torn apart by misery and war, their ancestors used their gifts to build the great city of Arkspire, a bastion of peace and learning. They sacrificed their own wants and needs to ensure the people of Arkspire were protected and that the terrible curse of the Betrayers was kept at bay.

They will never abandon us. Not even in death. When an Arcanist's time comes to an end, they choose another to pass their powers on to. A child whose heart is pure enough to accept the gift of magic. A child who proves themselves as worthy as those who came before. A child who swears to defend Arkspire with all that they have until the day comes for them to pass on their powers to another generation.

And so it is that the legacy of the first Arcanists continues to this day, a legacy of compassion in an uncaring world, of magic in the face of despair. Their names are eternal.

The Tempest.

The Maker.

The Watcher.

The Enigma.

The Shrouded.

Under the eyes of the five great Arcanists and their illustrious Orders, Arkspire will always stand.

Hail to the Arcanists!

Hail to our saviours!

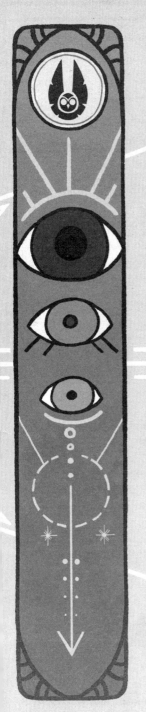

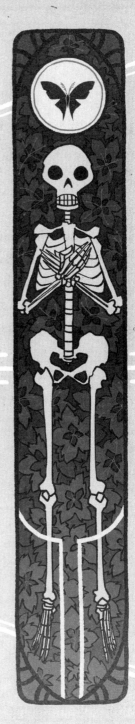

THE GREAT CITY OF
ARKSPIRE

INVENTION DISTRICT
Home of The Maker,
leader of
the Order of Invention

RADIANT DISTRICT
Home of The Tempest,
leader of
the Order of Radiance

IRIS DISTRICT
Home of The Watcher,
leader of
the Order of Iris

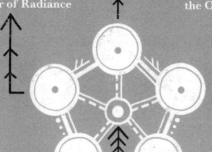

THE CRUX

GATEWAY DISTRICT
Home of The Enigma,
leader of
the Order of Gateways

MIDNIGHT DISTRICT
Home of The Shrouded,
leader of
the Order of Midnight

PROLOGUE

The alleyway didn't stand a chance. Juniper Bell cleared it with one giant leap, breaking into a roll as she landed.

Her mama smiled with pride. 'Ain't no question you're a daughter of mine.'

Grinning, Juniper turned back, hoping to see her twin sister following close behind. Instead she saw Elodie stranded on the rooftop on the other side of the alley, knees trembling as she peered over the edge.

Juniper had been afraid this would happen.

'You've got this, El!' Mama called. 'It's not as far as it looks!'

'I – I don't know if I can . . .' Elodie's eyes watered with frustration.

'You could totally clear that with one leap,' Juniper said encouragingly, 'and you'd need to as well, otherwise you'd fall and die.'

'Juni!' Elodie squealed.

'C'mon! What's the worst that can happen?'

'Erm . . . That I fall and die?! We're not even supposed to be up here! We'll be in so much trouble if we're caught.'

The Bell family were from the Iris District, ruled by the Arcanist known as The Watcher. But they were currently in the neighbouring Midnight District, home to The Shrouded and her Order of Midnight. It wasn't against the rules to cross districts . . . but, on a special night like this, there was no way lower-city Dreggers like them would be welcome to scurry about the Uppers. So what other choice did they have but to sneak across the rooftops? The chance to see an Arcanist in action was worth the risk.

'No one's catchin' us tonight,' Mama reassured Elodie. 'We'll be in and out like a shadow!'

'Just like The Shrouded!' Juniper said.

Mama laughed. 'But even more *shadowy-er*!'

Elodie still wasn't convinced, eyeing the army of wardens standing guard in the streets below, rifles resting on their shoulders.

'I should go back for her . . .' Juniper muttered to her mama.

Juniper had been born a whole fifteen minutes before her twin and took her job as older sister very seriously. The girls shared the same brown skin and dark-coloured hair as their mother. But whereas Juniper's hairstyle looked like it'd been hacked short with blunt scissors (because it had), Elodie's was tidy and neat. Still, Elodie had tried to put her hair into scruffy bunches to look the same as Juniper's. She always wanted to be just like her twin. It could sometimes be a bit much having a copycat follow your every step, but, though she would never admit it, it made Juniper as proud as pie.

'No. She can do this; I know she can,' Mama insisted.

Juniper nodded, deciding to try a different tactic. She wanted to help Elodie, but nothing would change unless Elodie stopped worrying about what might go wrong all the time.

'Look, maybe this was a bad idea,' Juniper called. 'You wait there. We'll go watch the amazin', marvellawesome Arcanist an' we'll tell you *aaaaall* about it when we get back. Shame you'll miss it, though – you'll probably be older 'n Mama next time there's an Inheritance . . .'

'So not *that* old,' Mama added.

Elodie's large eyes grew even wider at the very idea.

'No, please don't leave me! You were right – I can do this!'

Juniper smiled, triumphant. If there was one way to get Elodie to break the rules or make a death-defying leap between rooftops, it was by tempting her with the Arcanists. She was obsessed with them.

Elodie peered over the roof edge only to recoil. 'But what – what if I fall?'

'You won't!' Juniper and Mama insisted in unison.

'You don't know that!'

Juniper perched on the side of the roof and held out her hand. 'I'm here to catch you.'

'And you won't let go?'

'Never.'

Elodie studied her twin for any sign of a lie. 'You promise?'

'Promise.'

Elodie gulped, then stuck her tongue out with concentration. That's how Juniper knew things were about to get serious. Elodie readied her stance. Narrowed her eyes. With a deep breath, she took a run-up . . . and jumped! She cleared the alleyway below – *just* – and Juniper caught hold of her flailing arms and pulled her to safety.

Elodie looked back at the jump she'd just made, almost unable to believe it. 'I . . . I did it? I did it! I did it!' She bounced up and down, Juniper holding her hands tight.

'Ain't nothin' Jelliper can't do when they're workin' together,' Mama said fondly, using the nickname the twins had given themselves. She pulled them into a hug.

'Well, we can't turn back time,' Juniper said.

Elodie pulled a face. 'Why'd we need to do that?'

'Cos at this rate I reckon we might miss the Inheritance.'

Elodie's mouth fell open. 'Visitor beyond, we need to move, move, move!'

The large town square in the Midnight District was fit to bursting. The massive crowd bustled in the sticky evening air. Fancy folk, the lot of them, each wearing more snazzy threads than the last. The men, with their sharp coats and oiled hair, preened themselves; the ladies posed in the most fashionable dresses, their jewels glinting in the glow of the uncountable ether-light candles filling the square. Everyone was

enraptured by the haunting song played by an orchestra on the large outdoor stage in the square's centre.

The twins gasped. 'Whooooooooa!'

'Best seats in the house, or your money back!' Mama grinned, sitting down on a rooftop edge that overlooked the festivities. The twins sat beside her, Juniper's legs swinging over the edge, Elodie a little further back.

'This is amazing!' Juniper said, punching a fist into her palm, beaming. Elodie bit at her thumbnail, laughter threatening to bubble out of her.

'Not bad, huh?' Mama said. 'When the world gives you an empty bag, it's your job to fill it.'

No matter which Arcanist you were lucky enough to see, the spectacle never got old.

Witnessing the impossible happen right before your eyes was not something you ever forgot or ever got used to.

But tonight was extra special. It was the first time there'd been an Inheritance in the twins' lifetime. The moment an Arcanist's powers were passed on to their chosen Inheritor, a gift every child in Arkspire dreamed might one day be given to them.

Mama had said she'd take the twins to see the ritual a week ago (so long as they didn't tell Papa), and they'd been buzzing ever since, lying awake in bed every night, squirming in anticipation. Elodie had even put on her nicest jumper for the occasion. Sure, it was way too big for her, like all her clothes, but at least this one had no holes in it.

The orchestra suddenly piped down and an expectant silence fell over the square. The air was so electric that it was a wonder nobody was being shocked. You could almost taste it on the warm evening breeze, fizzling on the tongue, and the sweet scent of the black flowers the Midnight District was so famous for tingling the nose.

A lone lady stepped out from the orchestra. She began to sing. The song was beautiful but also sad, the kind that got under your skin and gave you goosebumps. It was a song of mourning. Two pillars of white ether-light flared silently behind her, illuminating something on the stage that, until now, had been hidden in shadow. It was an open coffin resting on a pedestal. Inside lay the body of an incredibly old woman, her eyes closed, her wrinkly white hands crossed over her black funerary robes.

Behind the coffin stood a young girl not much older than the twins. Her brown hair had been pulled back into two buns, a headdress placed above her forehead, gleaming in the ghostly light. Dozens of coins dangled from it – payment for the ferryman to take the souls of the dead to the Beyond. Her pale oval face could barely hold back a smile. Couldn't blame her, really, considering what was about to happen. Juniper would've broken into a jig if she'd been chosen to become an Inheritor.

A tall, gaunt-looking man from the Order of Midnight stood beside her. Both looked solemnly down at the coffin.

Once the song had come to an end, the man stepped forward.

'People of the Midnight District!' he declared in a dusty old voice. 'It is with great sorrow that we say farewell to our beloved leader, twenty-third of their name. But, as is custom, we have mourned this terrible loss during the searing light of day. Now, in the soothing darkness of night, we shall rejoice – for her legacy will live on! The Shrouded has chosen a child worthy to Inherit her gifts and become the next in their great line, as is the way! Chosen Inheritor of The Shrouded, please come forward and embrace your destiny.'

The girl nodded, stepping up to the casket. She seemed confident. Ready. She'd spent the last few years doing nothing but training for this moment, after all.

Elodie gasped as The Shrouded opened her eyes. She'd been so still, so peaceful, you would've been forgiven for thinking she was dead. That and the fact she was lying in her own coffin. Her misted eyes focused on the girl standing above her. She raised a withered hand that the girl took gently but with conviction.

'I, Nyx Neverbright, give myself to the power of The Shrouded. May my name be forgotten as I am born anew,' said the girl, before closing her eyes.

The crowd held its breath.

Juniper took Elodie's hand and gave it a squeeze. 'Here we *goooooo* . . .'

The shadows that danced in the flickering ether-light suddenly . . . *changed*. They moved with purpose, wisps of darkness leaking out of the woman in the coffin before coiling their way up Nyx's outstretched arm. They threaded over her shoulder; they cocooned her torso and reached for the place where her heart was. A

14

sigil inscribed on her hand began to glow.

That's when the ether-lights disappeared. Candles flickered out, every one of them. The glow of every streetlamp and every window vanished. The entire Midnight District went dark.

Elodie squeezed Juniper's hand even tighter.

The only light came from Nyx herself on the stage. More sigils had grown from the one already on her hand, spiralling up both her arms, strange symbols glowing bright white in the pitch-darkness. Her eyes shone as bright as flame. She raised her arms, weaving her hands as though she were dancing, the sigils blurring with the movement. Then she clapped her hands together.

And, just like that, the pillars of ether-light flared back to life, every candle reignited, and the streetlamps buzzed as though they'd never even considered going dark, not once.

Light returned to the district.

The ancient lady in the coffin had fallen still.

'The girl standing before you all is no longer Nyx Neverbright!' the girl shouted. 'I am now The Shrouded, twenty-fourth of their name, leader of the Order of Midnight and the Midnight District. And I swear, with the power gifted to me, to lead us to even greater heights than ever before!'

In eerie silence every person in the audience raised a candle, the square transforming into a sea of swaying stars. Bells rang out across the district.

The twins watched, spellbound. Beside them Mama's grin widened. Where they came from, down in the Dregs, wonder was in short supply. What they'd seen tonight would go some way to make up for that. But something niggled at the back of Juniper's mind. Despite all the celebrating, something felt off. Like a sudden chill on a summer's day.

Her breath puffed out in a cloud, despite the time of year.

It wasn't until someone screamed that it suddenly clicked. The bells weren't ringing out in celebration. They were ringing out in warning.

Almost immediately figures began rising up from the cobblestones, glowing as though lit by an unseen sun. They materialized out of thin air like a morning mist. They passed through walls as though they weren't there. Five of them. Unnatural twisted things, almost human, but with hideously stretched limbs and too-long fingers, their ethereal bodies transparent and coiling like smoke on a breeze. But worst of all was their faces – bottomless voids of nothingness except for the two bright eyes that burned with hateful fire. The things reached out towards the people around them, pointing to the new Shrouded on the stage.

'Shades!' Mama whispered in horror.

The Betrayers' curse.

The audience became a panicked rush of chaos. The crowd fled in terror, pushing and tumbling over each other in their eagerness to get away. And who could blame them – Shades leeched the life force out of anyone they came into contact with, leaving only lifeless husks behind. Wardens directed the crowd to a line of sigils etched into the cobblestone ground. The Shades stalked after them, but before they could snatch at any unfortunate soul, the sigils flared to life with a searing light. The Shades recoiled in agony – if such things could even feel pain.

'We've gotta go *now*!' Mama said, pulling the girls away from the square.

The family ran. Juniper leaped after Mama over the gap between rooftops, but Elodie skidded to a halt.

'El, you have to jump!' Mama cried.

'I can't!' Elodie whimpered.

'You can! I'll catch you!'

A glow began to radiate from the roof tiles below Elodie. She screamed, stumbling back as a Shade rose out of the roof in front of her, its pitiless eyes burning enviously at the life she had.

Juniper's insides froze. 'Elodie, *run!*'

But Elodie could only gawp. The flowers on the rooftop, once in vibrant bloom, withered and died in the thing's presence. It moaned low and desperate, its unnaturally long fingers twitching, ready to strike. If that thing so much as touched Elodie, it would steal the life from her in an instant.

'Elodie!' Mama screamed, leaping back over the gap. Juniper could only watch as her mama tried to reach her sister, but the Shade lashed out with frightening speed, Mama ducking out of its grasp by a hair's breadth. She tried again, but the thing was too fast.

Then, out of nowhere, something snatched at the Shade's wrist. It looked like some kind of rope, except it was made entirely out of twisting shadow. The Shade resisted, trying to pull itself free, but another shadow-tendril snatched its other arm, wrenching it back.

Nyx, or The Shrouded as she was now called, rose out of the shadows on the rooftop. The Shade screeched and struggled, but The Shrouded's magic held it tight. She rushed up towards it, drawing sigils in the air in front of its screeching, featureless face, the symbols hanging in the air, glowing bright. They grew bigger, joining together and spinning round the Shade like a lasso, before suddenly tightening together in a flash.

Then the fading wails of the Shade were all that remained of it, the thing itself banished back beyond the Veil.

'Baby!' Mama rushed to Elodie, cradling her tight. 'I'm sorry – I'm so sorry – I couldn't get to you! I tried, but I –'

But Elodie wasn't listening. Her eyes were wide and glistening. But it wasn't with fear, not any more. She was staring up at The Shrouded in complete and utter awe.

'Are you OK?' The Shrouded asked, her voice full of concern.

Elodie nodded.

'Thank you!' Mama whispered, tears streaming down her face. 'Thank you so much!'

The Shrouded breathed out in relief, then disappeared back into the shadows, off to deal with the remaining Shades in the square.

Juniper leaped to the roof, falling to her knees to hug her trembling sister.

'El! Are you OK?'

'That . . . was the most incredible thing I've ever seen,' Elodie said, her voice little more than a whisper. 'The Shrouded . . . Can . . . can you imagine having the power to protect people like that?'

'Come on – it's not safe,' Mama said, trying to lift Elodie – but her daughter resisted, unable to take her eyes off The Shrouded, now back down in the square.

'I want to help people like that,' she said breathlessly. 'I want to make a difference like they do. I want to become an Arcanist!'

Juniper made to speak, but her mama shot her a look of warning. They needed to get out of here.

'If anyone can become an Inheritor, it's you, El,' Mama said cajolingly. 'But we really have to go.'

Juniper swallowed hard. There wasn't a kid in Arkspire who didn't dream that they could become an Arcanist. All you needed to do was prove you had what it took: that you had the grit, determination and a pure soul. Anybody in Arkspire could become a *somebody*.

But Juniper knew the truth. Only kids from the Uppers were chosen, those from families with power and money. Dregger girls like the Bell sisters didn't stand a chance; even at her age, Juniper knew that. She knew their place, and it wasn't up in the towers of the Arcanists.

Even so, she couldn't bear to tell Elodie, not tonight. The Shrouded had filled her sister's heart with hope and inspiration, and Juniper refused to be the one who stole that from her.

She'd come to remember this moment in the years to follow.

1

ENEMY OF MY ENEMY

Two years later

Juniper Bell was being followed.

She'd clocked the man a few streets back. She'd tried her best to shake him, ducking and weaving through the press of people going about their busy lives in the bustling markets of the Iris District, but the man was sticking to her like a bad smell.

He knew what he was doing; Juniper had to give him that.

He was careful. He kept to the long shadows cast by the low-afternoon sun, avoiding the spears of sunlight that managed to sneak past the steep-stacked buildings that formed the canyon-like streets. He used the ramshackle market stalls for cover, slinking between barking merchants flogging their wares and the throng of potential buyers, obscured by the mingling smoke of cooking food and burning incense. His features were hidden by the wide hood of his long cloak. Probably had deep, dark eyes, Juniper reckoned, and a big ol' scar across his face, with a dagger at his belt too. All the usual requirements that came with such mysterious figures.

He knew what he was doing all right. It was just that Juniper Bell happened to know better.

No doubt he was a relic hunter, just like her, probably following her in the hope of stealing the juicy target she'd been tracking all afternoon.

Not on my watch, buddy, Juniper thought.

She looked ahead at her mark, a clockwork cart driven by three rough-looking customers. They kept their heads down, neckerchiefs pulled up over their noses and wide-brimmed hats dipped down low. Trying not to attract too much attention. But it was the way they clutched their revolvers, hidden under their duster coats, that struck Juniper. They were so tense and anxious, eyeing every passer-by as if they were some

24

long-awaited enemy. Juniper couldn't blame 'em. Word had it this lot had ventured out into the Badlands, the deserted ruins that surrounded Arkspire for as far as the eye could see. Everyone knew the rarest, most valuable arcane relics were found in those forgotten districts.

But good luck finding anyone willing to go out there and get 'em. You only went into the Badlands if you were (a) *seriously* lost or (b) had a *major* death wish. Seems that these guys had got out relatively unscathed, however (if you ignored the tormented, hollow looks in their eyes), and, judging from what she guessed was a big pile of loot under the cover on their cart, a little richer too.

Another sound began to join the clamour of the market: the crackling drone of the phonograph speakers fixed all around the city. '*Remember, citizens of Arkspire! Any arcane items or relics suspected of being magical must be reported to your friendly local wardens,*' came the posh announcer's voice, all too familiar to the residents of Arkspire. '*The wardens of the five Arcanist Orders are here to protect. It is better to be safe than sorry. Don't forget: contraband equals chaos!*'

A large armoured clockwork wagon chugged across a junction ahead of Juniper, the word REQUISITIONS painted on its side in swanky letters. A gaggle of heavily armed wardens rode the wagon, their long grey coats displaying the owl emblem of the Order of Iris, their rifles glinting in the dusty light.

Being caught with forbidden magical relics was a pretty serious crime in Arkspire. So the trick was not to get caught.

The smugglers Juniper was following knew this well enough. They slowed down to a crawl so as not to draw too close to the patrol. As Juniper got nearer, a girl emerged from the crowd, bumping into her. She wore a tunic that had clearly been stitched together from scraps with faded blue worker's trousers underneath. Her short-cropped black hair framed a wide, kind face and a small nose.

'So sorry!' she said.

'No problem,' Juniper replied, pulling the large cap she wore down low to hide her eyes, careful not to show she recognized the girl.

It was Thea, Juniper's best bud and partner in crime.

Juniper put her hand in the pocket of her long threadbare coat and retrieved the piece of paper Thea had dropped in there. It had been folded to look like a rat, the symbol of their gang, the Misfits. Sure, the gang currently only had two members, but that still counted as a gang, right? Juniper unfolded the paper and looked at the pictures drawn on it. There was a stick person with scruffy hair just like Juniper's, and another six stick men behind her, all with angry eyes and sharp teeth. Thea was warning her she was being followed by six people, not just one. It seemed like Juniper's target was more popular than she'd first realized.

Whatever was on that cart must be super-special indeed.

There was an arrow at the bottom of the paper too, indicating she should turn it over. On the other side was a picture of a friendly bear giving the Juniper stick girl a hug. Yeah, it was sweet, and, yeah, it was awesome.

Juniper pocketed the note. OK, six relic hunters, five of them hidden, all after the same score as her. She'd have to think on her feet.

Juniper slipped through the crowds as nimbly as a cat. Without making it obvious, she glanced in a shop window and caught sight of the reflection of the cloaked man behind her. He was still shadowing her and getting closer. She spotted another figure standing by a market stall, all shady and mysterious, and another pretending to read a newspaper. She made out the tattoo of a shark on one, a bull-head pendant on another. Rival gangs, the lot of 'em, and each unaware of the other, as far as she could tell. Scarves were pulled high up to their noses, hoods or hats hiding their faces.

This could get interesting, Juniper thought. But she reckoned she could make it work for her.

Taking a deep breath, she rushed towards the clockwork cart. The closest smuggler didn't see Juniper reaching for his sleeve; he was too busy eyeing the Requisitions wagon as it disappeared down the street. His eyes widened at her touch, his gun hand twitching.

'Whaddya think yer doin', kid?!' he spat. 'Get outta here!'

Juniper's heart thrummed in her chest, but she tried to keep her cool.

'Please, mister, I'm here to warn you!' she said in the most concerned voice she could muster, making her eyes as big and shiny as a kitten's.

The smuggler looked as though he was preparing to

boot her into the gutter, and his buddies shot her vicious glances. 'Listen, kid, I ain't gonna warn you again –'

'Please, he's over there!' She pointed at the cloaked figure, who stopped in his tracks in the middle of the street. 'That man in the hood, he's been followin' you!'

'What're you yammerin' about?' But the smugglers looked at the hooded figure, trying to suss him out.

'I saw he had a shark tattoo, an' my mama always told me to stay away from people with shark tattoos,' Juniper insisted.

'Shark tattoo?' a smuggler repeated, narrowing her eyes.

That got their attention.

Juniper had no idea if the guy following her was part of the Sharktooth gang, but at least one of the creeps in this market was, and she already knew that these smugglers were Tungsten's crew. Boss Tungsten, kingpin of the relic black market, hated the Sharktooths more than anyone.

The hooded figure began backing away, only making Juniper's accusation more believable.

Big mistake, buddy, Juniper thought. *Should've played it cool.*

The smugglers raised their revolvers, watching the man suspiciously, just as Juniper had hoped they would. She'd been relying on the smugglers being as jumpy as they'd looked.

The hooded man bolted.

A smuggler opened fire.

And all chaos broke loose.

Splinters of wood and plaster exploded into the air as bullets began tearing across the street. The other five hidden relic hunters had pulled out pistols and opened fire in return on the smugglers. The market crowds erupted into panic. The smugglers dived behind their cart for cover, firing back at their attackers. Juniper followed, pressing her back against the cart as bullets ricocheted off the metal.

'I hate to say I told you so, but I totally told you so,' she said to the smuggler she'd tried to warn.

'Get lost – I ain't gonna tell you again!' He held his gun over the cart and fired without even looking.

'Kuh . . . *Fine!*' Juniper said. 'I dunno . . . You try to help a guy . . .' She hopped up, clambered into the cart and dropped on to the hessian cover that hid the loot.

'Hey, get outta there!' the smuggler cried.

Just then the cart's mechanisms belched white steam, the sigils on its engine flaring to life – as Juniper knew it would. Thea had used the distraction to hop into the driver's seat and push the ignition levers. The Misfits worked like a well-oiled machine – in and out, no time for hesitation.

The cart lurched obediently forward with a squeal of grinding gears.

Roaring in fury, the smugglers began to give chase – but the puffs of bullet dust all around soon reminded them of how much danger they were in and forced them to take cover again.

'Come back!' a smuggler shouted, as if that had ever worked.

'I thought you wanted me to get lost?!' Juniper called back.

The smugglers yelled after her as the cart tore down the street, but their voices were drowned out by the noise of the engine; Juniper assumed they were sending kind words and good wishes. She gave the smugglers a little wave of thanks just before she lost sight of them round a corner.

2

UNDER THE OWL'S EYE

A few streets away, a large wooden sculpture of an owl stood proudly beside a quiet, dusty alley. Candles had been placed at its feet, as well as bronze coins, apples and other such offerings. It was a shrine to The Watcher, the Arcanist ruler of the Iris District. It was a place of peace and contemplation amid the hustle and bustle of the markets. At least, it had been, until the cart tore past it, skidding into the alley and clipping the corner of a building as it did so. The cart spluttered to a stop in a cloud of steam and broken brickwork.

'Oops,' Thea said, dropping out of the driver's seat. 'Someone put a wall there.'

A dank odour hung in the dark, narrow alleyway, but even that couldn't wipe the smile from Juniper's face. 'That wall should be minding its own business, an' don't let it tell you otherwise. You were amazing, Thea!'

'Nothing I could've done without your quick thinking,' Thea said, as the two friends did their elaborate and perfectly choreographed celebratory handshake, which involved lots of quick hand motions, hopping on one leg and high-fiving while facing in opposite directions.

Juniper grinned and placed her hands on her hips. 'Think I'm gonna call that little scam: *The Enemy of my Enemy Equals Friends (Kind Of)*.'

Thea nodded. 'Oh, I like it. Catchy.'

'But *what – a – getaway*, Thea!' Juniper stepped back to inspect the cart, impressed they'd only dented it a little. 'The way you swerved round all those people . . . You were all, like, *swooooosh*, *brrrrrruuum*!'

'There was a lot of screaming, wasn't there?'

'Hey, they all leaped outta your way, didn't they? There *waaaaaas* a lot of screaming as a whole today, though,' Juniper admitted, 'even more than in Rust Lanes last week . . .'

'At least today didn't involve nearly as many bloat toads,' Thea noted.

'Yeah, true. I'm *still* finding slime in my boots.' Juniper shuddered at the memory of that mess of a heist. 'Anyway, shall we see what we bravely risked our necks for?' She pulled the cover off the back of the cart and gestured to Thea. 'After you, m'lady.'

'Oh, so kind.'

Thea climbed into the back of the cart and gave a low whistle when she saw what was inside. It was absolutely rammed full of contraband. Books, scrolls, bottles and relics, most supposedly having once belonged to the great (yet terrible) Betrayers, hot out of the Badlands. Legend had it that The Visitor had blessed one hundred people with the power of magic, but only five of them had proved worthy of such a gift – the Arcanists. The other ninety-five . . . *well*. Stories told of all the despicable, evil things the Betrayers did, how fearful their arcane weapons were. They were truly the stuff of nightmares.

Juniper couldn't wait to see 'em.

Without wasting another moment, the girls began sifting through it all. Juniper picked up a couple of bottles: one with a picture of an eye on its label, the other with a star. Uncorking both, she took a whiff and screwed up her face.

'Fake. Worthless. Looks like our smuggler friends musta done a bit of shopping downtown . . .'

'Never fails to amaze me what people will buy to feel more like the Arcanists,' Thea said.

Juniper tossed the bottles behind her and lifted

another labelled with a heart. 'Ah, a home-made love potion. Knew I'd find at least one of you. Y'know what I'd love? To stop findin' these things! Think this potion'll work for that?'

'*What is life but love and sandwiches?* as my grangran always says,' Thea quoted.

Juniper nodded, as if she ever understood what Thea's grangran was going on about. 'So wise.'

'I wonder what this is?' Thea held up a short pointy stick. 'It is beautiful. Could it be some kind of magic wand?'

'That's Primrose's Patented Pimple-Popper,' Juniper said, rummaging through another box.

'How do you know?'

'Cos I saw him give a demonstration the other week.'

Thea considered if that was gross or not, then happily slipped it into her bag. Juniper lifted a glass globe to her face and gave it a shake. Two globules of light ignited as if from nowhere, merging together to form the shape of a dragon that shone as bright as the sun. It flew about the globe with an eerie grace, the relic letting out a faint pulse with each beat of its wings.

'Now *this* relic has magic coming out of its ears!' Juniper said. 'Doesn't seem so dangerous either. Get in my bag!'

'This is authentic too,' Thea said, holding up a

vibrating clay necklace with a crystal in its centre. 'It's got a nice vibe about it.' The crystal suddenly spat out small sparks of green energy. 'Ow,' she said, as it stung her. 'Ow. Ow. Ow. Ow. Y'know, maybe I'll put this one down.'

Juniper's grin grew wider as they sorted through the loot. An ever-burning candle whose flame was cold to the touch. A book that contained smells rather than words. A spyglass that when looked through showed a different location altogether. Incredible, impossible things – the likes of which Dreggers rarely saw thanks to the watchful eyes and snatchy fingers of Requisitions.

'What. A. SCORE! An' these don't seem all that terrible – I dunno what people are so afraid of!'

But there was one item that really caught Juniper's eye.

Packed away in a straw-stuffed crate all on its own was a little worn chest. Juniper opened it – expecting treasure – and was surprised to discover a broken piece of mirror inside. She frowned. It was about the size of her hand, its glass old and dusty. Pretty boring compared to the rest of the haul . . . but, still, something about it grabbed her attention and wouldn't let go. She examined it closely, the glass reflecting her face and the dingy alley behind. Kind of what you expect a mirror to do really.

But, wait – what was that?

In the reflection – a shifting shape . . . Something moving behind her? She spun round, worried they'd been found. But all she saw was Thea poking a ring with a flower embedded in it and the empty street beyond. Juniper looked back at the glass, but there was nothing there either. She could've sworn she'd seen something . . .

She shrugged, wrapping the shard in some cloth before slipping it into her coat pocket. She'd think about it later. For now, they had a job to complete.

'I reckon this is the biggest haul we've ever taken!

It's gonna bring in some *biiiiig* coin. No wonder the other relic hunters were so eager to blast each other for it!'

'Almost makes you feel bad for stealing it all . . .' Thea said, packing her own bag. *'Almost.'*

'I like to think we rescued it,' said Juniper. 'Better with us than the greedy black-market gangs or rotting away in the Requisitions vaults while we're all starving at home. So, I say the more tasty relics, the better, num-num-num-num!'

Thea nodded. 'Oh, I agree. Particularly with the "num" part, but I can't imagine your sister will be too pleased about this.'

Juniper's smile faltered. 'Don't worry about Elodie. She can't get upset if she doesn't know.'

The girls ducked out of the alley, bags bulging. They crossed a ward-point, the sigils etched into the cobblestones humming gently. Thankfully they concluded the girls weren't Shades and let them rejoin the busy market streets, the late-afternoon sun warming their faces.

The sound of a phonograph notice rose above the murmur of people trading and dealing. *'Though the Betrayers are gone, it doesn't mean their followers are too. Always be on the lookout for anything suspicious. Remember: a watchful eye uncovers the spy!'*

Each district in Arkspire was built directly on to the

gargantuan tower of its ruling Arcanist – colossal structures miles wide and so tall they gave the bellies of the clouds a little scratch. Juniper looked up at the huge iron plate that held the Uppers aloft high above, doing its very best to block out the sky for those below.

As for the lower levels of the city, or the Dregs as they were (kind of) affectionately known, they clung to the towers like barnacles to a boat, like fungus to a tree or like a big heap of rubbish dumped at the base of a beautiful marble statue.

Juniper and Thea walked past a load of merchants standing outside their stores and hollering up a storm. 'Legal relics right here! Treasures the Arcanists *want* you to have! Talismans that can't be beat!'

'Sigil chalk! Get ya sigil chalk! Shades getting you down? Show them their limits with our patented sigil chalk! Proven to offer greater protection against Shade attack or your money back!'

'Wanna show yer true loyalties to The Watcher? Get yer limited-edition owl brooches here!'

A cat dashed past the girls, chased by a particularly brave rat.

The Invention District had its workshops and manufactories, the Radiant District its shiny lights and libraries. The Iris District had wild animals roaming its streets.

Packs of stray dogs, gangs of curious cats, swarms of chittering rats, crows cawing and pigeons cooing. Most districts tried to discourage such residents, but not the Iris District. The Watcher could see through the eyes of others, especially animals. Just because she hadn't been seen for decades didn't mean she wasn't there. Least that's what the old folks said. They even told tales of how you might be lucky enough to spot it: a cat looking back at you with a glowing glare, a violet glint in a gull's eye.

Juniper wasn't so sure. She'd never seen it in all her thirteen years, and she'd learned to trust her own eyes over some fable an old granny told her grandkids to scare them into behaving themselves. Still, the animals of the Iris District were treated well. Food was left out for them, water too, just in case The Watcher saw the kindness in her people and decided to bless them.

It made people feel secure. Like they were being taken care of, like their protector always had an eye out for them, keeping them safe from the Shades.

Juniper chuckled as a dog joined in with the chase, and only just caught sight of the Requisitions wagon ahead. It was packed with the smugglers who'd been arrested for starting the shoot-out. Wardens marched alongside the slow-moving vehicle, searching the market for any other ne'er-do-wells who needed a lesson from the firm hand of the law. And they were heading straight towards the girls.

'*Psst*, dead ahead,' Juniper said under her breath, focusing on her boots but indicating with her eyebrows. The wardens didn't know the girls had been involved in the shoot-out, but the smugglers did, and Juniper didn't want to be recognized.

'Oh dear,' Thea whispered. 'How do you want to do this? *The Check and Checkmate*? *Slippery Jelly*? *Schmoozing Butler*?'

'Why don't we try *Innocent Civilians*?' Juniper suggested.

'Simple but effective,' replied Thea. 'Whatever you do, I've got your back.'

Juniper didn't need to be told. She could always count on Thea.

'I mean, what's the worst that could happen?' Juniper said, adjusting her cap and pulling her tattered scarf over her nose. The Misfits knew how to blend in. If they didn't want to be seen, they could make themselves disappear.

Juniper was good at being a nobody. Perhaps a little *too* good, she sometimes thought.

Keeping their heads down, the girls walked right past the patrolling wardens without so much as a second glance. Juniper blew air from her cheeks with relief.

That was until something in Juniper's bag pulsed with a loud rumble. She felt it vibrate through her bones and into the ground at her feet. She nearly tripped from the shock but managed to keep moving, trying to hide her surprise. Thea gave her a curious look, as did some of the closest passers-by.

'Are you hungry, Juni?' Thea asked.

'Keep *moving*,' Juniper urged, picking up the pace.

But it happened again. A deep, reverberating pulse, like someone had struck a massive drum she'd forgotten was in her bag. Was it one of the relics? This time more people looked around, confused, alarmed even. Juniper dared to peek over her shoulder and saw what she'd dreaded: the wardens had stopped in their tracks and were looking in her direction.

'Nothing to see here, guys. Just keep moving . . .' Juniper whispered, trying to lose herself in the crowd. The next pulse was less a rumble, more a deep boom, and people jumped away from Juniper in fright, leaving her all too exposed.

'You there! *Stop!*'

Juniper cringed at the sound of the warden's voice.

'Don't even think about running!'

'Too late,' she said, and the girls tore off down the street.

3

GIVING IS ITS OWN
REWARD

The girls ran hard at the nearest shop wall and used their momentum to launch themselves upwards. Thea grabbed a low awning while Juniper caught hold of a windowsill, flaking paint raining down on the warden just below her.

'Come back!' he cried, snatching at her foot, which she pulled out of his grasp just in time.

Gripping the sill tightly, Juniper pulled her feet up close to her chest, then vaulted up to the next sill, then the next, before leaping over the ornate railing that bordered the edge of the roof. Thea was close behind, holding on tightly to her satchel straps. The wardens backed away into the startled crowd below, eyeing the girls closely as they considered their next move. The girls bolted across the higgledy-piggledy maze of rooftops, and the wardens dashed towards the nearest crossroads in an effort to cut them off.

They could certainly try, but the Misfits were in their element now.

Roof-running's what they did, and the Misfits knew this district like the back of their hands. One thing was for sure, though: they'd never get away with all the racket coming from Juniper's satchel. Another pulse echoed out over the rooftops, making the tiles shudder as Juniper swung her bag off her shoulders and began sifting inside. She found the culprit soon enough. The dragon globe was glowing bright and trembling with manic energy, the dragon inside roaring with each pulse.

She didn't know what she'd done to set it off, but she couldn't be having this, no, sir. She dropped it as she ran, the globe rolling down the sloped roof and into the street below.

'Be free, noisy ball!'

'We'll miss you!' Thea added.

As if in answer, the globe let out another booming pulse – this one so loud it cracked the surrounding windows.

OK, so maybe these relics were *slightly* more trouble than Juniper had given them credit for.

They ran on, bounding over narrow alleyways and sliding down sloped tiles, but whenever Juniper peeked into the streets below she could see the wardens still hot on their heels. Most would've given up ages ago.

'Someone should give these guys a raise!' Juniper said, before turning to look for the source of the music drifting on the air.

A pounding of drums, a flurry of wind instruments. It was a parade in a nearby thoroughfare. A unit of wardens escorted a super-swanky carriage carrying another shrine to The Watcher. A marching band led the procession slowly down the road, a group of ten uniformed children walking alongside it, holding out baskets to the gathered crowds. The people were placing gifts in the baskets, all watched over by stern magisters from the Order of Iris who rode on the carriage.

'Magister' was the title given to the high officials of the five great Orders, and, as far as Juniper could tell, the main requirement of the job was an inability to smile. 'Arkspire is strong because we stand together,' one of them declared. 'Give generously, good people, and your charity shall be rewarded!' It was a Procession of Giving, when people made offerings and gave thanks to their Arcanist ruler, hoping to aid in their bitter battle against the Betrayers' curse.

'There, into the crowd!' Juniper said, swinging over

a roof edge and using a drainpipe to shin down to street level. A man poked his head out of a window just as Juniper passed him. 'Life on the go, right?' she said apologetically. 'Who's got time for all those crowds?'

The man could only watch as Juniper slid down to the street, Thea a heartbeat behind her. They dashed through a clothing stall, the merchant too busy haggling with a customer to notice. Juniper emerged with a new cap that was a few sizes too big, but she hoped it offered her some amount of disguise in case the wardens found them.

Thea, on the other hand, now sported a big pink hat with so many flowers on it that some might've even called it excessive. Juniper looked at her, an eyebrow raised.

'Fashion,' Thea simply said.

The girls pushed into the crowd, worming their way as deep as they could into the press. Good timing too, as Juniper spotted their pursuers skidding round the corner, chests heaving with the effort of the chase. They stalked down the edges of the crowd, searching for the girls while keeping out of the way of the parade.

'Uh-oh, I think we might have a problem . . .' Thea whispered.

'Yeah, I see 'em. Don't think they see us, though,' Juniper replied.

'No, I mean, I think that noisy ball might've been more of a trendsetter than we first realized . . .'

'What do you mean?' Juniper asked, taking her eyes off the wardens for a second and seeing that Thea was holding her satchel open. It was a ruddy riot of activity in there. Relics were sparking, trembling, smoking.

'Looks like the globe might've set them off?' Thea suggested.

Panicked, Juniper opened her own bag, and saw it was much the same situation. A carved bone hummed an eerie song, a stone amulet was in the process of duplicating itself, a wooden frog carving was becoming slimier by the second. Juniper whipped off her scarf and shoved it into her bag, hoping it might muffle the sounds. Thea hugged her satchel tightly to her chest, hoping for the same thing.

Didn't work all that well, truth be told.

Green smoke was beginning to leak out of Thea's bag.

The stupid bone was humming louder in Juniper's.

'I know the Betrayers were evil and all,' Juniper hissed, 'but what reason could they possibly have had to make a bone sing?!'

They were getting sharp looks, people growing agitated by all the commotion. Juniper shrugged apologetically, trying her best to keep the movement in her bag out of sight.

'Visitor beyond, there's gotta be a way outta this!' Juniper said, fretting. Thea sat on her bag, wisps of green smoke curling round her backside. They couldn't get rid of the loot, could they? Not after all the hard work they'd put in to get it. But the wardens were getting closer, and there was no doubt the girls' boisterous bags would give them away.

Suddenly a hand reached out and grabbed Juniper's satchel.

Juniper pulled it back, snapping round. It was one of the uniformed children holding out the offering baskets as part of the procession. The girl looked small for her age, which was about thirteen years old. White hair

clips kept her fashionable wavy dark hair out of her eyes. She wore a smart charcoal-grey uniform with bright golden buttons running in two rows down the middle. The emblem of the Watcher's owl was embroidered on to golden epaulettes at her shoulders. She was a Candidate – a child who'd been selected from countless thousands to train in their district's Academy. Every Order had an Academy, a place where Candidates were taught about their ruling Arcanist's unique abilities and how to use them, all in preparation for whichever one of them was given the honour of being chosen to Inherit the Arcanist's powers once they died.

And Juniper knew exactly who this Candidate was.

It was Elodie, her sister.

'Thank you so much for your *generous* contribution, citizen,' Elodie said, her words sounding angry despite her bright smile.

'Sorry, not offering today,' Juniper replied, holding tight and unwilling to give up her loot. People closest tutted at Juniper's lack of generosity. Elodie's eye gave an involuntary twitch, but she didn't let go.

'I *really* think you should *reconsider*. Such weighty possessions can prove to be a burden, and I'm sure The Watcher would be gladdened by your generous contribution.' Again Elodie smiled brightly, but her glare was full of meaning, hidden to those gathered round but all too clear to Juniper.

'Nope, it's no burden! It's *exactly* what my family needs, in fact, so . . .' Juniper clenched her teeth, refusing to give up the bag. The wardens were just a few steps away now.

'You wouldn't want to risk putting yourself and your family in unnecessary *danger* by not receiving a blessing from our revered leader, would you?' Elodie asked, her smile faltering.

'I'd be in no danger if you just *let it go*,' Juniper shot back. The people around her were gasping at her rudeness towards such an authority in the Order of Iris.

'The Watcher works in mysterious ways, and, who knows, perhaps she can help you with your *problem*? Like, *right now*?' Elodie practically growled the last words, holding Juniper's gaze, her eyes widening with suggestion.

To be fair, at this point, Juniper's bag had caught fire. The magical flames were cold thankfully, but, hey, a fire's a fire. Sometimes you gotta know when to let go, and fire's generally a good sign.

Juniper released the bag and Elodie shoved it into the large basket, trying to smother the flames without anyone noticing. 'And might your friend want to do the same?'

'Oh yes, I do! I don't usually have anything to donate,' Thea said, handing over her satchel quite happily, smoke still spilling out of it.

'Thank you very much. The Order of Iris will take this from here,' Elodie said, before moving away. Thankfully the wardens paid no attention to two girls donating to a Candidate, and so they continued on, searching for more suspicious activity.

'Welp –' Juniper sighed – 'that's the last we'll see of the greatest haul we've ever taken. It was sweet while it lasted.' Elodie was a total stickler for the rules, and Juniper knew that once her sister had properly put the cold fire out those relics were going straight into the Requisitions vault.

'Yes, but the memories will last,' Thea said, placing a reassuring hand on Juniper's shoulder. 'Elodie may've actually helped us there, to be honest. I don't think we were getting away with that lot, what with all the fire and smoke.'

Juniper supposed Thea was right, but it didn't stop her fuming. After all that work. After smoothly pulling off *The Enemy of my Enemy = Friends (Kind Of)*. After escaping that shoot-out and a chase with the wardens. All that for nothing, thanks to Elodie. She stared after her sister, trying to shoot daggers out of her eyes.

Annoyingly it didn't work. But, as if sensing the attempt, Elodie glanced back, and the look she gave Juniper was truly one of barely restrained fury. Juniper wouldn't have been surprised to actually see daggers flying towards her. Yet another thing her sister was better at than her.

4

HOME SWEET HOME

Sometimes you have to know when you're beat.

Juniper had decided this was *not* one of those moments.

Stupid Elodie, acting all high an' mighty all the time. Even growing up, whenever the twins had played Arcanists, Juniper would always have to be a Betrayer. She got tired of being the baddie, always having to lose – but she knew how upset Elodie would get if she couldn't be an Arcanist. They were her idols. And since The Shrouded had saved them, all Elodie thought about was becoming an Arcanist, just like her. Elodie made it her business to tell people how they could be better, as though everyone should listen to her.

Juniper's mind raced, plotting how the Misfits could reclaim the loot, the loot that would've fetched the kind of coin you just didn't see down in the Dregs. They could sneak on to the back of the procession carriage and grab the bags when no one was looking? All they'd need was a warden's uniform to blend in. Sure, it'd be way too big for them, but if Juniper were to stand on Elodie's shoulders . . . *maybe* . . .

Nah, too risky.

What if they caused a big enough distraction, then got everyone looking one way while the Misfits nabbed the loot?

I wonder where that dragon globe landed, Juniper thought. *Maybe we could still find it . . .*

Might even have time to graffiti a picture of Elodie with stink lines coming off her on the carriage. Juniper grinned at the idea. She looked across at Thea, who was humming a jolly tune to herself, apparently having already got over losing the biggest, bestest take they'd ever had. Never-not-chill Thea.

Juniper sighed. Maybe she should take a leaf out of Thea's book. Maybe she was getting too hung up on this. There'd be other relics. There always were.

Just not from the Badlands. Juniper winced, feeling the sting of their loss once again.

They were already almost home now, descending a large rickety staircase that wound its way down one of the support struts of the vast district-connecting iron bridge above. Evening had arrived; you could tell by the deeper shades of gloom that hung over the streets as thick as the smog.

Without The Watcher around, The Maker had vowed to help the Iris District and had brought his giant manufactories into the district, as well as the jobs that came with 'em. People thought such a move might've brought The Watcher out of hiding, fists swinging, ready to take her district back, but apparently not. The manufactory fires were always burning down here in the lowest levels now, clunking machinery churning out marvellous mechanical marvels night and day.

The twisting streets were busy with a shift change, exhausted labourers making their way home, nodding to those heading in for the night. Soaring cliffs of ramshackle shacks, scrap cabins and junk heaps sprawled out in all directions, built on top of each other like massive insect hives in a competition to escape the filth and muck that passed for streets below. A mess of ropes and pipes criss-crossed between the shack-stacks like the cobwebs of some giant spider that had gone well and truly insane.

'No place like home,' Juniper said.

'*Ahhh*, breathe it in,' Thea said, taking a deep breath. The air was thick with the smell of hot metal and the delightful, distinct notes of a recently used chamber pot.

A man with a white eye scowled at the children as they passed, more blades than any one person needed sheathed at his belt. A group of cloaked figures whispered in the shadows of an alley opposite a beggar cooking an old boot over a fire. The woman next to him was trying to flog the other. The Dregs were home to the desperate and lost, those who had less than nothing but would still fight you for it. It was the same story in every district. Every one of them had their lower levels, their Dregs.

After making their way through the warren of streets, the girls finally arrived at their destination. Corroding pipes feeding all the way down from the Uppers plunged into the muddy ground. Water poured out of them like waterfalls into a large crack in the earth, moss and algae growing round the edges. It was kind of beautiful in a grim leaky-drainage-pipe kind of way. Within this space was a building that was much smaller than the mega shack-stacks that made up most of the Dregs. But what it lacked in size, it more than made up for in something else, something the rest of the Dregs was sorely lacking. An inviting appearance.

It had been built from wood, fairy lights hanging from its awning. The apartments that Juniper and Thea lived in were on the floors above a shop, warm light spilling out of the windows that were filled with displays of vials, jars and bottles of all shapes and sizes. A sign hung at the door. **Adie's Apothecary**. A small oasis amid a sea of decay.

A bell rang as Juniper pushed through the door, the protective wards sketched on the door frame humming as she entered. The store was a wonder, the walls made of dark-wood cabinets and cubbyholes filled with countless herbs, ingredients, remedies and potions. Juniper took in a deep breath, eagerly anticipating the mysterious, enchanting aromas of incense and herbs – a relief from the stench outside.

Instead a powerful punch of liquorice stung her nostrils.

'Urgh!' Juniper blew out through her nose.

Wisps of smoke clung to the ceiling.

'Oh dear . . . has Grangran been experimenting with new recipes again . . .?' Thea wondered aloud.

'Uhhh . . . Madame Adie . . .?' Juniper tried.

A door behind the counter slammed open, and an old lady burst out, hacking and spluttering, chased by a great plume of greenish smoke. OK, now it *really* stank of liquorice.

'Curses! Confound it! Blast, bother and other such terms of irritation!' the lady yelled, holding a rag to her face and opening a window.

'All good, Madame A?' Juniper asked.

The lady spun round, staring at the children through her thick glasses, cocking her head to the side as if she barely recognized them. Despite being from the Dregs, she looked very stylish. Her grey hair was pulled up into an impressive explosion of tangled shagginess. Her neck was wrapped in many decorative scarves from which hung all sorts of charms and pendants, some clattering against the gleaming stone brooch she always wore pinned to her luxurious shawl. 'Girls! You want to be careful, sneaking up on an old lady like that!'

'A glorious sundown to you, Madame Adie!' Thea sang.

'Do you . . . need a hand?' Juniper asked.

'A hand?' Madame Adie blinked, barely visible through the smoke. 'Ah, these noxious fumes!' She chuckled. 'No, no, it's nothing. Simply my latest project refusing to dance to my tune, *as per usual*!' She yelled the last bit at the door, as if her experiments had ears. Maybe they did for all Juniper knew. 'Oh, and don't breathe in the fumes, darlings. It's Moon Kiss, the smallest whiff of which will put you to sleep for hours.'

The girls shoved their noses into the crooks of their elbows. They were used to this kind of thing.

Madame Adie dabbled in something she called *alchemy*. She had a whole workshop back there in her private quarters. It was some kind of 'science magic'; least that's what Madame Adie said. A magic anyone could use, not just the Arcanists. She tried to keep it on the down-low, however, in case the wardens caught wind of her experiments and decided to take a dislike to it. Not that you'd know it from all the explosions she caused.

'Well, s'long as you're sure,' Juniper said, stepping up to put out a small flame that had caught on one of Madame Adie's scarf tassels.

As she did so, there was some movement within the scarves, and a little whiskered snout poked out from the folds, sniffing the pungent air. It was McGrubbins, Madame Adie's faithful pet rat, and the inspiration for the Misfits' very own gang emblem.

'Don't you worry about me,' Madame Adie said. 'Why, if anything, I feel like it is *I* who should be worried about *you two*. Word is there was a little *hullabaloo* in the higher markets this afternoon, and perhaps my memory deceives me – I am getting so forgetful these days – but weren't you girls planning on going up there today?'

Juniper and Thea shared a glance. *Busted.*

5

RELIC RECOVERY

'You already heard about that?' Juniper asked.

There was a mischievous glint in Madame Adie's old eyes. 'Darling, it's the Dregs. Word travels fast.' She wasn't wrong. 'Course, I imagine all that fuss had nothing to do with you two now, did it?'

'Not us, no,' Thea said, skipping over to Madame Adie and taking McGrubbins in her arms. The Dregs had no shortage of rats, but this one wasn't nearly as ferocious or hungry-looking as the others. He squeaked his approval as Thea gave him scritches behind the ear.

Once the fumes had gone, Juniper listened carefully to make sure the coast was clear. When she was satisfied it was, she spoke in a low voice: 'Even though we absolutely, positively had nothing to do with that crazy shoot-out in the market, we *did* happen to stumble on the most major relic haul *ever*, straight outta the Badlands . . .'

'Oh?' Madame Adie's eyes lit up. Though she had a well-earned reputation for being a kind, caring old sort who sold miracle medicines and tinctures at a fair price, she wasn't all doilies and teacups. She'd been around long enough to get to know people, to make certain *friends*. These *friends* had their fingers on the pulse of the undercity, and from the shadows they saw things. Things like when and where certain forbidden relics were being moved through the city. They'd share these interesting titbits with Madame Adie, who would pass them on to the Misfits – not to encourage them to steal, of course, but just in case they might find such information . . . *of interest*. And should those treasures make their way back to her apothecary – well, you can't have that kind of contraband sitting around the place, can you? So she might as well sell them on to collectors who happened to be passing through.

'We're talkin' real rare items, the likes of which I've never seen before,' Juniper said. Madame Adie rubbed her hands together with glee. 'Thing is,' Juniper continued, 'we bumped into Elodie and she kinda . . . took it all from us.'

Madame Adie's shoulders slumped, and she blew a hair out of her eye. 'Oh.'

'Still, we got to run around a lot, which is always

nice,' said Thea, still stroking McGrubbins, who'd nestled into the crook of her arm.

'Now, why would Elodie do such a thing?' Madame Adie asked. 'She knows how much your papa needs the money . . . and it's not like those Arcanists need any more trinkets. They're already nose-deep in magic; maybe it's time to share the goods with those who would really benefit from it.'

Juniper bit her lip. Unlike everyone else, Madame Adie wasn't exactly the Arcanists' biggest fan. Her jabs and jibes tended to put Juniper on edge, like the Arcanists might somehow overhear her. 'You know Elodie –' Juniper shrugged – 'if there's a hair outta place or a picture frame that's crooked, she's gotta set it right. No way was she gonna let us walk outta there with illegal relics.'

'Also, our bags were literally morphing into other-worldly horrors in our hands, so –' Thea shrugged too – 'could be she saved us from certain arrest, or some kind of hideous inter-dimensional mutation at the very least.'

Juniper glared at Thea. 'Did she, though? Did she *really*?'

Thea thought on it, then gave a nod. 'Yes.'

'I suspect you're right,' Madame Adie said. 'We should give poor Elodie a break. Ain't easy to be a

Dregger in an Academy. She works so hard and truly has the weight of the world on her shoulders. Though joining the Orders is a choice I'll never understand, ain't no doubt her heart's in the right place.'

'An' doesn't she let you know about it . . .' Juniper mumbled, shoving her hands into her coat pockets. She was startled to find something inside one of them, an object wrapped in a cloth. Juniper perked right up as she remembered what it was.

'Hey, y'know, might be that today wasn't a *total* bust, after all . . .' She unwrapped the cloth and held up the mirror shard she'd found on the cart.

Thea clapped with joy. 'You managed to keep something?'

'Not just something, the *best* thing! Er . . . whatever it is . . .' She placed the shard on the counter in front of Madame Adie, the glass gleaming in the dim lantern light.

'Oooooh,' Thea said, drawing closer.

Madame Adie cocked her head to the side, her brow creasing as she focused on the relic. 'My, my. What a thing, indeed . . .' With great care, she lifted the shard to inspect it. 'And, you know, I suspect I know *exactly* what this is . . .'

'You do?' Juniper asked, hoping she'd say as much, her jaw clenched in anticipation.

Madame Adie nodded. 'I do. This shattered piece of mirror glass . . . is an absolute mystery. I've never seen anything like it.'

Juniper blew air out of her cheeks and rolled her eyes. '*Seriously?!* You're gonna joke around after the day we've just had?!'

'Allow an old lady her fun, will you? Truthfully this is a unique item – you don't find relics like this just lying around Arkspire any more, not with Requisitions combing through the city. Incredible . . . You can almost *feel* its power.' Madame Adie gazed at the shard with the same fascination as Juniper, her face reflected back at her.

'It's clearly very shiny and special,' Thea said, 'but . . . what does it do?'

'That I do not know,' Madame Adie said. 'Looks like it might've come from a larger piece that, alas, I suspect is lost to time. But if it came from the Badlands, there's a good chance it's very, very dangerous . . .'

'Yes,' Thea said, nodding. 'Probably very good at helping you to brush your hair too.'

Madame Adie beamed. 'Excellent work, girls, excellent work indeed! We can all look forward to a nice healthy payout from this, I don't doubt. Certain customers of mine will be tripping over themselves to get their hands on such a find, and I'll be sure to give you both your cut once they do.'

She began to wrap the shard back in its cloth, but as she did Juniper thought she saw it again. Movement in the glass. Like a flicker of colour, a shift in the light. She looked over her shoulder, but, as before, there was nothing there.

What *was* this thing? What kind of dark magic had the Betrayers poured into it? As Madame Adie placed the shard in a drawer behind the counter, locking it with a small key so that it was safe and out of sight, Juniper supposed she'd never find out. Perhaps it was just as well.

6

JELLIPER

The sudden sounds of a ruckus came from outside. A load of shouting and jeering, enough to make those inside Adie's Apothecary rush to the windows to see what was causing it. Juniper was surprised to see Elodie walking towards the shop, flanked by two wardens from the Order of Iris. Her chin was raised, head held high, despite the less-than-warm welcome she was getting from a gang of kids perched on top of the shacks either side of the road. They threw insults at her like stones, sneering and pulling faces.

'Look who's come crawlin' back . . .'

'Smellodie Bell!'

'What happened? You finally realize you're the worst person to rep us Dreggers at the Academy?'

'She ain't a real Dregger – nothin' that weak could be . . .'

The wardens reached for the truncheons at their belts, but Elodie laid her hands on their arms, signalling for them to stand down.

'Hey!' Juniper yelled, bursting out of the shop door.

'Oh, look, the loud one's here,' said the biggest of the kids. 'Right on cue.'

'Don't, Juni,' Elodie pleaded as her sister drew near. 'The last thing I need is for people to see a Candidate involved in a petty street fight.'

'I'd get outta here if I were you,' Juniper continued to shout, regardless, 'before anyone sees that big lump on yer head!'

'What? You stupid as you look?' the kid shot back. 'I ent got no lump!'

'Really?' Juniper said, scooping up a pebble from the ground. 'Then what's *that*?' She pulled back her arm, but something grabbed her wrist before she could throw anything. She turned round to see Papa, his hand easily big enough to hold her entire wrist, his heavy eyebrows furrowed, hiding his small, tired eyes.

'There's not a problem out here, is there?' he asked the kids. 'Nothin' I need to let yer parents know about?' Papa had once been a bouncer at the Swig 'N' Swill and knew most people in the area. The kids flinched at the

71

sight of him, despite the frilly apron he wore over his manufactory overalls and the wooden spoon he carried.

'We'll see you later, Smellodie,' the ringleader spat, motioning for his gang to leave. 'You can't hide behind others forever.'

'Shoulda let me do it,' Juniper said, watching them scramble away. 'You'd be amazed how a pebble between the eyes can really change how people look at you. Kinda like this.' She crossed her eyes and stuck her tongue out. 'You gotta stand up to them one of these days, El. I showed you how to throw a punch; you just gotta –'

'Not get into pointless fights?' Elodie interrupted. 'I appreciate you standing up for me, but I have more important things to worry about than name-calling.'

'That's my girl,' Papa said, drawing her into a hug. 'We're all Arkspire, after all.'

Juniper furrowed her brow.

'It's good to see you, Papa,' said Elodie, smiling. She then turned to her warden guards. 'Can you wait for me here, please? I won't be long.'

The wardens bowed, then took up position either side of the shop door, truncheons grasped in their fists as they looked out at the disordered tangle of shacks around them.

'Wasn't expecting you back for another few weeks,'

Papa said, leading them into the apothecary. 'Thought you'd be busy with training up at the Academy?'

Madame Adie gave Elodie a welcoming smile; Thea held up one of McGrubbins' paws and gave her an energetic wave.

'I am, but it's been so long, I thought I'd come visit,' Elodie said, waving back. 'I hoped to have a word with Juni too.'

Juniper froze. *Uh-oh.*

She didn't like the sound of that. She shared a glance with Thea. Had Elodie come all this way to grass them up for earlier?

'Good thing I made a stew, then,' Papa said. 'Reckon there's just enough for all of us.'

Juniper followed her family up the stairs at the back of the store, feeling like she was being led to the gallows. The Bells' home wasn't much to look at, little more than two tiny rooms they rented from Madame Adie. The main room consisted of a threadbare couch and an old creaky table decorated with the scratches and stains it'd collected throughout the years. The twins pulled up two stools and sat at the table while Papa returned to the pot bubbling away in the corner. As always, he looked comically large next to the tiny stove, with his tree-trunk arms and huge hands tenderly sprinkling some salt into the pot.

Juniper tried to read her sister and work out why she'd shown up out of the blue. Elodie wasn't revealing anything; she simply traced a wiggly line scored into the table with her finger. Juniper had made it when she was only little. Elodie had helped, even though she'd worried it was wrong to damage furniture. They'd been trying to write the name *Jelliper*, but had been stopped before they could finish by a very angry Mama. Elodie had cried for ages after, despite all the excuses Juniper had made for them.

'Here we go,' Papa said, placing a bowl of stew in front of the girls. Juniper's belly rumbled. It smelled great. You could tell Papa was real proud of this one; his moustache was twitching with excitement.

'Thanks, Papa,' the girls said together.

'And a special treat for a special occasion,' he said, passing a breadboard to Elodie. A tasty loaf rested on it, its crust golden and crispy. 'Did a favour for old Laurent down the way, and he baked this as thanks.'

'Whatta guy!' Juniper beamed, mouth watering.

'So, tell us, how've you been?' Papa asked Elodie, as she started to tear a hunk from the bread.

'It's been crazy. This is a secret, but The Watcher's current Inheritor has become too old to Inherit magic, so the Order are preparing to hold another choosing ceremony any day now. They have us training even harder than before.'

'Can't have an Arcanist dying without an Inheritor at the ready,' Papa said, eyeing the bread as eagerly as Juniper. 'Can you imagine losing a whole Arcanist line on top of everything else?'

'And you know what really gets in the way of us preparing for the choosing, of doing something useful with our time?' Elodie said, the loaf still in her hands. 'Having to deal with all these relic hunters breaking the law and making our lives more difficult.'

Juniper and her papa both straightened at Elodie's words. So she had come to snitch.

'They've . . . been a problem?' Papa's voice was low, almost sad. Mama had been a relic hunter. Though he had never approved of it, the words still reminded him of her.

Juniper's pulse quickened. As twins, the girls had a special connection with one another, a deep understanding of each other's expressions and movements, a shared language no one else could begin to understand. Juniper shot Elodie the briefest glance, but the look said it all.

Please don't tell.

Elodie ignored her and went on. 'We had a few today, in fact. Careless, selfish individuals who had no idea what they were carrying – how dangerous the relics were. One of them could set fire to anything . . .'

'*Anything?*' Juniper asked. That sounded awesome. She regretted losing the loot even more now.

'Anything. Even water! I wish there was some way I could reach these people. I feel like grabbing them by the cheeks and shouting in their face, "The Betrayers were evil! You cannot mess with their magic – no good can ever come from it!"'

'Suppose some people just won't listen,' said Papa.

'I dunno,' said Juniper. '"When the world gives you an empty bag, it's your job to fill it."'

Elodie dropped the bread as fast as her jaw. It was one of Mama's sayings. Juniper knew it would get a reaction out of her sister, and she used the opportunity to snatch the breadboard. Elodie was taking way too long with it. 'I reckon the relic hunters know the danger, but they're so desperate they don't have any other choice. There's big business in relics; least that's what I hear.'

'While I do feel sorry for them,' Elodie said, snatching the breadboard back, 'and understand what they're going through, they're wrong.'

'They sound pretty cool to me.' Juniper reached for the board, but Elodie held it out of her grasp.

'There's a reason the relics of the Betrayers are forbidden – it's to keep everyone in Arkspire safe. You know Shades killed three people last week? *Three!* Betrayer magic is ruining lives, and to think people are still willing to mess around with such magic – magic they can't hope to understand.' Elodie really emphasized this last bit, staring right into Juniper's eyes.

'Three deaths . . . ?' Juniper's belly twisted at the thought.

Nobody actually knew what Shades were. Ghosts? Demons? Other-worldly entities? But then all you really needed to know was that if you saw one, you stayed the heck away from it. Shades first appeared centuries ago, during the war between the Arcanists and the Betrayers. There were only a few at first, but their numbers grew till the Badlands outside the safety of Arkspire's wards were swarming with them. A terrible curse had been placed on the land by the Betrayers in a last-ditch attempt to win the war. Shades were drawn to life like moths to a flame – only these particular moths snuffed out the flame as soon as they touched it.

'Still, I thought it was the Arcanists and their Orders who were meant to protect us from the Shades?' Juniper swiped the breadboard from Elodie.

'We're doing our best!' Elodie said, grabbing the board's other end. 'You have no idea how bad the Shade curse is getting!'

A game of tug-of-war started, the two sisters staring each other down, unwilling to let go.

Papa cleared his throat. 'Well, isn't this nice?' In one smooth move he yanked the breadboard away before the bread went flying. 'The family all together. Doesn't happen too often these days. Precious moments these. No place for hot tempers.'

'You're right,' Juniper said, sitting back on her stool, but it was too late – her temper *was* hot. 'I shouldn't blame you, El. It's not your fault the Order you work for is ruled by the worst Arcanist of them all.'

'Juni!' Elodie and Papa cried together.

Juniper gave a small smile.

'You can't say things like that!' Elodie insisted.

Juniper knew it. The words felt wrong coming out of her mouth, like she was somehow placing a curse on everyone in the room just by speaking them. But she was getting angry and tired of being spoken down to.

'Am I wrong?' Juniper asked. 'Sure, The Watcher's power's impressive enough, but it's not much use in a fight, is it? What's she supposed to do – stare the Shades to death?'

'At least she's not putting her district at risk by stealing deadly contraband from dangerous criminals!' Elodie retorted.

'No, she wouldn't do that – she's too busy hiding while the rest of us have to fend for ourselves! Being able to see threats coming from afar has made her a coward!'

'OK, that's enough,' Papa warned, but Juniper wasn't done, not by a long shot.

'The Watcher spends her days hiding while the other Arcanists risk their lives defending us all! Is that the kind of Arcanist you want to become an Inheritor to?!'

'The Watcher does care,' Elodie said, quiet now. 'It's just . . . she sees things we don't; she has visions of possible futures we could not understand. If she's hiding herself away while the city suffers, there must be a very good reason. But that's why it's so important I try to get chosen. We need someone from the Dregs to become

Inheritor. Someone who knows what it's like to live down here. Someone who can make a difference.'

Juniper studied her twin sister. They were the same age, yet Elodie spoke like someone way older. It felt like just yesterday they were scratching scribbles into the table – now Elodie was talking about changing all of Arkspire?

'You're wasting your time,' Juniper said. 'Dreggers aren't welcome up there. They never are, an' never will be.'

Elodie let out a little hiccup of indignation, but didn't argue. Instead she clutched the lucky coin Mama had given her the day she'd applied to the Iris Academy, tied to a cord around her neck. Elodie knew how fierce the competition to become an Inheritor was better than anyone, and nobody doubted her more than herself. But still she looked at Juniper with a sad expression, full of infuriating sympathy. 'So you'd rather I sit back and accept everything as it is? I'm doing all I can to make things better for us, and I wish you'd do the same! What else do you want me to do?'

'How about not abandoning me an' Papa down here for a start!' Juniper snapped, the words leaving her lips before she could stop them.

Elodie made a sound like a small gasp, clearly hurt. Papa flinched, his mouth moving as he tried to think of what to say, something that might calm the situation.

Elodie scraped her stool away from the table and stood up straight. 'Oh, grow up, Juni!' she cried. 'One of us has to!' Light glinted off the tears welling up in her eyes. 'Dinner looks delicious, Papa, but I'm afraid I've lost my appetite. I – I'm sorry.'

And, with that, Elodie turned on her heel and headed straight out of the apartment, slamming the door behind her.

Not to be outdone, Juniper thundered past her speechless papa and into the bedroom, pulling back the ragged patchwork hanging that gave her section of the room a meagre amount of privacy. She dropped down on to the bed and buried her face in the pillow. It was only then, as her belly groaned, that she wished she'd thought to grab a hunk of that bread.

7

SELF-REFLECTION

Sometime later, the curtain was pulled back, its rings scraping along the wooden pole. Juniper sensed the large presence of her papa standing beside her bed. She didn't look up, her head still in her pillow. Tough to breathe, sure, but it somehow helped the simmering frustration gnawing inside her. With a sigh, Papa sat on her bed. The springs creaked under his considerable bulk. After a moment, he placed a hand on her arm. It was Juniper's turn to sigh then, and her fists unclenched.

They sat together in silence. Not much for words, her papa.

'Take it you had a rough day?' he said at last.

'It might've hit a little snag,' Juniper said, resting her chin on her pillow.

Papa rubbed his eyes. 'And every other snag on the way down, it sounds like.'

'It's not like I'm gonna use the relics for some big evil plan,' Juniper protested. 'I can get so much more money from relics than from runnin' around doing some stupid delivery job or whatever. We need the money, right? So I'm doing everything I can to help us!'

'And we love you for it, Juni,' Papa said, 'but you have to stop an' think about how your actions might affect others. Slow down an' use your head. I know you have one on yer shoulders, an' it's a good 'un at that. What if you'd been caught today? What if they discovered you were El's sister? She could've been thrown out of the Academy!'

'What else can I do? They already work you to the bone in the manufactory an' we still barely scratch a living.'

'If Elodie gets chosen as Inheritor, everything will change for us.'

Juniper growled under her breath. Why did everything have to rely on Elodie? It sounded like that mirror shard alone could fetch more coin than Papa could hope to make all year, not that she could tell him that. 'I know you're tryin' your best, Papa, but we're desperate, an' you know it. If El doesn't get chosen . . . well, people pay good money for relics and –'

'And it's my job to look after us all,' Papa interrupted, 'and I will do my job.' He lowered his eyes, knowing full well that it wasn't enough. The Bells had never had it easy, but ever since Mama had passed it was almost impossible to make ends meet.

Juniper swallowed hard. She hadn't meant to make him feel ashamed.

'El needs you, Juni,' Papa continued. 'We all do. An' you'll be no good to us in jail. I want you workin' for somethin' bigger. Somethin' worthy of you. You *have* to be better than this place.' His voice almost sounded pleading. 'We all do. Otherwise the Dregs'll eat us whole.'

Juniper buried her head back into her pillow. The silence dragged on. Finally Papa stood. 'I never want to hear that you've been stealing again, understand? We are *not* a family of thieves.'

Not with Mama gone, we're not, Juniper thought. Instead she just said '*mmmf*' from the pillow.

'Juniper?'

'Yes, captain!' she said, throwing her hand into a mock salute without lifting her head. She heard Papa leave. She opened an eye, looking at the weathered old red chest that sat at the foot of her bed, the chest that held her most precious keepsakes, the few things she had left to remember her mama by.

She missed her desperately. Mama had always been so very proud of Juniper. So impressed with her roof-running, her nimble feet and quick wits. These were the things Juniper was good at. Why shouldn't she put them to good use?

It felt like sleep was going to be a stranger that night. The small bedroom trembled with Papa's snoring, loud as a manufactory. Juniper lay under her tangled bedcovers, staring up at the ceiling. Years ago, the twins had tried to spruce it up a bit, decorating the plaster with paint and crayons. Elodie had done drawings of the family, of the Arcanists helping the smiling people of Arkspire. She'd painted trees and flowers, forests and animals, things you just didn't see in the Dregs. Hopeful things. Beautiful things.

Juniper had used up the red paint on particularly gruesome scenes of monsters biting people in half and Arcanists blowing people's heads off.

Maybe the idea of Jelliper had always been a childish fantasy . . . Maybe they'd always been as different as cats and dogs, just Elodie hadn't been brave enough to admit it till now . . . Maybe the Academy had brought out her true self . . .

Juniper turned her pillow over. If Elodie was chosen to Inherit The Watcher's power, everything would change. Their family would be raised to the highest levels of society. Juniper and Papa would be allowed to join Elodie in the Uppers. They'd be given a mansion in the shimmery neighbourhoods of the Order of Iris's magisters; they'd have servants who'd attend to their every need.

And yet . . .

If Elodie was chosen, what would that make Juniper? She'd definitely have to stop being a relic hunter. Then who would she be? Just the older sister of the future Watcher? Why would anyone care about who she was when her sister was an Arcanist?

She knew how hard Elodie had worked for this. If anything, the harder her training had got, the harder she'd knuckled down. If anyone deserved to become The Watcher's Inheritor, it was Elodie.

And yet . . .

And yet Juniper found herself wishing The Watcher would pick anyone but her sister. Shame gnawed at her for the thought, but, whatever, it was the truth.

Juniper sighed, rubbing her face. Her thoughts were buzzing round her head like a bee that had forgotten which way it needed to fly. Sometimes you just have to accept sleep isn't going to come, no matter how much you toss and turn.

As silently as a mouse, Juniper crept out of the

bedroom and opened the door to their apartment with barely a creak. She'd see if Thea was awake. Thea always knew what to say. They could sneak up on to the roof like they sometimes did, chatting away till the sounds of the city lulled them to sleepiness. But to Juniper's surprise she saw the glow of a light in the apothecary downstairs. Madame Adie would usually disappear into her private quarters when she closed the shop, especially this late. Curious, she tiptoed down the stairs.

The apothecary was lit by a single lantern, the shadows long and deep. Thankfully the smell of liquorice had disappeared and had been replaced by the earthy scent of herbs. Madame Adie was using goggles with many adjustable magnifying lenses to

inspect something she clasped with large tweezers. McGrubbins sat close by, busy grooming his whiskers and letting out the odd squeak.

Madame Adie glanced up at the sound of Juniper's arrival, the goggles making her look like some giant insect. 'Juni! You're up late.'

Juniper shrugged. 'Can't sleep. Guessin' you can't either?' She approached the counter to see what Madame Adie was looking at. It was the piece of mirror glass she'd found that afternoon.

'It's this curiosity you brought back for me – or should I say *cursed* me with? Quite the riddle. You know relics are a bit of a speciality of mine . . . and yet, for the life of me, I can't figure out what this thing actually

does, or which Betrayer it might've once belonged to. Nibbling away at my mind, this infernal thing, like an itch I can't scratch . . .'

Juniper cocked her head, taking a closer look. There was definitely something strange about the glass, no matter how ordinary it first appeared. She narrowed her eyes. She thought she caught another flash of movement reflected back at her, but she couldn't be sure it wasn't just the flickering of the lantern.

Madame Adie leaned back in her chair, lifted her goggles and raised her arms in a big stretch. 'No good work was ever done while half asleep, eh? I should probably hit the sack.'

She took one last, lingering look at the shard, clearly frustrated. She placed it in the drawer at the back of the counter, which she locked shut, dropping the small key in her pocket.

'I suspect bed wouldn't do you any harm either, young treasure seeker.' Madame Adie smiled, pushing herself up from the seat.

'Yeah, I guess,' Juniper said, but then she grabbed Madame Adie's wrist. 'Wait!'

Madame Adie looked surprised. 'What is it?'

Juniper paused, as if unsure what to say. 'It's nothing,' she said eventually. 'I'm gonna head up. Goodnight!'

'Sleep well.' Madame Adie gave Juniper a strange look. She allowed McGrubbins to climb up her arm before shuffling into her private quarters. Juniper climbed the stairs, but stopped at the top, sitting on a step with her back against the wall.

She held out the small key she'd slipped out of Madame Adie's pocket and grinned.

8

MIRROR'S TRUTH

Normally she'd feel guilty for pickpocketing a friend, but she was only borrowing the key. Besides, Juniper was the one who'd found the shard. She just wanted a closer look to see if she could glean anything from it herself – maybe even discover the source of the movements she swore she saw in the glass. What was the worst that could happen? She wouldn't get another chance once the thing was sold.

Positive that Madame Adie had gone to bed, Juniper crept back down into the apothecary, careful to avoid the creaky floorboards. She knew them by heart, each one – this wasn't the first time she'd sneaked about at night. The shop was entirely dark now. The countless jars and pots stood to attention on the shelves like silent guards. Luckily jars have no eyes, or voices either, for that matter, and Juniper was able to sneak behind the counter without Madame Adie becoming any the wiser. Carefully, Juniper slid the key into the drawer's lock. Holding her breath, she turned it. The lock clicked.

Juniper grimaced. It sounded as loud as a gunshot in the still silence of the shop.

Thankfully no one came to investigate, and Juniper pulled the drawer open, the mirror glass glinting inside.

She held it up to the dim light that spilled in from the street outside, her own reflection staring back at her. Her hazel eyes. Her dark raggedy hair framing her round face. Nothing out of the ordinary. Same ol' Juniper – nothing magical about that reflection. So what did she keep seeing in this thing? Was it really just a trick of the light?

She shifted the shard around, gazing into the glass at different angles, but she only saw reflections of the apothecary – so far so normal.

'What *are* you?' Juniper whispered. 'Reveal to me your secrets, O strange mirror!'

That was when she spotted the door.

She could see it behind her in the mirror's reflection, set between two cabinets on the opposite side of the shop.

A door she didn't recognize. A door she was pretty sure she'd never seen before, and she'd lived above this shop all thirteen years of her life. Juniper glanced over her shoulder, and a cold shiver ran down her back. There was no door – only a plain dark-wood wall in between the two cabinets. She looked back at the mirror shard. There it was, as clear as day. The door was only showing up in the mirror's reflection!

'What the . . .?'

She rushed round the counter and over to the wall, feeling for any hidden cracks, searching for any concealed hinges or handles. She felt nothing but the rough texture of wood. She turned her back to it and held the shard up over her shoulder. She wasn't going mad – there was definitely a door in the reflection. A door with an ornate iron handle.

Using the mirror as a guide, Juniper reached down to where the handle was in the reflection. To her amazement, not only did her hand grasp the handle within the mirror but she felt something in her hand in the real world too. She hadn't felt the handle before . . . Was the mirror's magic at work here? Did you have to look through the mirror?

Juniper's nerves buzzed with excitement and not the smallest tickle of fear. Was she actually going to do this? Open an invisible door to who-knows-where that you could only see within a magical mirror once belonging to one of the evil Betrayers?

Darn right she was.

She pushed down on the handle and pulled it towards her.

It was the strangest thing. Juniper could feel a door opening, could feel the change in the air on her face, and yet her eyes saw nothing of the sort. The wall before her remained exactly what it had always been – a solid wall. And yet, by looking in the mirror, Juniper could clearly see that the door was opening. Light spilled from beyond, leaking out into the room in strange, complex, magical sigils, as though some invisible hand was drawing them with blue fire.

Juniper yelped and dropped the shard as it gave her a sudden shock, her nerves tingling unpleasantly. She stared, aghast, as the sigils began to seep out of the shard into the real world, the strange lines burning their way across the shop floor. Juniper jumped from foot to foot, trying to avoid them, unsure what they might do if they touched her – and not really wanting to find out. They grew in speed, spreading like wildfire, over the counter, up the walls, weaving and overlapping and creating intricate patterns.

OK . . . how hard can it be to close a magic-barfing door? Juniper thought, just before she was blasted off her feet by a massive invisible force. She hit the counter hard, knocking the air from her lungs. Gasping for breath, her eyes widened as she realized her hands had landed on some of the shimmering sigils. They prickled, like she'd somehow managed to grab hold of lightning. The sigils wound themselves over her hands in an instant. Juniper pulled away in fright, and watched in horror as the lines continued to crawl up her forearms like snakes, drawing glowing arcane symbols right up to her elbows.

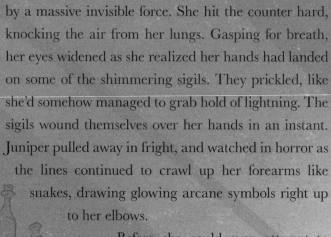

Before she could even attempt to understand what was happening to her, an explosion of blue light erupted from the shard, bursting in a beam through the ceiling and up into the floors above. The light somehow grew brighter and brighter until Juniper was forced to close her eyes and look away. She was hit by a fierce cold; every one of her nerves tingled, crying out at the chill. She realized she was screaming, though she couldn't hear it over the roar of the magic spewing out of the shard.

What was *happening*? Was she about to die?

Then, just as quickly as it had started, the chaos came to a sudden jarring end. It was as though it had realized it didn't belong in this world and had jumped back through the doorway it had come from.

Juniper dared to open her eyes. Her breath became ragged. Her eyes squinted, still sore after the blinding brightness. Particles of light drifted around her like pollen on the breeze, fading into the air. After all the noise, the world suddenly seemed very quiet. Paper and dried herbs fluttered about Madame Adie's room, which now smelled like the damp aftermath of a storm. There was a smoking hole in the ceiling, embers burning red in the darkness, glowing sigils seared into anything the mirror magic had touched.

But the strangest thing of all was the fact that Juniper was no longer alone.

Something was wreathed in the smoke billowing round the mirror shard – now little more than a pile of ash. It was the shadow of a monstrous creature, its body sleek and predatory. The thing grew bigger and bigger.

It flexed its claws; it opened its massive jaws, long fangs sharp and deadly.

Every one of Juniper's muscles screamed at her to run. Was it a Shade? Was it something even *worse*?

The creature turned to face her – its features still hidden by the smoke. She tried to scramble away, but her back was already against the counter. The thing rumbled and hissed – low and deep in its gullet – before lurching towards her with a blood-curdling snarl.

9

PRISON BREAK

The thing lunged out of the murk – and Juniper realized the smoke may have *slightly* exaggerated its size. The beast was tiny, about the size of Juniper's forearm. It appeared to have a small snout, pointy ears and a long swishing tail, but it was hard to tell. It was like a living shadow, shifting and coiling like a black candle flame, its eyes glowing a bright, fierce turquoise. It fell forward on to its front claws and opened its jaws wide – a blue light coming from within – then wider, wider still, as though it was about to unleash a spine-chilling roar . . .

. . . but instead it coughed and spluttered. And spoke.

'Something . . . stuck . . .' The creature coughed again, pointing into its open jaw, its long, luminous tongue lolling.

'What. The. *Heck*?!' Juniper squealed.

She'd had the misfortune of seeing many Shades in her time, but she'd never, ever heard one of them *talk*.

The thing hacked and heaved, before spitting something on to the floor. Slimy. Lumpy. Gross.

The creature looked at the ectoplasmic gob, considering its handiwork, before it raised its glowing eyes towards Juniper. 'No, no, don't get up to help . . . Just choking over here. Please don't trouble yourself.'

Juniper's eye twitched. She'd seen quite enough, to be honest. And, judging from the thumping footsteps and raised voices beginning to echo through the building, she was about to have a lot of company,

asking difficult questions she didn't particularly fancy answering.

With the smallest of yelps, she scrambled across the shop floor and flung herself into a cupboard, slamming the doors behind her just as footsteps came tumbling down the stairs. Juniper squidged up tight against the vials and jars stored inside, hoping her racing heart wouldn't give her away.

'*What the* —' came Papa's voice, stunned by the sight that welcomed him. 'What *happened* here?!'

'My goodness . . .' gasped Madame Adie. 'How *extraordinary*!' Her voice sounded more awestruck than frightened, like someone admiring a pretty painting.

'Have you seen Juniper?' Papa asked.

'A while ago, yes. She couldn't sleep, but she went back to bed, I —'

'But she's not upstairs!' Papa panicked. 'Visitor beyond, where is she?'

'The rooftop maybe?'

'Juni?' Papa called. 'JUNI?!'

Incredibly neither of them seemed to have noticed the talking *shadow-monster* that had popped into the shop.

More thundering footsteps went up the stairs, as Papa and Madame Adie raced to find her. Juniper felt bad for making them worry like this, but what was she supposed to do? Tell Papa she'd messed with a forbidden relic and opened a doorway for a monster right below their home?

She frowned, remembering El's words from earlier. But this didn't prove Elodie right! Relic hunting wasn't dangerous. Relics didn't usually do . . . this.

Juniper's chest was heaving. She stared wide-eyed at the sigils scrawled across her hands and arms. Their glow illuminated the dark cupboard. She scratched at them, but no matter how hard she rubbed, the marks remained.

'I'm assuming your arms don't normally look like that?' said a voice beside her ear. The creature!

Juniper jumped and scrambled deeper into the cupboard. She snatched for something to defend herself with, bottles clinking and tumbling with her movements.

'What – what *are* you?' she demanded, wishing she'd picked up anything other than the ball of string she was currently holding out in front of her like a weapon.

'What am I? What *am* I?' The creature looked down at itself, its vivid eyes and glowing maw the only sign it was anything other than a shadow. It paused. 'Quite frankly I'm not entirely sure. A being of great power, I've no doubt. More importantly, *where* am I? What is this place?'

'A-Adie's Apothecary,' Juniper said, not taking her eyes off it. 'In the city of Arkspire.'

The thing tilted its head. 'Never heard of them. Are you sure you didn't just make them up?'

'How could you not have heard of Arkspire? It's the biggest city in the world, and the only place of safety left!'

'*Safety?*' The creature chuckled, flexing its claws. 'It is danger itself that should fear me, not the other way round.' Its voice sounded male, full of arrogance but with a splash of confusion.

At least it wasn't attacking her; that was a plus. Not yet anyway . . .

'What about these sigils?!' Juniper urged, holding her glowing arms up.

'*Sigils?*' The creature looked her up and down. 'Is that what they are? Didn't you have them before? How dull. Your arms look utterly majestic now. A touch of brilliance amid an otherwise bland exterior. You should be thanking me.'

'You have to get rid of them! I can't go around looking like this. People'll think . . . Well, I dunno what they'll think. But it won't be good!'

'Oh, I can't do that,' the creature said smoothly.

'What?! Why?!'

'I do believe we've bonded.'

'*Bonded?*' Juniper blinked. Her mind felt like it was wading through sludge, struggling to keep up. 'Look, I'm flattered. I'm sure you're real nice an' all, but I think it's *waaaay* too early to tell if we're buddies yet, and –'

'Gah, no, not *friends*!' The creature gave her a disgusted look. 'Urgh. Heavens. A being from the Other Side needs to tether itself to the world it's visiting – find an anchor, if you will.' It spoke slowly, as though explaining itself to a little child. '*You* are that anchor, strange little girl. Without you, I will be dragged back to the Other Side.'

'So . . . you're from the Other Side, then?'

Just like the Shades.

The creature blinked, as if it had just realized the fact itself. 'Oh! Why, yes . . . I suppose I am!'

Juniper swallowed. This was bad. This was really, *really* bad. *Still* didn't mean Elodie was right, though.

'Look, I don't care – just get rid of the sigils!' Juniper insisted. 'You know how much trouble I'll be in if someone sees me like this?!'

The creature sniffed. 'I fail to see how any of that's my concern. After all that time trapped in that diabolical mirror, I quite fancy stretching my legs.' Its tongue flickered out of its snout like a snake. 'I do believe I've been to this plane before. I recognize its flavour, and, as I recall, I rather liked it here . . .'

Juniper did *not* like the hunger in its voice.

'Is that what the mirror is? A doorway to the Other Side?'

The creature winced. 'No, I think not.' It clenched its fangs as if struggling to think. 'It was an accursed place I've been trapped within for . . . for . . . How long has it been?' It screwed up its eyes and started banging its head with its small fists, shadow-stuff swirling with each strike. 'Think! Think! Why can't I remember anything?' Its eyes shot open, focusing on Juniper, who recoiled at the burning ferocity she saw there. 'Was it *you*, foul trickster? Was it you who put me in there?'

'Me?! I didn't do anything to you! And, anyway, if I had put you there, why would I release you now?'

The thing narrowed its eyes, considering her carefully. 'Hmm, yes. Perhaps I am giving you too much credit. My broken memories must've been caused by all that time spent in such a cramped little place. Such an ordeal can fragment a mind. But you just wait – my memories *will* return, and I *will* get to the bottom of this! Boden and I both will, you . . .' The creature's eyes suddenly widened. 'Wait!' It pulled at its long ears, concentrating, then pointed a claw at Juniper. 'Who is Boden? I demand you tell me!'

Juniper pulled a face. 'No idea! You're the one who said it!'

'Urgh, useless! But I do remember him.' The creature frowned. 'And I remember something else too: a group of people. My *enemies*. They stood in a circle, chanting . . . casting their pathetic little spells in an attempt to defeat me, as futile as such a thing may be.'

'The Arcanists?' Juniper offered.

It had to be them. The Arcanists were the only people who could wield magic. It was their job to defend the world against the dangers that leaked through the Veil, and if they had trapped this thing in the mirror, that meant it was an enemy of Arkspire aka Very Bad News.

'Why would they trap you?' Juniper asked, her throat tight.

'Wouldn't you like to know?' the creature retorted, then thought on that. 'I'd quite like to know myself, truth be told.'

'I reckon they imprisoned you,' Juniper said, frowning, 'because you did something bad. Because you're dangerous.'

'*Imprisoned?* Like some common criminal?!' The creature tutted, disgusted at the very suggestion.

'Well? Were you? *Are* you?' Juniper pushed.

'Quite possibly, to be honest. My incomprehensibly fabulous mind feels a bit like soup at the moment. Ah! Soup! I recall that, at least!'

Juniper nodded. 'I mean, soup is pretty important, to be fair.'

There was a sudden noise outside the cupboard. The creaking of a floorboard. Juniper froze. Had Papa come back?

'Anyway, I –' the thing began.

'Wait – shhh!' Juniper hissed.

The creature raised a brow. 'Don't shush me!'

Juniper tried to grab its snout to keep it quiet, but it was like trying to grab water – you could feel it there, but it fell through your hands before you could do anything with it. The shadow-stuff the creature was made of wisped faintly round her grasping hands.

'How *dare* you!' it growled, just as the cupboard doors were pulled open.

'Hello!' Thea said, looking as though finding Juniper wrestling with an other-worldly creature inside a cupboard was exactly what she'd expected to see. 'Quite the exciting night, isn't it?'

'Oh, good, more of you,' said the creature. 'It's not like this was already confusing with just the two of us, is it?'

Juniper gasped. 'Thea – thank The Visitor! Have you seen Papa and Madame Adie?'

'Oh, they're on the roof, looking for you. Grangran sent me to see what all the hubbub was about. You know what she says: *get no sleep and miss the worm.*' Thea considered the devastation around them. 'I don't suppose you know what happened down here, do you? I'm guessing you might have a clue, seeing how your eyes are glowing and all.'

'They're *what*?!' Juniper leaped out of the cupboard and checked her reflection in the dark shop windows. As might've been expected when a huge magical beam had burst out of the building, the spectacle had attracted some attention. A crowd had gathered outside the apothecary, people trying to peek through the windows while others rattled at the locked door, searching for answers. But more disturbing was what Juniper saw in her reflection: her eyes were glowing bright blue, just like the sigils on her arms. She dropped low and out of sight, dragging her hands down her cheeks in exasperation.

'Don't get me wrong – I'm very jealous,' Thea said, ogling them.

'Don't tell me that's something your eyes don't normally do either?' the creature said. 'Honestly, what a bland creature you must've been before I arrived.'

'Hello there,' Thea said politely to the creature. 'What's your name?'

'Ah, at last! Someone with the manners to ask!'

'Oh, I'm sorry, how terribly rude of me!' Juniper said sarcastically. 'I clearly got a little hung up on the fact you're currently *ruining my life!*'

'Apology accepted. As for you, strange child, my name is . . . well, you know, it's . . . probably something very impressive and mighty . . . likely to provoke awe and fear in equal measure . . .'

'You don't even remember your name?!' Juniper said.

'Who needs a name when they're as unforgettable as me?'

'Well, I'm happy to give you one if you'd like?' Thea offered.

'I'd rather you called me "Lord" or "Master" or "Highness".' The creature sniffed. 'But if naming me will still your tongue, please, by all means.'

Thea pondered for a moment, looking at the creature and the devastation it had wrought. She suddenly raised a hand, slashing it in its direction like a sword. 'I hereby dub thee "Cinder", for you have surely ignited our evening with adventure. And a little fire.'

'I hate it,' the creature said. 'But there's little you humans do that pleases me.'

'Cinder it is!' Thea clapped happily, then offered her hand. 'It's nice to meet you, Cinder!'

Cinder gazed at her hand dubiously.

'He came from inside the mirror shard,' Juniper explained. 'I saw a door in the reflection that wasn't really there, but actually it was, and I . . . well, I kinda opened it. This thing bampfed into the room in a blast of light and did all *this*!' Juniper pointed frantically at the sigils around the room and on her arms.

'Classic,' Thea said. 'Also, do you know that you blew a hole through the roof?'

'I didn't do anything! *You're* the one who did this!' Juniper accused Cinder. 'You have to put it right!'

'I have bigger matters to attend to,' Cinder said loftily, 'things that your puny mind couldn't comprehend.'

'Like *what*?!' Juniper sputtered.

'Why, revenge, of course. Against the people who did this to me.' Cinder's eyes gleamed with gleeful malice. 'Your Arcanists deprived this world of my perfection for too long. For such a crime, they must be obliterated.'

Juniper's jaw dropped. He wanted to go after the *Arcanists*?

She took a deep breath, trying to compose herself. She could deal with that bit of nonsense later. 'I'm sure you've got very big plans. But –' Juniper gestured at the shop, then at her sigils and eyes – 'you can't just leave me like this. If the wardens come, we'll all be in deep trouble!'

'"We"?' Oh, there's no "we",' Cinder sneered. 'Apart from your body serving as my anchor to this world, I'm afraid you're nothing to me. Less than really. Now, if you'll excuse me, I'm off to serve some well-deserved revenge.' He bowed before trotting towards the front door. 'Farewell, strange, ugly creatures.'

'No, not out there!' Juniper cried, leaping after him. But before she could stop him, Cinder's shape changed. He . . . *flattened*.

At first Juniper thought her eyes were playing tricks on her, until she saw him slide under the gap at the bottom of the door as though he were no thicker than paper. He'd become a literal shadow. With no time to be amazed, her pulse pounding in her skull, Juniper fought to unlock the door. She swung it wide, the people gathered outside jumping back in surprise. She looked about the busy street, hoping to catch the creature before too many people saw him. But what she saw was even worse than she'd imagined.

She was standing face to face with a group of five wardens, large and broad-shouldered, rifles in their hands, staring down at her with emotionless goggles.

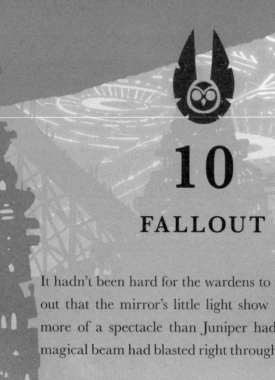

10

FALLOUT

It hadn't been hard for the wardens to find her. Turns out that the mirror's little light show had been even more of a spectacle than Juniper had thought. The magical beam had blasted right through the roof of the

apothecary as well as the Uppers high above, before exploding in the night sky. There, a storm of crackling blue energy illuminated the entire city, and sigils the size of marketplaces were scrawled across the black sky, washing the city in a strange other-worldly light.

Juniper tried to swallow the lump building up in her throat, but it wasn't easy. Crowds of people gazed at the sky-sigils, whispering in frightened voices. The whole neighbourhood reeked of a lightning storm, even though there wasn't a cloud to be seen.

As for Adie's Apothecary itself, the glowing sigils that had leaked out of the mirror had crept into the streets beyond, etching themselves into the muddy ground, over pipes, up neighbouring walls. Juniper's location had basically become a glowing target. She'd been hard to miss, all things considered.

The wardens marched Juniper through the murmuring crowd towards a Requisitions wagon, Thea at her side. Juniper tried to shift the heavy metal cuffs biting into her wrists into a more comfortable position, but it was no use. The fact that she was still dressed in her pyjamas didn't help her feeling that things were not exactly going her way.

'*This is an Order warning,*' crackled the street phonographs. '*All citizens must clear the area. Unauthorized magic has been detected. This area is unsafe and potentially life-threatening. For your own safety, clear the area!*'

Many Dreggers left in a panic, but a lot more remained, stepping away from the girls yet still eager to see who had caused such chaos in their district.

'The Betrayers are back!' some gasped. 'They've infiltrated our walls!'

'Right in our neighbourhood, no less. Always thought she was a bad 'un . . .'

'Traitorous scum,' one particularly nasty man spat.

Juniper flinched. Their words hurt, their spiteful gazes and snarling faces even more so. Some eyed the sigils on Juniper's arms, thankfully no longer glowing. They'd turned a darker shade than her skin colour, almost as though they were strange burn marks or tattoos. She saw some people noticing these markings, so similar to those of the Arcanists themselves, and she couldn't help but cringe.

Then some of the crowd did something entirely unexpected.

They bowed.

Not just a dip of the head or a doff of the hat. They fully went down on one knee and bowed.

'The Visitor is great! The Visitor is good!' some were whispering in awe.

'The Visitor's sent the Dregs a new Arcanist to stand for us all!'

'She'll raise us from this place; she'll make things safe for us again!'

The wardens quickly pulled Juniper's sleeves down, and she tucked her hands under her armpits to hide the rest. She didn't know what to make of it.

Was she a Betrayer? Or an Arcanist? All she'd done was open a door . . .

'Juni!' yelled a voice.

She spun round, catching sight of Papa and Madame Adie lurching through the crowd. The terror in Papa's eyes hurt Juniper more than the handcuffs wringing her wrist bones.

'Don't worry, Papa!' she shouted as she was bundled

into the back of a clockwork wagon, trying to sound confident. 'I'll sort it out! It's all under control!'

'Stop! That's my daughter!' he cried, fighting against the wardens who were forcing him back. Then Thea was thrown in after her, and the wagon doors were slammed shut, leaving the girls in darkness.

'It's all under control . . .' Juniper repeated quietly.

The wagon's engine rumbled, the vehicle trundling away from the noise of the crowds, away from Papa, away from home. The girls squinted at each other through the gloom, unable to believe what was happening.

'Well, what a pickle,' Thea said calmly.

'It's OK! It's OK!' Juniper blurted, pacing from one side of the wagon to the other. The light from the sky-sigils leaked through the wagon's narrow slotted windows, shimmering blue as if the whole city were underwater. 'We'll sort this out; we always do.'

'I just hope they let us talk to family before sending us to jail,' Thea said. 'I need to make sure Grangran won't try to break me out. I've seen her when she's angry, and the wardens just aren't prepared for that kind of carnage.'

'No one's going to jail!' Juniper insisted. 'I've just gotta come up with a plan.' She dropped on to the wooden bench that ran round the wagon's interior, tapping at her head, trying to encourage the plans to rise up like bubbles.

By now the wagon had reached the Skyline, a network of giant cable-car gondolas that transported people, vehicles and cargo between the Dregs and the Uppers. The wagon drove into a gondola large enough to hold it, and, with a clunking shudder, was lifted off the ground towards the upper Iris District.

Juniper rarely went to the Uppers. It wasn't a place for the likes of her. Visits there usually ended with the wardens chasing after the Misfits, deeming them too unsavoury for the rich magisters who lived in its many mansions and swanned about in its fancy establishments. Elodie had fitted right in, of course, what with all her proper manners, pronunciations and high-falutin' Academy buddies. Juniper's stomach lurched at what Elodie would say about all this.

As the gondola rose out of the smog of the Dregs, an incredible view of the city emerged. The five unimaginably large Arcanist towers stood proudly in a circle, connected by vast interweaving bridges. Each tower formed the bones of a district, and looked different from the others, built to represent the Arcanist who lived in its highest levels. The top of The Watcher's Iris Tower, for instance, was made of glass, and hundreds of telescopes poked out of it like a pincushion, scanning the heavens for portents and signs. The Shrouded's Midnight Tower, in comparison, resembled a cathedral spire made of ivory, draped in creeping black flowers and flickering candles, and was topped with a large bell tower. But the one thing the towers had in common was the way they loomed over the city, watching over it like protective guardians. Juniper could almost feel the arcane power washing out of them like a wave.

She bolted forward, raising a finger. 'Wait!'

Thea froze, as still as a statue.

'They must be taking us to the top of the Iris Tower, right?' Juniper said.

'Right!' Thea agreed. 'That is the headquarters of our district, after all.'

'But our district doesn't have an Arcanist! Least not one who actually shows up for work . . .' For once, The Watcher's cowardice might actually help them. 'Arcanists can sense magic, but the magisters can't! Specially those from the Order of Iris – they're all half asleep as it is!' Even Elodie would sometimes complain that she wished they were a bit more . . . *competent*. 'Here, do you have a pen on you?'

'Always,' Thea said, pulling one out of her pyjama pocket.

'Trace over the sigils on my skin!' Juniper urged, exposing her forearms. 'We'll just tell 'em we were messing around playing Arcanists – they won't know these are real! And it's not like there's any evidence left to pin the blame on us either. The shard turned to dust and that weird Cinder creature did a runner.'

Thea gasped. 'We could do *Pass the Buck*! Or *Pointy, Pointy, Finger, Finger*! Oh, or *Escape Goat*!' She could barely contain her excitement. 'We could tell them some petty rival sent Madame Adie a relic in a package, rigged to explode when she opened it –'

'All innocent and unsuspecting!' Juniper added, liking the plan more and more.

'Which would explain the sigils around the shop and

in the . . . well, in the sky. It's just a bit of magic gone wrong! No harm done.'

Thea set to work tracing over Juniper's sigils, the two girls beaming all the while. They'd be OK. They'd talk as fast as they could, bombarding the poor old magisters with information, and they wouldn't know which way was up or down. Madame Adie would definitely back up their story – she had no love for the Order – and the magisters would send them on their way, probably happy to see the back of them.

'Juni . . . can I ask you something?' said Thea, now inking over the symbols on Juniper's left hand. 'What *was* Cinder?'

'I have no idea,' Juniper admitted. 'Something horrible from the Other Side, I think. Like a Shade, but *way* more annoying.'

Thea nodded thoughtfully. 'Dangerous, then. I liked his ears, though.'

'They were very pointy,' Juniper agreed. Her belly tightened. She couldn't get

his threat of revenge out of her head. What had she unleashed upon the world? Upon the Arcanists? Some evil ally of the Betrayers imprisoned for terrible crimes against humanity? Guilt wriggled in her insides, but she tried to smother it. What was the worst that could happen? The Arcanists were like living demi-gods. They'd trapped Cinder before, so they could do it again. He'd be like an insect to them, ready for the smooshing.

Cinder wasn't her problem. Not any more at least.

Apart from a few smudges caused by the moving wagon, Thea had done an amazing job tracing over the sigils on Juniper's arms. They now looked like they were just part of some kid's game. Juniper grinned widely, feeling more confident than ever they could get out of this.

Just then the wagon juddered to a stop. The back doors were flung open, the light of the sky-sigils and streetlamps pouring into the small space.

'Out,' a warden said, motioning with his rifle.

'Since you asked so nicely,' Juniper replied, stepping off the back of the wagon. She looked up at the building that loomed high above her – and her stomach dropped like a stone.

They weren't at the Iris Tower. Instead of that gleaming palace, the girls were faced with a different imposing building, an ancient circular theatre as old as the city itself with grand stone walls and a large domed roof. The front courtyard was heaving: fancy clockwork carriages clustered together in a fight for parking spaces; armed wardens guarded the flustered-looking magisters who stepped out of them, red-eyed and ruffle-haired, groaning about the hour. Their colours showed them to be magisters from all five Orders, not just the Order of Iris. And presiding over it all were five ginormous statues, each one faceless, representing the ever-changing bodies of the Arcanists.

Juniper felt as though she'd slipped into a pool of ice-cold water. This was the Crux, where the biggest, most important matters of the city were discussed. She gulped. 'Why – why are we here?'

The warden laughed. 'You think what you've done warrants a little slap on the wrist from some magisters? Nah. This is bigger than that.' He pointed up at the sky-sigils, still crackling like some mad lightning storm. Then he leaned in, real close to Juniper, the shimmering blue light reflecting off his goggles. 'The Arcanists wanna judge you for themselves, face to face.'

11

CRUX OF THE MATTER

The *Arcanists*? Surely the magic in the sky wasn't that serious? But, judging from the number of bigwigs, it really was. No way was Juniper's plan going to work now! The Arcanists would see right through it – they'd *sense* the magic in Juniper's sigils. Juniper felt sweat beading on her back even as a chill ran down her spine. She had to think of something else, *fast*. But her thoughts were galloping too quick to grasp.

'Keep moving,' the Warden Captain ordered, encouraging the girls with his rifle.

They were led up the large staircase towards the entrance. If the city of Arkspire was shaped like a wagon wheel, then the Crux was the hub at its centre. Every district had bridges leading to this central tower. It was said to be built above the very crater The Visitor had created when it had first crossed through the Veil to bless the Arcanists with its power. It was a sacred, neutral place, which none of the Arcanists ruled, but where they met to talk city stuff and make all the big decisions. Decisions like what to do with an insolent little relic hunter like Juniper.

As the girls reached the top of the stairs, they found someone waiting for them in the large doorway.

'Juni!' said Elodie. She'd clearly just leaped out of bed; her face was puffy, her hair a mess, her clothes scruffy, but her big eyes were alive with alarm. The wardens gave Elodie a curt bow as she approached but didn't allow her to get too close to Juniper and Thea. 'I was hoping I'd catch you out here,' Elodie said, following them inside. 'All the Orders have been gathered; everyone's waiting for your trial inside!'

'*Trial?*' Juniper grimaced. They really weren't messing around.

Thea smiled, jingling her handcuffs. '*Judgement comes for us all*, as Grangran always says.'

Juniper couldn't deny she was relieved to see her sister. Elodie knew what made the Orders tick, and they could sure use that know-how right about now. Plus, she seemed to agree with Juniper that now wasn't the time to pull out the ol' 'I told you so's.

Almost immediately Elodie's worried expression

disappeared, replaced with outrage. 'Juni, what did you
do?! I told you that messing with relics was dangerous!
I told you it would end up getting us all in trouble!'

OK, maybe not. Juniper wondered if she should start
a mental tally of how many times Elodie would say 'I
told you'.

'It wasn't my fault!' she said.

'It wasn't –' Elodie broke off as she saw the pen marks
all over Juniper's arm. 'Wait, what's that?'

'Nothing!' Juniper said, hiding her arms behind her
back.

'You're *trying to pull a trick*, even at a time like this?!'

Especially at a time like this, Juniper thought.

'You have to tell the truth, Juniper!' Elodie said, as the wardens led them down elegant corridors busy with magisters, each of them eyeing the prisoners with open distaste. 'The Arcanists themselves will judge your crime. This is serious! Really, really serious!'

'Well, I think they've been very kind so far, inviting us to this lovely building at such short notice,' Thea said, looking about in wonder.

'I'm here to help you, but you have to tell me what happened,' Elodie insisted, ignoring Thea.

'I don't know what happened, El.' Which was partly the truth, she supposed. 'It was some relic in Adie's place. Just a tiny piece of mirror – it didn't even look magical! Can't you do anything to get us out of this? Pull out some sneaky Candidate privilege or something?'

'I'll try to vouch for you,' Elodie said, still looking at Juniper with disappointment, 'but the rest is up to you. The Arcanists are wise and kind, and will see that you meant no harm. They're the only ones who can get to the bottom of this, whatever –' she gestured at one of the large windows that lined the corridor and the flickering lightshow in the sky beyond – 'whatever *this* is.' It sounded like Elodie was trying to convince herself more than anyone else. 'Just . . . just let me do the talking. Unless they talk to you, of course, then *definitely* answer, but only about what they've asked you. Don't talk about anything else. Or for too long. And please, *please* don't lie – the Arcanists will see right through you. Do you understand?'

'But I –'

'Just don't, OK?' Elodie held Juniper's gaze, trying to hammer home the point. 'And whatever you do, do *not* tell them about the brown thing you found in the back alley that one time . . .'

'But people love that story!' Juniper said.

'Quite the adventure,' Thea agreed.

'Absolutely not!' Elodie insisted. 'And don't stare! But make sure you look at them when you speak, to show respect. You must bow when they address you, but don't grovel, and –'

'Elodie, I get it!' Juniper snapped. 'Follow your lead an' be about as interesting as a stone. I reckon I can just about manage that.'

Elodie sniffed. 'I'm just trying to help.'

Juniper screwed up her eyes. She could have sworn that Elodie was getting a kick out of this. In places like this Juniper was a fish out of water. For once, Elodie got to be leader of the pack. Then again, maybe she was imagining it. Juniper's nerves were on edge. Her heart was keeping pace with the quick steps they were being forced to take down the corridor. She took a deep breath, trying to calm herself.

Maybe Elodie was right. She was always going on about how just the Arcanists were. What was the worst that could happen? The Shrouded had been so kind when she'd saved Elodie and Mama years before. She'd see this wasn't Juniper's fault. Juniper would get a little telling-off, then be sent on her way.

At worst a brief spell in a jail cell.

Or a few weeks in a prison.

Months.

Years.

Visitor beyond, they're going to execute me, aren't they?!

'OK, here we go,' Elodie said, as they arrived at the doors to the main hall, brushing Juniper's messy hair and trying to straighten her ragged pyjamas. 'And perhaps try just a little bit to not look like you've crawled out of a hole in the ground.'

'But, Elodie,' Juniper said, managing a smirk, 'we *have*.'

Elodie sighed, already sensing how well this meeting was going to go. 'Just promise me you'll try not to mess this up. You know you go too far.'

Juniper wanted to object, but, considering she was being escorted to face judgement from the all-powerful rulers of Arkspire for releasing a vengeance-obsessed magical creature upon an unsuspecting city, she couldn't deny she might've gone a *tad* too far this time.

12

THE ARCANISTS

The doors to the main hall rumbled open, and the two wardens standing on either side of it banged their ceremonial spears on the ground. Nerves tugged at Juniper's insides as she entered the vast hall beyond, the dancing blue light from the sky-sigils shining through a large glass-domed roof above.

In fact, jangling nerves barely covered it. Juniper felt like she was seconds away from throwing up.

Magisters had already filled the stepped seats that encircled the hall. Each Order had its own section, marked by large banners displaying their Order's emblem. The young Candidates to each Arcanist were present too, all straight backs and wide eyes. Wardens stood guard at every exit.

Elodie gave Juniper's arm a squeeze. 'Good luck,'

she whispered, before rushing off to join her fellow Candidates in the Order of Iris section.

Juniper was separated from Thea and ushered to a stand in the middle of the vast circular hall. The warden who'd arrested her pulled up her sleeves, revealing the pen-covered sigils running along her arms. Gasps came from the magisters, followed by looks of fear and disgust (and the odd bit of mockery).

So many people. The high and mighty of Arkspire were all looking at her. Juniper felt as though her heart had somehow climbed into her mouth, and she wasn't a fan, not one bit.

'I'm right behind you, Juni,' Thea called. 'Literally!'

Juniper managed a smile in reply. She was struggling to resist the instinct to leg it the absolute heck out of there. She hated not having escape routes.

The crowd suddenly fell still as if by some silent command. It was as if the entire hall was holding its breath, waiting for whatever was to come next. Juniper feared they'd be able to hear the pounding of her heart.

There was a sudden flash of blinding light and a thunderclap that shook the building. There, up on an ornate balcony above the Order of Radiance's section, a young, handsome man had appeared, and was gazing down at her. He wore a suit that seemed normal enough, if incredibly swish and expensive, but it was the strange umbrella he held that set him apart. It looked like a jellyfish, its tassels swaying as if underwater. It glowed brightly with magical light, the brightness dimming now but still hard to look at.

Juniper had no idea why you'd need an umbrella indoors, but just as she thought it, she swore she could smell rain, and a damp breeze rustled through her hair. Orbs of light floated lazily about the young man's head, their luminous tentacles drifting in an invisible current. They merged together behind him, forming the jellyfish emblem of his Order in pure white light. He was The Tempest, Arcanist leader of the Order of Radiance.

Then came movement on the next balcony along. A doorway that hadn't been there before opened in the wall, revealing a forest that simply should not have existed. Afternoon sunlight shone on a lush canopy and over the snow-capped mountains in the distance. A red-hooded figure whisked through the entrance, as nimble as a dancer, leaves swirling around him as if part of the dance. His face was hidden by a white mask, plain except for a few arcane symbols etched in red round the edges. Keys hung from bracelets, belts and necklaces all about his person. The Enigma, leader of the Order of Gateways and the Gateway District.

Something scuttled over the balcony as the Arcanist took his seat, something large and reptilian. Juniper blinked, only to find the creature gone and replaced with a red sculpture of a chameleon, the emblem and colour of his Order.

The next section, claimed by the green banners of the Order of Invention, had no balcony. Instead, there was a large bronze sphere at the top of the magisters' seating area. It had been making an ominous ticking sound since Juniper had arrived, but now that ticking become a frantic whirr. Steam jetted out of the machinery's seams, latches unlocked, and the sphere opened. Within were more metallic compartments, unfurling one after the other like the petals of a flower. With the sound of chugging pistons and clunking cogs, a platform rose out of the device, a metal balcony, upon which sat a man.

To call him big was doing the guy a disservice. He was *huge*, as big as a ruddy storm. His seat, massive for any normal person, could barely be seen beneath his bulk; it was all hidden behind the enormous coat he wore. Even now, he was busy tinkering away with something, a large wide-brimmed hat hiding his face. It didn't take any stretch of the imagination to guess this was The Maker. The spider emblem of his Order was wrought out of iron and topped the giant's throne.

The fourth Arcanist was one Juniper knew well, or didn't, as the case may be. Purple ether-light illuminated a balcony that was far more modest than the rest. It had no decoration to speak of, except for the large emblem of an owl set into the back wall. The throne sat empty, its magisters and Candidates, Elodie one of them, looking almost embarrassed to be there instead. It was the seat of The Watcher, leader of the Order of Iris.

No-show yet again, Juniper thought. *Well, least that's one less person who can find me guilty.*

Finally the air in the hall began to grow heavy, and the shadows of fluttering moths appeared on the floor, though the moths themselves were nowhere to be seen. A shiver ran down Juniper's spine.

All the shadows within the hall, those of the seats and banners and all the people inside, started to shift and move. They left their owners, merging together on the floor like a giant snake made of darkness, slithering towards the final balcony. There they pooled into a pitch-black mass, from which, like a ghost, The Shrouded rose, her arms crossed in front of her chest, her face hidden behind a black mourning veil. The pool of shadow rose with her, transforming into a hundred moths. They landed on the wall behind her, forming the shape of the Order of Midnight's moth emblem. Juniper saw that the other shadows were back where they belonged, as if they'd never been anywhere else.

Juniper's heart was pounding in her ears so loud she felt dizzy, like the whole Crux was spinning around her.

Be cool, she told herself. *Nothing says innocent like keeping it cool!*

But these were the Arcanists of Arkspire. They were the Inheritors of a great power, from those who'd stayed true to The Visitor's trust, who'd used their powers to save the world from the Betrayers. Juniper gazed up at the legends she'd been told tales of since she was a baby. The *actual* Arcanists. The actual, flippin' Arcanists themselves.

And there was Juniper, standing before them in her pyjamas.

Juniper heard Elodie clear her throat. Juniper realized she was staring. Startled, she averted her eyes and managed to pick her jaw up from the floor. Everything had seemed so dreamlike up to this moment, but now it hit her at last how serious the situation really was. Under the Arcanists' gaze, she'd never felt smaller, or more insignificant. She could almost feel their power pushing down on her.

'This meeting of the Crux Council is now in session,' a magister announced.

'*Quite* the night we're having,' The Enigma crooned; his voice was as smooth as a quick-talking street hustler.

'Distracting is what it is,' The Maker grumbled, his voice deep and echoey, like he was speaking from within a metal drum.

'Juniper Bell,' The Shrouded said.

'That's me!' Juniper blurted. She still caught Elodie giving her a steely glance. 'Uh, that's me, m'lord,' Juniper said, correcting herself.

'*Worship*,' Elodie mouthed. '*Your Worship!*'

'Your Lord Worship, My Worship,' Juniper spluttered.

A murmur rose from the audience. The Arcanists considered her curiously. Clearly she wasn't quite the sinister renegade they'd been expecting.

The Shrouded nodded, as if she understood Juniper's nerves. 'The crimes you've been accused of are serious,' she said in a way that suggested she wished it wasn't so. 'Using forbidden magic . . . putting the entire city in danger.'

'We're lucky no one was hurt,' The Tempest added.

'Lucky as a horseshoe,' The Enigma agreed. 'You wouldn't mind tellin' us how it is you've managed to put on such a spectacular show now, would you, Ms Bell?'

'I . . . uh . . .' Juniper's voice died in her throat.

Elodie caught her eye and widened her own, saying all she needed to with her glare.

A soothing breeze radiating from The Tempest worried at Juniper's hair, carrying with it the scent of rain. She had a sudden urge to tell the truth, to reveal all. She was about to start spilling when something distracted her. Her shadow, it was *moving*. A piece of it tore away, slinking down the hall, apparently unnoticed by anyone but her.

She frowned. Was it The Shrouded's doing? But she didn't look as though she was controlling anything, sitting on her throne with her hands placed over her lap.

'I – I –' Juniper stuttered, watching in disbelief as the piece of her shadow rose up the wall towards The Shrouded's balcony.

'If there was a relic, you must tell us, so that we can undo its evil,' The Tempest urged not unkindly.

The shadow slithered on to the balcony and behind The Shrouded. It changed shape, growing two pointy ears and a long swishy tail.

Ice suddenly clutched at Juniper's heart. It was Cinder. The little creep had used her to sneak into the Crux, hitching a ride on her shadow!

Cinder's bright eyes flared at the sight of the Arcanists. He bared his fangs and flexed his claws.

Visitor beyond, what's he up to?

'You must understand, Ms Bell, that we're doing this for your own safety,' The Tempest continued, interpreting her silence as fear. 'The Betrayers corrupted everything they touched. Anything they once owned is tainted with their evil.'

But Juniper could barely hear him. Sparks had begun to ignite between Cinder's claws.

He was charging up a spell – and he was going to attack The Shrouded.

13

JUDGEMENT

'Stop!' Juniper yelled.

The hall gasped in shock. Even The Maker looked up from his gadget.

Cinder's sparks fizzled away to nothing, but, judging from his frustration and the way he was looking at his claws as if they'd suddenly given up on him, Juniper guessed it wasn't because of her words.

The Tempest blinked, confused by her outburst.

'I – I mean, DON'T stop spreading the word about how bad the Betrayers were,' said Juniper, chuckling nervously. 'It's important we never forget!'

Juniper could see Cinder trying again, but once more the sparks evaporated before they could do any damage. He flung his head back in a rage. The Shrouded turned round, sensing something behind her, but Cinder dissolved into a shadow just as quickly. It's not like there weren't enough shadows to hide in up there.

'I – I think Ms Bell has been ruffled by your glorious presence, Your Worships,' Elodie said, stepping forward and bowing so low her hair brushed the floor. 'If you'd allow, I would like to vouch for my sister.'

A murmur washed throughout the crowd. Elodie was taking a huge risk by admitting she was related to Juniper. Juniper would've been thankful were she not entirely distracted by Cinder, who was now slithering back across the hall towards her.

'If it'll help make sense of this, be our guest,' The Enigma said, flinging his legs over the arms of his throne and lounging like a cat.

'What my sister did was wrong,' Elodie began, 'but she would never choose to hurt others. She might sometimes make bad decisions, but I know she would never have messed with a relic if she'd known its true power.'

Cinder reached Juniper, merging with the shadows behind her.

'What. Are. You. *Doing*?!' Juniper hissed, moving her lips as little as possible.

'Trying to exact my revenge – what else?' Cinder whispered back.

'Well, stop it!'

'Seems that I have no choice in the matter. My inconceivable powers appear to have abandoned me.' He said it like it was the greatest tragedy to ever befall the world. 'I blame you.'

'*Me?*'

'You must've done something wrong – said the wrong word during the incantation when you summoned me or some other amateur mistake.'

'But I didn't say any incantation!'

'Well, there you go. Useless. You are the *worst* person I could've bonded with.'

'Then do us *both* a favour and unbond with me, you jerk!'

'*Gladly*, if only it were that easy. To sever a bond and tear a gateway between realms requires incredibly powerful magic. As much as it pains me to admit, I clearly am not at my full potential at the moment. Just as well, as I don't intend to go anywhere without getting my revenge.'

Juniper clenched her teeth. She turned her attention to Elodie, who was still going on about how many mistakes Juniper had made but how they were all out of ignorance – in other words, how stupid she was.

'Do you understand the damage your sister might've caused?' The Shrouded suddenly snapped. Her tone startled Juniper. It lacked any of the warmth or kindness it had had before. 'This is not some childish mistake, this is an attack on Arkspire! This kind of action cannot go unpunished – people look to us to keep them safe, and we must be seen to act!'

The Shrouded's magisters roared in agreement.

'My – my sister's choices may be questionable,' Elodie said, her voice barely louder than a squeak, 'but she makes them out of desperation, like many of those in the lower levels . . .'

'So you admit that your sister is a relic smuggler?' The Shrouded asked.

'No!' Juniper cried, just as Elodie said, 'Yes.'

The rumblings in the audience grew louder, magisters shouting their suspicions, their disbelief.

Elodie shot Juniper a warning glance, but Juniper steeled her resolve. She could tell the Arcanists weren't going to let her off the hook. They would make an example of her to teach any other would-be relic hunters a lesson. If she told the truth, she'd be spending the rest of her life in a jail cell, and the chances were that Elodie would be kicked out of the Academy too, leaving the Bell family with nothing. Elodie might not know this, but Juniper did.

As Elodie began making more excuses to the Arcanists, Juniper remembered what some of the Dreggers had said when they'd seen the sigils on her

arms, and it gave her an idea. It was a long shot, probably even stupid to try, but if it worked it might just save her.

'Can you do *any* magic?' Juniper whispered to Cinder.

'Well, I was able to snuff the protective sigils we passed in this building,' Cinder said. 'They would've fried us both otherwise if they'd detected me. You're welcome, by the way. But what good is that for revenge?'

'What about those?' Juniper ignored his comment about revenge, and bobbed her head up to the giant sigils still lighting up the sky beyond the glass dome.

'Why would I do something to them? They're declaring my glorious return to this world.'

'Because if you don't I go to prison, and you'll be left all alone!'

'Somehow I think I'll manage . . .'

'Yeah, yeah. Look, just follow my lead!'

She had to go for broke. All or nothing. The Dregs had taught her the best way to survive was to always act like you had the upper hand, even if the odds were stacked against you.

Pulling her shoulders back, she looked The Shrouded in the eye. Or the veil at least.

'There was no relic, Your Worships,' she declared, interrupting Elodie's attempts at saving her. The crowd quietened to hear her excuses. 'One thing you learn quick in the Dregs is to stay away from such trouble, 'less you want the wardens knockin' on your door. An', trust me, if you live in the Dregs, you *never* want the wardens knockin' at your door. No, what caused all this,' Juniper said, holding her sigil-inscribed arms up to the crackling sky, 'was The Visitor itself. It came to me in a dream, all spooky-like and big-voiced, an' said that the world was in a right state. Said you Arcanists had your hands full, what with the Betrayers' curse, and so it was gonna bless me with a sliver of its power to give you a helping hand. The reason the sky's flipping out –' Juniper took in a deep breath and steeled herself – 'is because I'm an Arcanist. An' I'm here to do whatever I can to help put things right.'

The breeze radiating from The Tempest stilled. The Maker stopped fidgeting with his device. The Enigma sat up straight. The shadows around The Shrouded shrank, as though they too couldn't believe what Juniper had just said.

The Arcanists stared at her, astounded.

Elodie let out a pained groan.

Juniper had been going for the shock factor, hoping to put the Arcanists on the wrong foot. It had been a gamble, but, judging from their reactions, it had worked.

'Heresy!' a magister screamed.

'Lies! Filthy lies!'

'How dare you!'

The Maker held up a hand, and silence fell again.

'This is an extraordinary claim indeed. Only we five have the blessings of The Visitor's gifts,' he said. 'The Betrayers proved that most people cannot be trusted with such power.'

'P-please forgive her,' Elodie began. 'She doesn't mean it, Your Worships –'

'I absolutely do mean it!' Juniper interrupted.

The Enigma leaned forward, examining Juniper closely. 'I sense *somethin'* of the Other Side about you, girl,' he said. He swished back the waist-long cloak he wore, revealing the sigils that ran along his hands and arms, just like hers. 'Though you may share our sigils, I worry yours look an awful lot like they've been drawn on.'

Juniper jumped, as The Enigma was suddenly standing behind her. She could feel Cinder pressing against the shadows at her back, doing his best to hide.

'You *might* be blessed by The Visitor – emphasis on the "might",' The Enigma said, leaning down closer to inspect Juniper, his mask hiding his expression, 'but that blessing's as frail as a lamb. Barely a trace.'

'Who're we to question The Visitor?' Juniper said, goosebumps rising at his closeness, only to find The Enigma was no longer next to her.

'Right you are. Full of mysteries, that one,' he said from back on his balcony, raising a hand to his chin, still considering her.

'If you truly are a new Arcanist blessed by The Visitor,' The Tempest said, his voice kind but inquisitive, 'perhaps you could show us some of your power? That'd settle this momentous matter, and just in time for breakfast.'

'Course I can,' Juniper said with a confidence she in no way felt. But she'd started down this road, and there was no backing up now.

Elodie looked at her like she'd gone mad.

'It's now or never,' Juniper whispered to Cinder, hoping he'd play ball. She stepped forward and raised her arms in the most flamboyant way possible. 'Prepare, Your Great Worships –' she paused for dramatic effect – 'to be amazed.'

The Arcanists leaned forward ever so slightly, eager – or was it nervous? – to see what she could do. She threw her hands up into the air towards the sky-sigils.

And nothing happened.

Juniper threw them up again, but still there was nothing.

'*Cinder, help me or we're finished!*' she said, pretending to cough. She raised her hands again and again, but by this point it just looked like she was doing some kind of desperate dance.

The silence in the hall was almost oppressive. Then, to Juniper's astonishment, the Arcanists began to laugh. It was slow at first, but it grew and grew into uncontrollable belly laughs. The Enigma was doubled over, The Maker let out short barks like the grinding of metal, The Tempest chuckled into his hand. The only one who wasn't amused was The Shrouded, who sat upright and tense, as though at any moment she might demand the wardens take Juniper to prison for the crime of wasting their time.

But worst of all was Elodie. She looked mortified. Her fellow Candidates practically rolled with laughter, nudging her and pointing at Juniper and her pathetic attempts to pretend to be something other than the lowly gutter rat she was.

The realization hit Juniper like a fist to the jaw. Elodie wasn't just embarrassed. She was *ashamed*.

Juniper could feel her face heating up, her limbs turning to jelly.

She was just a Dregger gutter rat. What possessed her to think she could pull this off? Her breathing became heavy, her brow twitching as she struggled to think

what else she could do – what else might work.

She clenched her jaw and closed her eyes. 'Please, Cinder,' she whispered. 'If . . . if you help me, I promise I'll help you get your powers back. I'll help you get your revenge.' Talk about making a deal with the devil.

Cinder remained quiet, most likely trying to work out whether or not she'd be capable of coming through for him.

One last-ditch attempt, Juniper thought – and threw her hands up a final time.

Then she felt it. There was a chill under her skin, running up her arms, down her fingers, then tingling at her fingertips, which began to fizz with lightning. Opening her eyes, she saw that the sigils on the backs of her hands were shining bright, burning away the ink that had covered them. A surge of energy pulsed into her back from where Cinder hid, his magic coursing through her and up into the sky above. She could feel his will like a voice in her head, using her to change the world around them. It was amazing. It was terrifying.

The laughter in the hall stopped immediately, especially when the sigils in the sky began to fade, the shimmering light disappearing like a dying candle. With a last crackle of energy, the sky returned to normal, the dark of night once again falling over the city of Arkspire.

Juniper smiled. There was no arguing with that display of magic, no, sir, and there hadn't been a relic in sight.

Tension returned to the hall, though whether it was because the Arcanists were impressed or considered her a threat, Juniper couldn't be sure. The magisters gawped at her. Even the wardens, usually as stoic as statues, had staggered back in shock. There hadn't been a new Arcanist in a thousand years – yet, as far as they were concerned, they'd just witnessed the arrival of one.

This was historical. Monumental. And all a big lie.

Juniper didn't know what Cinder was – or what magic he wielded – but she did know it wasn't a gift from The Visitor. And there was no way in heck she was an Arcanist. But she'd worry about that later.

The Arcanists shared uneasy glances, apparently unsure how to react. Then, to everyone's surprise, a slow clap broke the suspense.

It was The Tempest, sitting back in his chair with a broad smile. 'Impressive. Very impressive.' He turned to the warden guarding Juniper. 'And you say the people of the lower Iris District saw this magic being unleashed?'

The warden snapped to attention. 'They did, Your Worship.'

The Arcanists shared another glance.

'You make a good case, Juniper Bell,' The Enigma said.

'I . . . I do?!'

The Shrouded rose from her chair. 'You can't be *serious* . . .? This is an insult to everything we stand for!'

The Tempest gestured at the clear sky above. 'You can't deny Ms Bell wields the arcane.'

'Hardly,' The Shrouded scoffed. 'She could be a Betrayer fanatic, using tricks and out to cause chaos in our city. We shouldn't believe her lies!'

'Sadly The Visitor is no longer here to tell us one way or the other,' The Enigma said, spinning a key round his finger.

'But there are ways for us to settle such things,' The Tempest suggested. 'A test. Five challenges, one set by each of us. If Ms Bell successfully completes them, she'll prove what she says to be true – that she is favoured by The Visitor and a true new Arcanist.'

The Enigma chuckled. 'Oh, I do love a good game.'

Challenges? Juniper didn't like the sound of that, but she guessed it was better than a trip to prison.

'It's settled, then,' The Tempest announced. 'Complete our challenges, and we shall gladly welcome you as a fellow Arcanist!'

'But fail any of them, and we shall know you are a traitor to Arkspire, using the forbidden powers of the Betrayers,' The Shrouded added, her balcony growing so dark she was barely visible amid the shadows.

Juniper gulped, a sound thankfully hidden as all the magisters stood, signalling the end of her trial. She felt sick. She felt ecstatic.

Thea ran over and gave her a squeeze. Over her shoulder, Juniper spotted Elodie looking back at her. Her face was etched in shock, but there was heavy suspicion there too. She knew that where Juniper was concerned, there was usually more going on than met the eye.

Let her be suspicious. At that moment, Juniper didn't care. She'd got away with it. And all she'd have to do to keep up the ruse? Why, convince the entire city she was an Arcanist.

Piece of cake . . .

Right?

14

ROOM WITH A VIEW

There was a young man in front of Juniper.

He looked friendly. Big smile, curious eyes, the kind of guy you'd tip your cap to on the street. Juniper felt affection for him, as warm as a ray of sunshine. But it felt strange to her – she was so used to feeling cold and untrusting.

Wait. No she wasn't. Was she?

The man looked at her. Opened his mouth to speak . . .

And Juniper's eyes fluttered open, the warmth of the dream as cosy as the bedcovers she was snuggled up in. Had it been a dream? It'd felt so real.

She blinked into the morning sun streaking through the large bedroom window. There, perched on the sill, was Cinder, the shadow-wisps of his body dancing dark against the light. He was gazing outside, but his mind was clearly elsewhere. Almost like he was lost in memories.

Juniper frowned. Surely not. Could it . . . could it have been Cinder's *memories* Juniper had just seen?

The idea of being able to see into his mind wasn't that strange, right? He'd said himself that they'd bonded, and that she was mooring him to this world, whether she liked it or not. What shocked her more was the idea of Cinder having any affection in that black heart of his.

'Can I help you?' Cinder asked, becoming aware of Juniper's eyes on him.

Juniper lifted herself on to her elbows, a sly smile stretching across her face.

'What? You look like a loony lemur.'

'Oh, *noooothing*.' Juniper's smile grew. 'Except for the fact that I know you have very warm, fuzzy feelings for someone.'

Cinder's eyes widened, telling Juniper all she needed to know.

'So *waaaaaaaaaarrrm*, so *fuuuuuuuuzzy*!'

'How did you –' Cinder's shadow-wisps flared. 'Never look into my head again, do you understand?!'

'Hey, I didn't choose to; it just happened. You think I *want* to see inside that messed-up dome of yours?'

'Pah. My inconceivable thoughts would blow your puny mortal mind.'

'Mm-hmm. Sure. Well, at least your memories seem to be coming back.'

'I think I'd rather they stay forgotten if you're going to spy on them, uninvited.'

'I don't understand what you two are talking about,' Thea said, who was already up, and busy rummaging through various lavishly carved wardrobes and drawers. 'But I'm glad you're getting along.'

'Wouldn't go that far,' Juniper said, trying to bounce herself upright. To her joy, it worked. She still couldn't believe the bed actually had springs! She collapsed back down on to the mattress in a starfish pose, grinning from ear to ear. It was comfy as a cloud! She sighed deeply. 'I could get used to this.'

'Me too.' Thea smiled, pulling an old Candidate uniform out from a wardrobe. It was dark grey with shiny brass buttons running down either side of the jacket. 'So many fancy fabrics . . .'

It turned out the Arcanists weren't going to just let the girls waltz straight back home after the trial. They said they needed to watch them, just in case they really were part of some deranged Betrayer cult. But because they – and seemingly quite a few Dreggers – believed there was a chance Juniper really had been blessed by The Visitor, they couldn't exactly stick them in some damp jail cell either. Instead The Tempest had arranged for the girls to stay in a spare dorm room in his own Radiant Academy until they could figure out what to do with them next. Sure, it wasn't exactly rolling out the red carpet, and Juniper was more than aware of all the servants sent to 'check in on them' (aka spy), but, still, she wasn't complaining. Compared to what they had in the Dregs, the room was a palace.

Only thing missing was Papa. The wardens had

assured the girls their families were being kept informed, but Juniper knew how worried Papa would be, and she wished she could reassure him herself.

Outside, the street phonographs whined. '*Good morning, proud citizens of Arkspire! What weather we had last night, ha, ha! Never a dull day in the city of magic. But please, rest assured that our great Arcanist protectors have the situation under control. There is no danger to the public. I repeat: there is no danger to the public. In other news, the Order of Gateways have –*'

'They didn't even mention us!' Thea huffed.

'Probably want to see what we're about before spreading rumours there might be another Arcanist in the city,' Juniper guessed.

'So, if we're going to pull off this *Don't You Know Who I Am?* ruse and pretend you're an Arcanist,' Thea said, swishing the epaulettes on the shoulders of the Candidate jacket, 'can I pretend to be the head warden of your Order, captain of your guard?'

Juniper sat up, grinning. 'Can't think of anyone I'd rather have at my back.'

'Oh, thank you!' Thea clapped her hands together. 'You won't regret it. I may not have a rifle, but I assure you that when we get out of here, I'll find the best stick possible to defend you with.'

If a shadow could look scornful, Cinder was pulling it off with some skill. 'I'm less concerned with your childish game of make-believe than I am with how you intend to come through on our deal,' he said. 'When will we turn our attention to restoring my magic?'

'Don't worry – I got you, Cin,' Juniper said.

Cinder stared at her with those eerie glowing eyes. '*Never* call me that again.'

'Look, if we can convince the Arcanists I'm one of them, I'll be allowed into all sorts of restricted places full of tasty magical knowledge and delicious secrets. You'll *definitely* be able to find out how to get your powers back there. And, whaddya know, we're already halfway there! They already think it's *possible* I might be an Arcanist, so now I've just gotta prove it.'

'Prove that you're magic, even though neither of us are?' Cinder raised a brow. 'All so that I can *actually* get my magic back? My, what a foolproof plan you have there. You do know the Arcanists are going to set you five challenges deliberately designed to be impossible to complete unless you're truly an Arcanist?'

'Well, you can turn off sigils. So that's a start!' Juniper offered.

Another withering look from Cinder.

Juniper didn't need to be told she was treading on very, *very* thin ice. But if she could play her cards right and convince people she really was an Arcanist, well . . . not only would she not go to prison but there was a chance she could bring her family and Thea into the Uppers, dragging a win kicking and screaming out of this whole sorry mess. She had made a living out of pulling off tricks – why should this be any different?

'We'll figure it out. We always do,' Juniper said. 'What's the worst that could happen?'

'Has anyone ever told you that if you have to ask that question then you're bound to find out?' Cinder rubbed his snout. 'Why? Why did it have to be *you* who found the shard?'

'Admit it: you wouldn't be having nearly as much fun if it'd been someone else!'

'*A pain in the butt can grow into a swell of the heart*, as Grangran likes to say,' Thea said, rummaging through a stationery drawer.

'Your grangran is just a fountain of wisdom, isn't she?' Cinder said.

Thea nodded. 'She is, and a two-time cockroach-racing champion.'

Cinder pulled a book from a bookshelf, but Juniper wasn't done with him yet.

'If you get your powers back –'

'*When* I get my powers back,' Cinder corrected.

'When you get your powers back, what will you do to the Arcanists?'

The question had been bugging Juniper all night.

She couldn't go ahead with this whole scheme without at least asking what he intended to do. Maybe it wouldn't be so bad. Maybe in creepy shadow-being land revenge meant something like playing a funny prank on someone? Y'know, balancing a bucket of water on a door or making a fart noise when someone sat down.

The devious look in Cinder's eyes told Juniper that he did not, in fact, mean that kind of revenge.

'I've already told you – I'm going to obliterate them.'

'*Riiiight*. Except . . . you know they're not the same

people who actually imprisoned you, don't you?' Juniper questioned. 'The Arcanists pass their powers on to a new child when they die. You'll be takin' out your anger on innocent people who have never even heard of you!'

'Yes, I read about that in this tome last night.' Cinder pointed to a book titled *A Brief History of the Arcanists*, though the size of the book suggested it was anything but brief. 'Rather dry, but very informative. Something about adults being too closed-minded and world-weary to Inherit magic?'

'Exactly,' Juniper said. To be honest, she wasn't entirely sure how it worked either, despite Elodie explaining it to her numerous times. But it was something to do with that for sure.

'Hmm, perhaps that does change things.' Cinder fell quiet for a moment, deep in thought. 'Oh, wait, no. I don't care. *Someone* needs to pay for what they did to me, and if the Arcanists responsible are dead and gone, well, their Inheritors will have to do.'

Juniper felt her cheeks flush. He really was a nasty little thing. 'Look, no hurting people, OK? That's the only way we'll help you.'

Cinder's eyes blazed with barely hidden fury, but he almost immediately calmed himself down. 'OK, I won't,' he promised, his clenched jaw curling into a grin so sinister he might as well have been hurting someone there and then. 'You can trust me.'

Nice try, bud. Never try to trick a trickster.

Juniper trusted him about as much as she trusted Madame Adie's alchemy not to explode. She didn't like this, not one bit. Cinder was a snake, no doubt – and a problem she was going to have to deal with. But that was a future Juniper problem. Right now, she needed him as much as he needed her.

'OK then. In which case, we should start with this Boden fella you mentioned,' Juniper suggested. 'He's the only lead we've got, and maybe he'll know more about your past, why your powers have gone and, most importantly, how I get rid of you.'

'For once, we're in agreement,' Cinder said, pouting.

'Is there any chance Boden could still be alive?' Juniper asked. 'Do you have any idea how long you were imprisoned for?'

'No. Could be decades, could be centuries. All I know is that it's been long enough for this world to become a very different place. It's more cluttered. Smelly.' He looked the girls up and down. '*Severely* lacking in interesting company.'

Juniper rolled her eyes and looked out of the window. The upper Radiant District gleamed outside. Extravagant mansions, beautiful fountains gushing water enchanted to shine as bright as fire. Ether-light lanterns lined the streets and hung from boutique entrances, washing the whole town in glorious shimmering light, no matter the weather. The way the light pulsed gave the whole district the appearance of being underwater. The potted plants and swaying trees even moved as though in an ocean current. It didn't look too bad to her. If anything, she felt almost ashamed to be there, like the district was some perfect painting

and she was a blemish in the corner.

'As for Boden?' Cinder shrugged. 'He had a face, that's all I remember. At least, I think he did. That or he had a very nice hat.'

'Important clues,' Thea said, attaching sticky tape to the jacket.

'So basically you have no idea where we should start looking for him?' Juniper asked.

'I'd imagine in one of these places of magical secrets and knowledge you seem so sure you'll have access to,' Cinder replied.

Juniper groaned. Arkspire was huge. Looking for Boden would be like trying to find a needle in a pile of straw, if he was even still alive. 'Do you at least know if *I'll* be able to use your magic once you get it back? Seein' how we're bonded and all, and I seem to be getting a peek into your horrible little brain.'

It was Cinder's turn to peer at her suspiciously. 'I don't know . . . Can you? Maybe you're secretly sapping my powers without telling me?'

Not that she'd ever admit it . . . but Juniper had certainly tried. But arcs of lightning hadn't crackled at her fingertips again, no matter how hard she had wiggled them. She couldn't even seem to muster the smallest sparkle of light. At one point she had burped so loud she could've sworn she was about to belch out a fireball, but, alas, it had just been (incredibly impressive) gas. She was about to answer Cinder when there was a knock at the door. Cinder's ears pricked up before he disappeared into the shadows. Juniper opened it to find a giant of a warden from the Order of Radiance.

'Ms Bell,' the warden said in a deep voice, 'your presence has been requested in the Academy training hall.'

'Finally realized we're innocent, huh?' Juniper said, nudging the man with her elbow.

The warden remained silent.

Tough crowd.

'Then by all means lead the way,' Juniper said, bowing low.

'Perfect timing!' Thea said, swishing the Candidate jacket over her shoulders – if it could even be called a jacket now. She'd cut away the lower half and hacked the sleeves. She fastened the button at her neck, wearing the thing like some kind of poncho over her pyjamas, the tape stuck on the back in the shape of the Misfits' rat emblem. She floofed out the epaulettes and stood to attention, saluting the others. 'Thea Tumbledown, Warden Captain, ready for action!'

15

THE CANDIDATE

The warden opened an umbrella and handed it to Juniper.

Juniper gave him a look. 'Isn't it bad luck to open an umbrella indoors?'

True to form, the warden said nothing.

It wasn't until they entered the Radiant Academy training hall and were hit by a wall of torrential rain that the girls understood. The Radiant Academy was less a building and more a storm encased in glass. Churning clouds swirled round a sphere of light that floated above the cavernous arena like a small sun. As she huddled with Thea under the umbrella, the salty scent of the sea filled Juniper's nostrils, along with the earthy smell of rain and the electric tang of lightning. It smelled of energy and excitement.

The Academy had many floors: huge gangways where dozens of children, all dressed in Candidate uniforms, trained hard for the chance of becoming The Tempest's next Inheritor. Some Candidates braced themselves in huge glass containers, gale-force winds lashing round them. Some dashed across the raised gangways near the ceiling, deftly avoiding the crackling lightning that speared down from the blustering clouds. Others practised choreographed movements, drawing sigils in the humid air as they moved with focused discipline.

The training looked hard.

It looked dangerous.

It looked *fun*.

Juniper couldn't help but feel a twinge of jealousy. She wondered what kind of things they were teaching Elodie at The Watcher's Iris Academy. Looking out of windows? Trying on different spectacles? She realized she'd never actually asked.

The warden left the girls on a balcony on the third level overlooking the training grounds. It was empty except for a metal table surrounded by a flurry of lights gracefully gliding through the rain like schools of fish.

Juniper was too excited to sit. 'This place is incredible!'

'It's quite something, isn't it?' Thea agreed, smiling at the fish light she was twirling round her outstretched finger.

'It's all right, I guess,' Cinder grumbled, one with the shadows beneath the table and chairs, the two glowing dots of his eyes the only sign he was there. 'The powers of this Tempest definitely feel familiar to me . . . like I've seen them before . . .'

'Probably from that time an old Tempest kicked your ghostly little butt?' Juniper suggested.

Before Cinder could retort, they spotted a group of five wardens heading down a gangway towards them. One of them held a large umbrella over a Candidate, a boy about the same age as Juniper. He had tanned skin and straw-blond hair that looked like he'd just got out of bed, tousled up in a way that seemed almost *too* perfectly messy. He wore his grey-blue Candidate uniform as if he didn't care, or at least as

though he wanted it to seem that way. A few buttons had been left undone at the top, his collar slightly ruffled, a few choice rips in the fabric here and there to make him look dangerous – but Juniper knew rips, and these looked purposely made. The jellyfish emblem of the Order of Radiance was emblazoned proudly on his chest. Stepping ahead of the wardens, as graceful as a dancer, the boy bowed low to Juniper, smiling the biggest, cheesiest grin she'd ever seen. She half expected one of his teeth to sparkle.

'Ms Bell,' he said in the posh accent of the Uppers, 'it is truly a . . . a –' he struggled to find the word – 'an *experience* meeting you. Your high jinks are the talk of the town!'

'Oh, that little magical storm last night? You noticed that?' Juniper asked, pretending to be modest. She held out her hand.

The boy eyed it, but didn't shake it, instead looking Thea up and down. 'I see you brought a friend too, *despite no invitation*.' He said the last part under his breath.

'Hello there,' Thea said, giving him a little wave.

'And, my, I'd heard you were a striking bunch, but I never expected you'd be so . . . so . . .' He gestured at them both, as though the word he was looking for was obvious. 'Tell me, where did you find such *fascinating* clothes?'

Juniper looked down at the pyjamas she was still wearing. 'These are my jim-jams. But this –' she gestured dramatically at Thea, who struck a pose – 'this is a Thea Tumbledown spesh, my butt-kicking Warden Captain and stitcher extraordinaire!'

'It's part of my summer collection,' Thea added. 'Got some pretty toasty ideas ready for winter too. Have my eyes on some cosy-looking scrap in a junk heap down by Seventh Stack.'

'You . . . made it?' The boy raised a brow. 'And here I was thinking you'd stolen a prestigious garment reserved exclusively for Candidates. Still, I, too, am not one for convention, as you have no doubt already noticed.' He pointed proudly at a particularly small rip in his jacket. 'Bit of a rebel myself. You don't become The Tempest's most promising Candidate without breaking a few rules! Though I'm sure you already knew that, seeing who I am.' He wiggled his eyebrows and folded his arms with a smile that couldn't have been smugger if he'd tried.

'I've decided I dislike this child,' Cinder's voice whispered in Juniper's ear.

'You're really the number-one Candidate around here?' Juniper asked.

'You mean to say that you've never heard of me?' the boy asked, sounding as though he thought he was being teased. 'You're pulling my leg, of course? Why, I'm Everard Allard Amberflaw the Fourth, star Candidate of The Tempest, top of the class in the Radiant Academy and son of the Viscount of Voice himself, Magister Allard Peregrin Amberflaw the Third!'

Juniper made an '*mmm!*' noise, and Thea smiled politely. It was clear neither of them had any clue what he was talking about.

'Oh, come now.' Everard's flawless smile slipped for just a moment. 'My father's the voice of Arkspire, the man behind all the announcements you hear around the city! Even Dreggers like you must've heard of him!'

'That guy constantly telling people what they should and shouldn't be doing?' Juniper asked.

'The very same,' Everard said proudly.

'His voice *is* quite soothing,' Thea acknowledged.

'Much like my own!' Everard said.

Thea shrugged. '*Weeeeell . . .*'

'Someone with as many names as you *must* be important!' Juniper said, her voice thick with sarcasm. She turned to Thea. 'Ain't this a treat for Dreggers like us to be taken to The Tempest by such a celebrity!'

'And his teeth are very shiny,' Thea noted.

'To The Tempest?' Everard chuckled. 'Aren't you a funny one! Goodness, no, His Worship is *far* too busy.

He gave me the, erm, *great* honour of talking to you in his place.'

'I definitely don't like him,' Cinder whispered. 'He smiles too much. His hair's too swishy. Shall I destroy him? I'm sure I can muster up the strength . . .'

Everard pulled up a chair at the table and gestured at Juniper and Thea to take a seat. His warden escort formed a circle round them, facing outwards. It was a wild guess, but Juniper felt Everard Lotsa Names wasn't all that impressed with her, and the feeling was mutual.

'The reason you've been called here is because you've . . . *intrigued* The Tempest,' Everard explained. 'He's interested in your powers, and how you gained them. Although your gifts *appear* convincing, you must see how hard your story is to swallow, especially to those of us experienced in the way of the arcane? As such, he's asked me, his greatest and most trusted Candidate, to observe you during the trials and in the lead-up to them.'

'You're gonna spy on me?' Juniper asked.

Everard blinked in surprise. 'Well, I . . . well, it's hardly spying if you know it's happening, is it?'

'I dunno, man; it kinda sounds like spying to me . . .'

'No! It's just . . . documenting, that's all! There has never been a new Arcanist, not since The Visitor's first blessings those many centuries ago, and His Worship is simply curious to discover why The Visitor has decided to gift its powers to someone new, and to someone so . . . *unrecognized* after all this time. Wouldn't you be? If, indeed, that *is* what actually happened.'

'It is,' Juniper said firmly. 'You're lookin' at the real deal, m'man.'

'Juniper would never dream of lying, I swear,' Thea lied.

'Perhaps. But I've been training in the Academy for five years. I've seen magic. And you . . .' Everard looked Juniper up and down. 'I don't know what you're up to, but I don't trust it. Still, who am I to judge?' said the boy, who clearly made a point of judging people. 'The Arcanists will decide your fate. I'm just here to watch. Observe. Report. We can't allow the terrors the Betrayers brought to the world to happen again; I'm sure even you can understand that.'

'Even me,' Juniper muttered.

'So, as of today, you may return home to the lower levels. But you're to report to me at sundown each day in the Radiant Academy with a full rundown of your day's activities.'

'But I live in the Iris District,' Juniper gasped. 'That'll take ages!'

'I imagine you'll make short work of such a journey

with your new powers!' Everard said, enjoying this far too much.

'You can't be serious!'

'You would know if The Tempest was joking, Ms Bell. Now, look, between you and me –' Everard leaned in as if to tell a secret – 'you could just take back what you said last night. You know, the whole thing about being an Arcanist? Then all this goes away. Me, the unwanted attention, the challenges . . .'

Yeah, and I get to spend half my life in jail. Juniper slapped her hands to her face and dragged them down as she groaned.

'Because, and I tell you this as someone who knows what they're talking about –' Everard grinned – 'I doubt your chances in the trials are very high. Next to none, in fact, for any them, let alone all five.'

Juniper's urge to punch Everard in the face was replaced with interest. 'The Tempest told you what the challenges will be?'

The question seemed to bother Everard. 'Well, n-no, he hasn't. But – but if Academy training is anything to go by . . . and from what I've gathered from you today . . .' Everard gave a sympathetic shrug, mouthing the word 'sorry'.

The urge to punch was strong. So strong.

Instead Juniper simply smiled her winning smile.

Sell the illusion, sell the grift. She spoke with her kindest, fanciest voice. 'I appreciate your concern, Sir Amberflaw the Second . . .'

'Fourth.'

'Exactly. But I have no doubt I'll do just fine in the challenges. And if it'll please The Tempest, I very much look forward to reporting to you. Directly. Every. Single. Day.'

Everard eyed her closely, deciding the idea wasn't as amusing as he'd first thought. He rose from the table. 'Well then, I look forward to seeing you in action. And I look forward to receiving your daily reports even more so! If the next few weeks are anything like the meeting we've just enjoyed, I don't doubt they'll be something to behold. The very best of luck to you all, though it sounds like you hardly need it!' He sniggered and made to leave, but a warden stepped in his way. 'Time to go, good sir!' Everard said, obviously a little annoyed his grand exit had been ruined.

'I've been given orders not to allow you back into the Academy, Candidate,' the warden said.

Everard forced out a laugh, looking back at Juniper and Thea as though it was a little in-joke they had. 'What do you mean you can't let me back?' Everard hissed under his breath. 'Says who?'

'The Tempest, sir,' the warden said.

'The – The Tempest? But I – I was meant to . . . Then . . . then where am I to go?' Panic was creeping into his voice.

Juniper would've felt sorry for him were he not such an arrogant, puffed-up bumface.

'With them,' the warden said, dipping his head towards Juniper.

'*Them?*' Everard sounded positively horrified.

'The Tempest needs detailed reports, Candidate, the kind that require eyes on the ground. Your eyes. You're to go to the lower levels of the Iris District, observe Ms Bell and send your reports back every two days.'

'*Go to the Dregs?!*' Everard's voice had reached a pitch Juniper reckoned only dogs could hear. 'But – but I'm an Amberflaw! I can't! I shouldn't! Does my father know about this? The Tempest gave you these orders? Are you sure? There – there must be some mistake! I can't, surely not . . . with *them*?!'

Yup, Juniper was pretty sure she heard some dogs barking in the distance.

'Oh, I'm glad I didn't destroy him,' Cinder whispered. 'Watching him squirm has been far more rewarding . . .'

'The Tempest's orders were very clear, Candidate Amberflaw,' the warden confirmed, closing the umbrella. 'Make sure you serve with honour and do the Order of Radiance proud.'

With a shriek, Everard spun round to face the girls, who both gave him their biggest, most welcoming smiles.

'Isn't this exciting?!' Juniper said, offering no space for him under her umbrella. 'We're gonna get along like a house on fire, I just know it!'

16

READYING A RUSE

Papa scooped Juniper into a hug the moment she stepped out of the Radiant Academy. Being crushed by a bear would better describe it, but Juniper was just as happy to see him.

'I'm so glad you're safe,' Papa muttered, his voice uncharacteristically wobbly.

'Glad . . . to see you . . . too . . . Papa,' Juniper said, gasping, 'though I'm . . . struggling . . . to breathe . . .'

Papa released her instantly.

'Ohhh, I was coming to get in on the action,' Thea said, her arms held out. Cinder remained hidden, no doubt watching such signs of affection with distaste.

'I'm sorry,' Papa said to Juniper, eyeing the people in the square outside the Academy. 'That was wrong of me. You've been blessed by The Visitor. I – I should've thought . . . with all these people watching . . . it's demeaning for me to hug you.'

'What?! I don't care about that – you're my papa!' Juniper said.

Papa looked embarrassed. 'Considerin' who you are now, I should show more restraint in public.'

The idea he would feel this way – that he'd hide his love for her because of some stupid title – turned Juniper's stomach.

'Not with me, you don't.' Juniper slipped her arm through his and Thea's and led them away, arm in arm, a ragged shadow darting unseen behind them.

They took the Skyline back to the Iris District. Papa couldn't stop staring at Juniper, both with relief and hesitation. Like he didn't know how to act around her any more.

'So . . . it's true,' Papa whispered, eyeing the sigils on her hands as though they were wounds. 'You've been touched by the Other Side. You really might be an Arcanist?'

Juniper wished she could tell him that nothing had changed, not really . . . but she stopped herself. This lie was big, even for her. She knew he'd be beyond disappointed in her.

So instead she just grinned, hoping to reassure him she was still the same ol' daughter he'd always known.

It didn't have to be a lie for long, after all. They'd get
Cinder his magic back, and then together they really
would have the power to change their lives.

'First Elodie, now you! Both my daughters in touching
distance of becoming an Arcanist?' He blew air out of
his cheeks. 'Yer mama woulda been over the moon . . .'

'Yup,' Juniper mumbled, pulling her sleeves over her
hands, 'she sure woulda been proud . . .'

Back home, Juniper was unsurprised to see Adie's
Apothecary still looked much the same as she'd left it –
like someone had thrown a stick of magical dynamite
at it. The sigils were still there, not glowing but scarred
into the building and its surroundings. A gaggle of

onlookers watched with curiosity as she passed, whispering to each other. Juniper's natural instinct was to duck and hide, to remain hidden, unnoticed. Keeping a low profile was how any relic hunter survived. But if her ruse was going to work, she had to play the part. The Arcanists were as showy as they come, and that meant Juniper would have to be too.

'S'up, citizens!' she cried out, giving them all a big wave. Some waved back, but most people averted their eyes, as if afraid to be seen even looking at her.

Regardless, it felt good to be home. Thea rushed upstairs to see her grangran, eager to tell her everything that had happened. Juniper was just happy to be able to change out of her jammies.

Everard arrived a few hours later, and Juniper and Papa went out to greet him. A convoy of three carriages pulled up, two of them just for the mountains of luggage Everard had packed.

'Yeesh, he's nearly as bad as you,' Juniper whispered to shadow-form Cinder.

'Please, even I would only demand two carriages.'

Everard's face was already sickly pale at the sights he'd seen travelling through the Dregs, but the last drop of colour drained from his face the moment he saw where he'd be staying. 'O-oh! How . . . rustic!'

It didn't help that a cluster of raggedy street cats

rushed past at that moment, chasing an even bigger swarm of filthy rats.

'Ahhh, how cute. And, my, I didn't realize how little sun you got down here . . .' Everard looked up at the shack-stack canyons towering above, flinching as if they were leaning in to crush him. They rose so high you couldn't even see the top of them – a chaos of buildings built atop buildings, a mad mishmash of materials, shapes and colours. 'I suppose that would explain the total lack of trees . . .'

'We have a lovely tree over there,' Juniper said, pointing to a yellow sapling barely clinging to life beneath one of the gushing waterpipes. 'It's got leaves and everything!'

'I can't imagine how I missed it,' Everard said. 'Not that I mind, of course! I'm a Candidate – top of my class! Adventure and hardship are what I breathe, what I live for!' He laughed in a way Juniper assumed was meant to sound brave, but it came out more like a strangled gargle.

'C'mon, lad – I'll show you where you'll be sleeping,' Papa said, grabbing hold of a suitcase some Dreggers had been helping themselves to.

'Thank you, good sir,' Everard said. 'I assume it'll be in the guest wing of your charming . . . erm . . . house?'

Juniper pulled a face. 'Guest wing?'

'What's that?' Thea said.

'Er, will a couch be enough?' Papa asked.

'A couch!' Everard's voice had gone very high. 'Ha! Now that *is* an adventure!' His smile was crooked, like he'd just caught the whiff of a bad fart.

One of the servants leaned in towards Everard. 'Remember what your father said, sir,' he murmured.

'Of course. I won't let him down; I never do.' Everard swallowed. 'My dedication to my Arcanist, my Order and the Amberflaw name will make him proud.'

'Very good, sir,' the servant said, bowing.

Everard watched as the procession of carriages drove away, looking as if his only way back to the Uppers was up a ladder that had just been kicked down, then set on fire for good measure.

Papa and Juniper had spent the rest of the day trying to find space in their two rooms for all Everard's luggage.

'Look at the size of this thing!' Juniper huffed, struggling with a mirror as big as her.

'Yes, it's rather small, isn't it?' Everard said, gazing into the glass and adjusting his hair. 'This is my travel mirror; I have many larger ones back home.'

Juniper's mouth fell open, watching as Everard pulled the plumpest pillow she'd ever seen from a case. Papa squeezed her shoulder. He'd been about as thrilled as Juniper to learn of their new guest, but was doing what he could to make Everard feel welcome.

'S'important we look out for each other,' Papa said, 'no matter where we come from. We're all Arkspire, aren't we?'

Juniper wondered about that. Sure seemed like some bits of Arkspire just looked out for themselves. Maybe it was time for the Dregs to do the same.

Juniper had a lot to do. First things first, she had a spiteful little shadow-monster to deal with. She reckoned finding this Boden person was one of her top priorities. The more she knew about Cinder and his powers, the better she could deal with him.

'Boden?' Madame Adie repeated, after Juniper had mentioned the name in passing. Madame Adie had *a lot* of contacts, after all. 'Never heard of him. Is that a first or last name?'

Juniper sighed. 'Y'know, I have no idea. Just a name I heard. Apparently he could give me advice on my new-found powers.'

'You don't say?' Madame Adie screwed up her face. 'A fellow historian of the arcane? Strange I haven't heard of him, then . . .'

It was a bad start, but Madame Adie wasn't the only one in the Dregs who had their ear close to the ground.

'We should ask Bleater!' Thea suggested when she was sure Everard wasn't around.

'You're right! "Need word on the street, talk to the Bleat,"' Juniper said.

'Asking a goat for help? This is a new low, even for you,' Cinder muttered.

'Obviously he's not a goat,' Juniper said.

'As amazing as that would be,' Thea added. 'He's a notorious ne'er-do-well, a roguish ruffian, a supreme scallywag, and he also has the nose to find anyone in the city.'

'That must be some nose,' Cinder said.

'Kinda medium, but his ears are big.'

The only problem was that it proved rather difficult to skip over to Bleater's with Everard watching Juniper like a particularly nosy hawk. What made it even worse was how much he clearly didn't want to be there; he was sulking the whole time like some sad little slug. Regardless, he was never seen without his notebook in hand, a pen in the other, ready and waiting for Juniper to slip up. He was bound to report the fact that Juniper was speaking to shady figures in dark alleyways, and it wasn't like she could explain it was to help her find a mysterious man who might've, probably, almost definitely been a Betrayer and possibly a friend of the little revenge-fuelled monster she'd brought through the Veil using a forbidden relic. That probably wasn't going to go down too well with The Tempest, no matter how she tried to dress it up.

There was nothing else for it: they had to lose the baggage.

'Remind me where we're going again?' Everard asked, following the girls through a dark, narrow street, looking at each passer-by as though they were about to mug him.

'Just fetchin' a few things for Papa,' Juniper said.

She shared a glance with Thea before they both clambered up a drainpipe. Everard had been so preoccupied eyeing a particularly menacing-looking man that the girls were already at the top of a stack by the time he realized what was happening.

'Hey!' he yelled, leaping at the wooden wall in an attempt to catch them. He caught one of the pre-made rips in his jacket, the sound of thread tearing lost under

Everard's high-pitched shriek. He dropped from the wall, patting his jacket as if that would magically mend it. He looked up at the girls, fury in his eyes. 'You need to learn your place!'

'*Excuse* me?!' Juniper said.

Other locals turned too, giving Everard rather unfriendly glares. He wrung his hands. 'I – I mean, the rooftops are no place for you! Use roads like normal people!' He pointed down to the filthy path they'd been following before letting out another wail as he noticed the muck that now caked his once pristine boots.

'Dregs are a little short on roads, as you can see,' Juniper explained. 'This is how we get around. Either keep up or go home! It's back that way!'

And, with that, they ran off, the sound of Everard yelling, 'Wait, don't leave me!' following their escape.

Cinder appeared on Juniper's shoulder, sniggering. 'That was cold, even for me . . .'

'Don't forget – I'm doin' all this for you,' Juniper said.

'For me?' Cinder feigned surprise. 'You shouldn't have.'

Without Everard, it wasn't long before they arrived where they knew they'd find Bleater – a small windowless building shaped like a dome, made entirely from stained copper.

The girls checked that the coast was clear. It was. The street was dark and easy to hide in, even for the Dregs, as it was draped in the shadow of a shack-stack overhang above. They leaned beside the metal door, all nonchalant-like, and, barely raising her arm, Juniper knocked on the door.

Clang-clang-clanggity-clang.

Bleater's special knock.

There was a moment of silence. Then a hatch hissed open in the door; two watery eyes peered out.

'Name?' Bleater whispered, fast and tense.

'Uh, Boden,' Juniper said.

'That it?'

'It's all I got.'

'Reward?'

Nothing was free in the Dregs.

'How 'bout a favour from the new Arcanist of the Dregs?' Juniper tried.

The hatch shut.

'No, wait, wait!' Juniper banged on the door again. 'What about a relic?'

The hatch slid open and a hand popped out. Juniper placed the relic she'd brought from her own personal stash, a glass bead that changed colour depending on the weather.

There was a moment's pause.

'Wait for word,' grunted the voice, the hatch shutting again.

That was as good as a handshake in Bleater's language. The girls shared a smile.

17

LIVING A LIE

Course, the real big thing Juniper had to worry about was the upcoming trials. The Arcanists still hadn't announced what challenges they were going to set for her, and it had nearly been a week since her hearing at the Crux. There'd been nothing printed about it in the newspapers, no phonograph announcements, nothing. It put Juniper on edge.

She suspected that the Arcanists were just waiting to see if she slipped up, so they could prove she was a liar before they made anything public. There was no need to add to the rumours going round of a new Arcanist – especially if Juniper was going to fall on her face without them.

It was a good thing she knew how to keep up a lie. Still, she reckoned she should try to get some idea of what she might be up against when the challenges were announced. And no one knew more about the Arcanists than the ultimate Arcanist geek, Elodie. She'd read every book on them, knew every story, could tell you all their tricks and what made 'em tick. If anyone would know what could be coming, it was her.

Juniper had sent a letter to Elodie a few days ago asking for her help. She'd written it in the doodle language they'd made up together when they were little, along with Thea. It was like the secret code of the Misfits, often scribbled on paper and folded into the shape of a rat so that they could send messages to each other across the rooftops and streets about potential pickpocket targets or watchful wardens.

But when Juniper tore open the letter Elodie had sent back to her, she was shocked to see it written in words. Actual, real words that anyone could read.

Dear Juniper,

Thank you for your letter. It was nice to hear from you. Even if I knew what the challenges might be, I could not tell you, as that would be cheating – which I'm sure you'd hate to do. If you would do me the great honour of listening to my advice, might I suggest spending more time doing some research, rather than playing celebrity? You might learn something new, like what it truly means to be an Arcanist, and why it would be a terrible idea for anyone to pretend to be one. The Arcanists are kind and forgiving – always remember that. I'm sure you'll do the right thing.

Yours sincerely,
Elodie

'I wonder,' Juniper said sarcastically, tapping her chin as if deep in thought, 'could it be that Elodie is trying to accuse me of something?'

'This sudden sibling rivalry in the race to become an Arcanist has blindsided her, that's all,' Madame Adie assured her.

Everard had listened carefully to Elodie's letter and now hastily jotted something down, as if inspiration had struck. He'd been really diligent with his note-taking, becoming particularly cheery whenever Juniper did something silly, writing it all down with renewed intensity, especially since she had ditched him earlier that week.

'No, wait! Don't write that!' Juniper said, worried that Elodie's letter more than hinted that something fishy was going on.

Everard scrawled even faster.

'Don't write that either! I'm just joking with you – no need to bore The Tempest with that!' Juniper swiped his notes away from him.

'Hey, that's confidential Order of Radiance documentation and not to be seen by the likes of you!' Everard snatched it back. He grinned wickedly. 'Besides, I can assure you it's only saying things His Worship will find *most* interesting.'

Juniper flicked a lock of his hair, and he recoiled as if mortally wounded.

'*Aaaaaaaand* breathe,' Thea said, massaging Juniper's shoulders, sensing her simmering frustration. Thea was wearing her self-made warden costume, now upgraded with a cracked pair of goggles she'd salvaged from a skip and an embroidered rat instead of one made from sticky tape.

'Let The Tempest read into it what he wants,' Madame Adie said, rubbing her hands together. 'I think the crowds you've been attracting speak louder than rumour or hearsay.' She gestured to the shop window. People filled the street outside the apothecary, shouting and calling for Juniper to show herself.

As if the mystery of the challenges and Everard's constant scribbling weren't enough, all the public attention was the third thing that Juniper had to deal with. The last week had been strange, to say the least. Who knew that becoming the first maybe – kind of – almost – new Arcanist in a thousand years might make you a person of interest? Juniper could barely go outside without being recognized.

There were no posters of her around the city, no statues or shrines in her honour, but it's amazing how fast word gets around, especially down in the Dregs. Adie's Apothecary had barely had a moment's peace since the trial at the Crux, with people desperate to see this so-called 'Arcanist of the Dregs' for themselves. Sure, most of them just wanted to accuse Juniper of heralding the second coming of the Betrayers, of being the bane of their city and the certain doom of them all, but, y'know – at least they still thought she was magical, which meant the ruse was working, right? Whenever Papa wasn't at work, which was rarely, he would follow Juniper around like a bodyguard, even when she said she could take care of herself. The last thing she needed was someone else watching her every move.

'Seems the least the Arcanists could've done would be to supply you with a warden for protection,' Papa had grumbled, looking out of the window at a group yelling about how little they thought of Juniper and her lies.

'Erm, hello?' Thea had protested, gesturing at her warden uniform.

Sure, some people were being jerks, but going from an urchin no one wanted to know to a celebrity overnight had its perks too. Bunyun's Bakery had given her more sourberry tarts and garglenut muffins than she could ever eat. Mr Lafayette in the lower markets had sorted her out with some new threads, one of which had no holes in it. Mrs Cleo from Scintillating Scents in the Uppers had even given Juniper a bar of soap, something Juniper had never owned before, which was now displayed proudly on the mantlepiece. The 'liar', 'fake' and 'Betrayer' graffiti that had started to appear around the neighbourhood kind of lost their edge when such gifts were piled at your doorstep.

But Papa was right to worry. The crowds outside the apothecary were growing every day, and they all wanted one thing. They wanted to see Juniper perform magic, to prove to them all that she was what she said she was. Which was a *bit* of an issue.

Try as he might, Cinder's powers didn't seem to be

increasing. And Juniper doubted that his ability to turn sigils on and off was going to impress the crowds all that much. They were getting restless. Their voices were getting louder. Their demands more insistent.

What if the apothecary was attacked? Juniper didn't want to put her family and friends in danger. She didn't particularly fancy the danger herself, truth be told. Juniper needed a plan, and fast.

Fortunately she reckoned she had just the thing, though she'd need Cinder's help. She'd had to take him to the outhouse round the back of the apothecary to get away from Everard's ever-prying eyes.

'You truly do take me to the nicest places,' Cinder commented. 'But I do hope you're not planning to use that thing while I'm here . . .' He eyed the toilet with suspicion.

'I have a plan, and I need your help to pull it off.'

Cinder had sighed. 'Why am I not surprised? It astounds me that you managed to do anything before I arrived.'

'Who are you talking to in there?' came Everard's voice from outside. He'd already caught Juniper speaking to Cinder a few times and, though he hadn't seen Cinder yet, he was getting suspicious.

'Myself,' Juniper said. Better he reported she was a weirdo than the truth. 'And do you mind? Can a girl not get some privacy round here?' She listened to the sound of Everard's footsteps reluctantly trailing away before she turned back to Cinder. 'So, my plan.'

'I can barely contain my excitement.'

'I asked myself: what would the Arcanists do? Well, they'd put on a show, right? So tomorrow, in front of the crowd, I'm gonna wiggle my fingers about, pretending to be all mystical, and you're gonna do your shadow thing, moving stuff while keeping outta sight.'

Cinder looked physically pained. '*That's* your plan?'

'People'll love it! It'll look like I'm moving objects with my *mind*.' Juniper raised her fingers to her temples to emphasize the point. Cinder did not seem impressed. 'Look, you got any better ideas?!'

'Many, but I suppose this one will do.'

'Trust me,' Juniper said. 'What's the worst that could happen?'

Cinder narrowed his eyes, but then shrugged. 'I suppose it *has* been a while since I've enjoyed a public beheading . . .'

18

MAKING MAGIC

Juniper woke to a belly twisting into knots. Her nerves turned her right off her breakfast, so instead she headed straight downstairs. Everard followed her with a spring in his step. Apparently he was as excited to see Juniper's powers as everyone else.

'A delightful morning to you, Juniper!' Thea said, beaming. She was decked out in her full warden costume, clutching the narrow plank of wood she'd declared was her Justice Stick.

'Your audience awaits you!' Madame Adie said, gesturing outside. As always, the street was rammed. 'Show 'em what you're made of and, once you've done that, point them to my door!'

While it may have taken a while for Juniper to get used to her new-found fame, Madame Adie had taken to it like a duck to water. A large banner now hung across the apothecary's awning, which read:

LIMITED-EDITION COMMEMORATIVE REMEDIES
IN HONOUR OF THE SIXTH ARCANIST!
BUY ONE, GET ONE SAME PRICE!

Juniper took a deep breath. *I am an Arcanist, I am an Arcanist,* she repeated to herself, trying to get into character. She pulled her shoulders back, stuck her chin up and strolled outside with particularly exaggerated arm movements.

The crowd hushed expectantly. Thea stood protectively at her side, Everard behind them, attempting to use them as cover against the unpredictable crowd.

Then, just as Juniper had cleared her throat and was about to give her best Arcanist speech, her voice was lost beneath a piercing squeal. It was the street phonographs screeching to life. To everyone's shock, the announcer's voice wasn't Everard's dad as usual. It was the voice of The Shrouded herself.

'Good morning, loyal citizens of Arkspire.' Her voice was so cold, so empty of joy, it seemed to chill the air. It couldn't have sounded more different from the kind, smiley girl Juniper had met years before.

'As most of you are no doubt aware,' The Shrouded continued, 'there is word of a sixth Arcanist within our city, a so-called "Arcanist of the Dregs". Were this to prove true, we will welcome our new sister with open arms, celebrating the ally we shall gain in our battle against the Betrayers' curse. However, the sole duty of the Arcanists is to keep Arkspire's citizens safe, and we would be failing in that duty were we not to make sure of this newcomer's magical abilities and her loyalties. Juniper Bell must prove her claim that she has been chosen by The Visitor, and, as such, each Arcanist will set her a challenge, a trial that only a true Arcanist of our glorious city would be able to complete.'

Juniper swallowed, aware of all the eyes on her. The Shrouded sure had good timing. She wondered how she'd known this was Juniper's big moment. She glanced at Everard, suspecting she already had her answer.

'I have the honour of setting the first challenge,' The Shrouded went on. 'It will take place in the Midnight District in six days' time. Juniper Bell, your challenge is as follows: at sundown of the sixth day, you are to use the bells at the top of the Midnight Tower to play the following melody, for all to hear.'

A simple haunting tune played over the speakers.

Five bell chimes.

That was it. And yet it somehow made the summer air feel all the colder.

The crowd waited, expecting more, but the phonographs had fallen silent. The bell chimes were replaced by a growing rumble of confused, excited voices.

'It's clear as day!' bellowed an angry voice. 'The girl's Betrayer scum! She's our enemy!' The voice belonged to a large man with a mighty moustache.

Many in the crowd backed him up. Everard was one of them, Juniper didn't fail to notice.

'Those of you comin' here to see her like she's some real Arcanist – what a joke!' Tash-face spat on the ground, flicking his cap up from his heavy brow. 'How can y'all sleep at night knowing you're giving attention to this imposter?'

Juniper tried her best to keep her cool. She refused to look intimidated. A real Arcanist wouldn't be. If she let the act slip, these snot-munchers would ruin everything.

'Have any of you actually seen her do any magic?' Tash-face growled. 'You're all betrayin' The Watcher, givin' this traitor even the smallest bit of your time!'

'What, the same Watcher who abandoned us and left the whole Iris District to fend for itself?'

Juniper was amazed to hear someone standing up for her, and even more bamboozled by the cries of approval that followed. The crowd was splitting in two, her supporters and her naysayers.

'At least the girl's a new start – the chance for something better!' another man said.

'Watch your mouth, traitor!' Tash-face roared, shoving the man hard.

'Visitor beyond, not again,' Juniper groaned as a scuffle broke out.

Cinder chuckled in Juniper's ear. 'Ahhh, the sweet sound of your adoring fans. Such a beautiful melody . . .'

'Shall I deal with it?' Thea asked, thumping her Justice Stick into her palm.

'Everybody, stop!' Juniper yelled. But the crowd ignored her, heaving and swaying with anger. 'I didn't ask The Visitor to bless me with its gifts,' Juniper tried to say, regardless of the noise. 'It just happened! I'm not trying to take The Watcher's position, and I'm definitely not a Betrayer! But I promise you this: if I pass these challenges, I'll make sure that life in the Dregs –'

Something soft, sticky and squelchy hit Juniper on the head. She wiped her hand over her face, slime trailing from her fingers. Probably best not to think too hard about what it had been.

'Oh dear, here come the vegetables,' Thea said, stepping in front of Juniper protectively.

She began batting the mouldy produce thrown by the angry crowd out of the way. Some exploded the moment they made contact with the bat. Despite Thea's brave efforts, the fruit and vegetables started raining thick and fast. The kids ducked round the corner of the shop.

'Where'd they find so much rotten food anyway?'

Juniper asked, her back against the wall. A particularly black-looking tomato splatted a hair's breadth from her face. 'You're supposed to eat it before it gets like that!'

Juniper searched for Cinder in the shadows and spotted his shape, lithe and snake-like, his eyes dim embers. She gave him a nod. It was time to put her plan into action. But Cinder simply gazed at his shadow-claws, completely disinterested in what was going on.

Frustrated, Juniper sidled over to him. 'Cinder, it's go-time!' she hissed out of the corner of her mouth. Everard was thankfully distracted, but she didn't want to take any chances.

'Not particularly sure why I'd want to set foot in that garbage storm,' Cinder said.

'Because this is where we win or lose 'em! You'll never get your answers if we don't make people believe our story!'

A brown blob hit the floor with a hearty plop.

'Still . . . I'd rather stay here where it's dry,' Cinder said, looking back at his claws.

Juniper growled with frustration – just as a melon exploded at Cinder's feet, showering him in chunks of foul-smelling mulch.

'RIGHT,' Cinder snarled, his eyes flaring bright (which had the curious effect of making Juniper's sigils glow). 'Who threw that?! Who do I need to obliterate?!'

He faded into the shadows just as Everard spun round at the sound of his voice, slime splatting to the floor.

Juniper followed Cinder, stepping out into the chaos, Juniper's supporters now in a full-on brawl with her detractors.

'Hey, Whiskers!' she yelled as loud as she could. The moustachioed man stopped his rabble-rousing long enough to look in her direction. 'You wanna see some magic? Well, watch *this*!' Juniper threw out her hand, making a real show of the whole thing.

The crowd stopped fighting, waiting anxiously or eagerly, depending on the side, to see what she did next. Juniper watched for the slight shift in the shadows that marked Cinder's location. He was hard to see, but she caught sight of him mostly thanks to the fact that he'd slid through a squished tomato and was leaving a kind of slime-trail of tomato juice behind him.

He was close enough to Tash-face now. So Juniper clenched her outstretched hand into a fist. At that moment Cinder leaped up on to Tash-face's back, pushing his cap over his eyes. Surprised, the man reached to lift it up, only for Cinder to jump over his head and grab hold of his moustache, swinging from it like a child. Totally unprepared, the large man lost his balance, toppling forward before falling flat on his face. And now was the time for the grand finale, the *pièce de résistance.*

Cinder gave the large burly man a major, merciless and entirely unflinching wedgie.

The onlookers goggled in disbelief before erupting into laughter. With Cinder being little more than another patch of darkness in a place already soaked in shadow, it had looked like the attack on the man had been all Juniper's doing.

Her supporters began cheering Juniper's name, throwing their fists up in support. 'Arcanist of the Dregs! Arcanist of the Dregs!'

Juniper gave them a flamboyant bow.

Tash-face scrabbled to his feet, barely managing to bring his underwear down to a place that wasn't eye-watering. His allies tried to help him, but he slapped their hands away. He shot one final hateful look at Juniper before hobbling away.

Juniper couldn't help but smile, and made sure to give Cinder a secret wink.

'Did you write *that* down?' Thea asked Everard. 'Make sure you note how Juniper masterfully controlled the unseen forces of the Other Side.'

'Oh, I've made a note,' Everard said. 'Quite frankly it's embarrassing how desperate people down here are to believe in your parlour tricks.'

Thea stuck her tongue out. 'If people down here are so gullible, why don't you explain how Juni did it, huh?!'

You could almost hear the cogs grinding away in Everard's head as he tried to come up with an explanation for what he'd just seen. It must've been a trick; he just had to work it out! But for all his trying, Juniper could've sworn she saw something there in his eyes.

It was the first wrinkle of doubt. Maybe, just maybe, she really was who she said she was.

19

A VERY SERIOUS HOBBY

Madame Adie chased away the last troublemakers with her broom. Clapping her hands together after a job well done, she turned to Everard. 'Now that that's dealt with, some wardens were looking for you, child.'

'For – for me?' Everard looked surprised. He clutched his notebook like a shield, eyes watching the skies for any sign of falling veg, clearly shaken up by the street brawl.

Juniper narrowed her eyes. She knew how gruelling Academy training could be. For someone who was meant to be top of his class, Everard sure was easily shaken.

'I think they have a message from The Tempest,' Madame Adie said. 'I told them to wait for you round back.'

Everard's fear evaporated. 'Visitor be thanked, His Worship has remembered me!' He practically skipped down the alley and round the corner.

'Now that he's out of the way, may I have a word with you two?' Madame Adie ushered the girls back inside. To Juniper's surprise, Madame Adie took them into her private quarters, a place she rarely let anyone else enter. It got Juniper's nerves bubbling.

It didn't help when Madame Adie locked the door behind them. Her quarters were even more jam-packed than the store itself.

Workbenches cluttered the room, each covered in weird devices, ticking machines, cauldrons and vials of every shape and size bubbling away in the cosy lantern light. Jars filled with strange colourful ingredients sat next to mortars full of smooshed pungent ingredients. Notebooks were strewn across the benches, pens dropped on their pages of half-scribbled notes and drawings.

'Oof, what a morning,' Madame Adie said, settling herself in an armchair. 'Glad your papa wasn't here to see all that, or we'd never hear the end of it.' She gazed intently into Juniper's eyes, as if searching for something there. 'Now, I'll only ask you this once, Juniper Bell, but is there something you wish to tell me? A little . . . secret you've been keeping?'

Even though a spark of shock jolted through her body, Juniper pulled her best innocent face. Visitor beyond, nothing slipped past Madame Adie. She stared deeply into Juniper's eyes.

She could stare all she wanted; Juniper wouldn't break.

No, sir.

Not a chance.

Although that stare *was* intense. It was like being glared at by a hungry 'gator. Juniper swallowed. Her palms were sweaty. She turned to Thea as if baffled by

Madame Adie's question, but Thea was busy poking a vial of bubbling pink liquid.

Juniper tried to stay as cool as a cucumber. 'Secret? Madame A, you know better 'n anyone I don't keep secrets. Clear as glass, me.'

Madame Adie sighed. 'You can come out from your hiding place. I know you're here. I've read enough to recognize signs of the Other Side when I see them.' For the longest moment, nothing happened. She tapped her foot impatiently. 'Well? I haven't got all day!'

The shadows behind Madame Adie grew thicker and deeper, flickering like a flame in the breeze. They coalesced into Cinder's sinewy form, his eyes burning menacingly into the back of Madame Adie's head.

'It is dangerous to assume you know another, old crone,' he said.

Madame Adie gave a little start when she turned to face him. 'My goodness. My, my. Here you are, as bright as a . . . well, as a dark shadowy thing.' Her small eyes were filled with wonder as she drank the sight of Cinder in, almost like she couldn't believe it.

'I can explain! It's not what you think!' Juniper began.

'He's just a figment of your imagination!' Thea said, waving her fingers mysteriously.

But Madame Adie wasn't listening. 'Remarkable . . .' she uttered, adjusting her eyeglasses to inspect Cinder closely, giving him a little poke.

'Indeed,' he said, poking her forehead and pushing her back.

Madame Adie seemed to come to her senses. 'F-forgive me! It's just your like hasn't been seen for centuries, since the war with the Betrayers! I've read so much about beings from the Other Side, but to see one in the flesh like this . . .'

'Well, at least *you* respect brilliance when you see it.' Cinder gave Juniper a glance.

Juniper sighed. 'He came from the mirror shard.' There was no point pretending now.

'I wondered where that had gone. So, a gateway of some kind?' Madame Adie looked utterly entranced. 'What powers do you have? What can you do?'

'Everything,' Cinder said, just as Juniper muttered, 'Nothing.'

'He's lost his memories, his powers, everything,' Juniper went on. 'We're trying to figure out how to get them back so that we can snip our bond and put things back to normal –'

'No!' Madame Adie snapped. 'You don't want to do that!' The very idea seemed to offend her. 'Unlocking his powers may be your only chance to complete the Arcanists' challenges!'

Juniper hadn't been expecting that. 'But aren't you afraid he might have been, y'know, *friends* with the Betrayers? He even said he wanted to get revenge on the Arcanists!'

Cinder gave them a wicked smile.

But Madame Adie didn't seem concerned. 'When something crosses from the Other Side, it is the one from our world who anchors them here and controls the bond.'

'You mean *me*?' Juniper asked. 'I'll be callin' the shots when he gets his powers back?'

'It's how the Betrayers were able to command such creatures in the war,' Madame Adie said.

Now it was Juniper's turn to give Cinder a wicked smile. He looked most perturbed.

'You mean you know what Cinder is?' Thea asked.

'Not exactly,' Madame Adie replied, adjusting her spectacles. 'Many strange and other-worldly creatures leaked through the tear The Visitor opened in the Veil, things of terrible power that the Betrayers sometimes bonded with and used to wreak havoc upon the world.'

Juniper gasped. 'Bonding with these creatures could give someone extra powers? Why've we never heard about this?'

'I can't imagine the Arcanists are too keen on it getting out,' Madame Adie explained. 'People might get ideas, and the Arcanists have already had one civil war to deal with.'

'You mean people like me,' Juniper said.

'You're not gonna grass up Juni, are you?' Thea asked.

Madame Adie looked shocked at the suggestion. 'Of course not. I think this is marvellous news! I've no doubt you would be a change for good in this city, Juniper. You might not be an Arcanist, but you are someone who would remember the little guy for once. But your powers are – hmm, how do I put this? – somewhat *underdeveloped.*'

'Well, I'm new to this,' Juniper explained. 'I haven't had Academy training, and I don't really know what my powers are, and I'm tired, and I kinda needed a wee when it kicked off and I –'

Madame Adie held up a hand. 'Darling, it wasn't a criticism. It all makes sense now. You don't have the powers of an Arcanist, but you *could* be almost as powerful as they are with some help . . .'

'Climbing a tower and ringing some bells doesn't sound too hard,' Juniper said.

'Kind of fun, if anything,' Thea added.

Juniper couldn't deny she'd been relieved to hear what the challenge actually was. She'd been expecting something really awful, like playing tag with a Shade or a race across the city strapped to a lightning bolt.

'We both know you're not that naive, Juni,' Madame Adie said. 'If you think The Shrouded won't have a few surprises in store for you, then you're sorely mistaken.'

Juniper knew she was right. She'd just wanted to enjoy the few moments when this whole thing might not have been a complete headache. 'Don't suppose you have any ideas?' she asked.

'As it happens, I might have just the thing.' Madame Adie's eyes shone with excitement. 'As you know, I do take my hobby very seriously –' she gestured at the alchemy equipment all around them – 'hoping it might help those of us without the knack for magic. Sounds like that very moment has come, don't you think? It would be my pleasure, no, my *honour*, to help you in your challenges. I could brew you up treats that would seem like magic to anyone who didn't know! At least, of course, until you can help poor . . .' Madame Adie looked to Cinder for his name.

'You may call me "Overlord",' he said. 'Or "Your Majesty", or "Your Imperious, August Magnificence" –'

'His name is Cinder,' Juniper said. 'Cinder the Stupid.'

'Well, until you can help Cinder regain his powers. Then the two of you will be a *real* force to be reckoned with.'

'You'd be willing to break the law like that?' Juniper asked, even though she wanted Madame Adie's help more than anything. 'We could spend forever in jail if they find out . . .'

'Oh, to see those smug posers get some egg on their faces!' Madame Adie rubbed her hands together. 'It'd be a win for the Dregs!'

Juniper was grinning widely, her belly doing rolypolies. After all the years of being a thief, a gutter rat, of living in the shadow of Elodie's achievements. At long last, with Adie's knowledge and Cinder's powers at her command, Juniper could actually prove she was a *somebody*!

Someone suddenly began rattling the door handle.

'Hey, why's the door locked?' came Everard's voice. 'Hello? Are you all in there? Can you let me in, please?' There was a pause, and then he began pounding on the door again. 'I demand that you let me in!'

At a glance from Madame Adie, the girls hid themselves as the old woman unlocked the door.

'At last!' Everard said, looking past her for any sign of Juniper. 'I couldn't find the wardens you spoke of! I'm sure there must be some kind of mistake, because I

know you'd *never* try to have a secret conversation without me, knowing full well The Tempest himself demanded I be witness to all your actions!'

'I get that you have a job to do, child,' Madame Adie said, reaching for her broom and grasping it in both hands, 'but if you ever try to burst into my chambers uninvited again, I'll show you just how little power The Tempest has down here. Do you understand?'

Everard had seen what she could do with that broom. He gulped and nodded.

Yup, at that moment, Juniper was sure of it. With Madame Adie on her side, there was nothing that could stand in her way.

20

THE STORM

The next day, the sky above Arkspire was so dark it could've passed for evening. The heavy slate-grey clouds unleashed torrential rain upon the city. Gushing waterfalls fell from the Uppers into the Dregs, turning its muddy streets into rivers. Everard was staring outside as the rain hammered on the living-room windows.

'Some storm, huh?' Juniper said, watching him. 'I hope Papa got to work OK . . .'

'I've never seen such floods before. Does it always do this down here?' Everard didn't take his eyes from the window.

'Yeah,' Juniper said, pulling out two bowls from the cupboard and placing them under a couple of leaks dripping from the ceiling. 'Dreggers are always asking the Orders to do something about it, but nothing ever gets done.'

Everard sat quietly. Bags hung under his eyes, as heavy as the rain. It hadn't escaped Juniper's notice that his note-taking had slackened over the last few days. The kid had been buzzing around Juniper like a fly she couldn't get rid of, but, still, Juniper found it hard not to feel sorry for him.

'You . . . er . . . sleeping OK?' Juniper asked, scratching the back of her head. 'I know our couch isn't the squishiest, and the springs are a killer. You can kip on my bed this afternoon if you need a nap?' she offered.

Everard held up his hands. 'I have a duty to fulfil! Besides, it's a bit hard to sleep with all those grinding noises I keep hearing.' As if in answer, a low grumbling sound, a bit like thunder, came from somewhere high above. 'What is that anyway?'

'The shack-stacks groaning under the weight of the water. Happens every storm.'

'It *does*?' Everard blinked. 'Are we safe?'

'We are.' Juniper nodded, then paused. 'Least I think we are. The level above our street is made of solid iron – ain't no way that's comin' down anytime soon, and if it does, ha, we'll be crushed before we know what's happening.'

Everard gasped. 'The rain makes buildings collapse down here?!'

'All the time,' Juniper answered, just as a knock came at the door and Thea skipped through.

'A delightful rainfall to you, Juniper!' She beamed, holding up the list of ideas they'd been drafting, trying their best to prepare for The Shrouded's upcoming challenge. So far they had come up with the following ideas:

Walk up the tower.
Run up the tower.
Climb up the tower.
Ride Everard up the tower. I think not. — Everard
Ride Cinder up the tower. NO. — Cinder
Make a human pyramid to reach the top of the tower.
Offer The Shrouded a sandwich and hope she lets the whole thing slide.

'You know, I think we're gonna nail this,' Juniper said, admiring their work.

The sound of a mocking snigger came from the corner of the room. All the children looked in its direction, but only Juniper and Thea knew it had been Cinder.

'Those bells are *so* getting donged,' Thea agreed.

'Everard – have you ever been to the Midnight Tower?' Juniper asked.

'I, um, well, yes, I have.' His eyes did that darty thing they did when he was nervous.

'And? What did you think? Anything I should know?'

He sniffed. 'I'm not here to give you my expert advice, but if you must know . . . it's my least favourite of the towers.' He seemed reluctant to continue. 'It's just – the other Arcanists inspire such hope. The Tempest brings us his guiding light, The Maker creates, The Watcher keeps us safe, The Enigma offers endless possibilities, but The Shrouded?' Everard swallowed.

'She deals with the dead,' Thea finished.

Everard looked positively panicked. 'O-of course, she's absolutely brilliant, and glorious, and I don't mean anything by that. It's just –'

'She's creepy as heck?' Juniper said.

'Yes! Especially those moths of hers. So quiet, so silent, guiding the spirits of the dead to the Beyond . . .' He gave a little shiver. 'Anyone else feeling a tad chilly?'

'It is quite cold, isn't it . . . ?' Thea said, having a little shiver herself.

Juniper felt it too. The already meagre lantern light seemed to dim and seep away, chased by growing shadows. Her breath puffed out as tiny clouds. The children shared a look of growing unease.

There was a sudden commotion from downstairs. Raised voices and thumping footsteps. Then someone knocked frantically on the door.

Juniper opened it to find a startled stranger waiting on the other side – a man whose soaking-wet hair clung to his shiny scalp, his long nose red from the cold, his cheeks puffing out as he breathed heavily.

'Arcanist!' he gasped out. Madame Adie stood behind him, looking just as anxious as Juniper felt. 'You must come quick! Shades have broken through the wards!'

The man led the way through the warren of twisting avenues to where the Shades had been spotted. Every bit of Juniper wanted to turn back, but what choice did she have? Arcanists were meant to defend the people against Shades, and she was meant to be an Arcanist.

'Running towards an invincible enemy, entirely unarmed,' Cinder whispered, clinging to her shoulder as little more than a wispy slither of shadow. 'I can't see how that could possibly go wrong.'

'Not completely unarmed,' Juniper declared, brandishing a paper ward she'd once kept from a relic haul for emergencies. Cinder eyed it dubiously. She pointed back at Thea, who was clutching her trusty

Justice Stick. Cinder's expression remained unchanged.

'OK, point taken,' Juniper groaned, all too aware that she had no plan for whatever came next.

Nothing could hurt a Shade. Nothing could even *touch* 'em. The only defence the people of Arkspire had against such nightmares were the Arcanists, who could banish Shades back beyond the Veil. But they couldn't be everywhere at once, no matter how powerful they were, and so they'd drawn magical warding sigils around the city, protected areas through which the Shades could not cross. But sigils grow old and wear away. Maintaining the sigils was an Arcanists' most basic duty.

Stupid flippin' Watcher, Juniper cursed to herself, dashing through the rain-slick streets. 'You can turn sigils off, but do you know how to turn sigils *on*? Could you redraw the wards?' she asked Cinder.

Cinder thought. 'I suspect I could, but I have no memory of how.'

'Helpful as always,' Juniper said.

'I try.'

They dashed past an unfortunate few still out in the storm. 'Get behind the East Stack wards!' Juniper shouted. 'Get to safety!'

'Aren't their homes warded?' Everard asked.

'Only those that can afford it have home wards,'

Thea replied, 'which is basically no one.'

Everard wrestled with this idea, almost unable to believe it. 'But – but that's so dangerous!'

A thunderclap roared from above, as the man skidded to a stop at the entrance to a market square, or at least what had once been a market square. A mighty torrent of water now crashed down from the levels above, rushing through the square like a raging river, tumbling over the edge down to whatever unfortunate buildings lay below. Wooden shacks had collapsed with it, their broken shapes jutting out of the water like wooden bones, people's meagre possessions floating over the edge.

'Th-there!' The man pointed, rain flicking from his lank hair. 'The Shades . . . they attacked, and . . .' The children stared at the scene before them, rain dripping off their caps, noses and chins. On the opposite side of the square a group of people clustered together on a rooftop as the debris-ridden rapids lapped hungrily at its edge.

Juniper gasped. 'They're stranded!'

Their fearful faces filled with hope at the sight of her. Hope that they, at long, long last, had an Arcanist in their district who had actually shown up, who was there to protect them. They were shouting something, but the roaring sound of the rushing floodwaters drowned their voices.

Juniper's insides felt heavy, her mouth dry. This was it. Her lies had finally caught up with her. People were relying on her magic to win the day. The magic she didn't have.

'You have to do something!' Everard urged.

'I know!' Juniper said. She felt Cinder coiling his tail round her arm, as tense as everyone else.

'Use your magic to help them!' came a voice. Juniper found the source – people were hanging out of their windows in the buildings above the square, watching with wild eyes.

'I – I can't . . .' Juniper whispered. She tried to push back the awful thoughts filling her head, the memories of the last time this had happened so close to home.

The pouring rain spattering on the dirt roads, crashing on the tin rooftops.

The shoving, panicking crowds.

Her mama's voice, yelling at her to get to safety.

The long, grasping fingers of the Shades curling round Mama's arms.

Juniper's breath quickening; her limbs growing as heavy as lead.

She flinched when Thea placed a hand on her shoulder. 'I'm here with you,' she whispered, giving it a gentle squeeze.

Funny how such a small gesture can fill you with courage. With a deep, shuddering breath, Juniper stepped forward. A tiny raft was caught in the flood, bobbing violently in the water.

'I'm gonna use that raft to fetch as many of them as I can,' Juniper explained. 'Thea, Everard, I need you guys to pull the rope tied to the raft and make sure we don't go tumblin' over the edge . . .'

Thea snapped into a salute, while Everard gave a nervous nod.

'I need you down here!' Juniper shouted to those looking out of their windows. 'Gather as much wood as you can from the wreckage! We have to make more rafts!'

'But the Shades!' a woman whimpered.

'They're not here any more, and those people need our help!'

Heads disappeared from the windows, racing to do as they were asked. Though frightened, they weren't going to argue with someone who might've been an Arcanist.

It felt weird people doing what she said. People who'd never have given her a second glance any other day. That was the true power of an Arcanist. Respect. Well, that and their all-powerful world-bending magics.

'I can't believe you're dragging me into this suicidal

scheme of yours,' Cinder complained, as Juniper pushed the raft out into the turbulent waters. It was tough-going. The current snatched at the raft, trying to steal it away, but Thea and Everard held the rope taut.

Slowly Juniper made her way across the flooded square – and as she did the voices of the stranded become clearer.

'Water,' she thought she heard them saying. 'Under the water!'

But it wasn't until she drew up alongside the rooftop that she could hear what they were saying properly.

'The Shades are under the water!'

A chill ran down Juniper's spine. She spun round, feeling like something was creeping up on her, but all she saw was the rushing water, too dark and dirty to see through. One thing was for sure, however – the water level was rising, and was now lapping over the edge of the roof. These people didn't have long before they'd be totally submerged.

'What we can't see can't hurt us, right?' Juniper said, trying to sound cheerful. 'I'll take as many of you as I can, but more help is on the way!' She gestured to the other side of the square, where thankfully people were roping planks of wood together into makeshift rafts as fast as they could.

Juniper tried to keep the raft steady as the first

passengers were lowered on to it. She was surprised to see Tash-face among the stranded, the man who'd been so outspoken against her a few days back. He helped people on to the raft in silence, unable to meet Juniper's eye.

'Bless you, Arcanist!' a mother said, holding her children tight.

Juniper gave a brief nod, then pushed away from the roof.

It was then that she saw it. Lights rising up from under the water.

They were dim at first, barely visible under the turbulent current, but they grew larger and brighter.

One of the kids screamed. Juniper knew how they felt.

Impossibly gaunt torsos rose from the waters like puppets on strings. The rain fell through them as though they weren't even there. The slender claws twitched like spider legs. And, worst of all, the voids where their faces should've been were endless pits of darkness, broken only by searing-white eyes that stared out at the living with a deep hunger.

Five Shades floated above the floodwaters, blocking the raft's way back to land.

21

A BEACON IN THE DARK

The Shades floated in silence. Then one reached out for the raft with a hungry desperation. With a cry, Juniper staggered back into her fellow passengers, whipping out the paper ward she'd brought with trembling hands. But to her horror she saw that the heavy rain had dissolved the paper; the magical sigil was vanishing into a squishy mulch.

'What are you waiting for? Banish them!' an old man blurted.

'I – I don't know how,' Juniper croaked, panic rising. 'Cinder . . .?'

'I can sense the old wards under the water,' Cinder whispered, little more than a shadow on the back of her coat, his eyes flashing briefly with icy fire. 'But they're too messed up to work.'

'Erm, we might have a much more immediate problem . . .' Juniper said.

'What are you doing?!' the mother cried, her children huddled close to her and crying into her arms. 'You're bringing them this way!'

The Shades were drifting towards them. Cinder was like some kind of Shade-lure, attracting each and every one of them.

'Your magic!' Juniper said to Cinder. 'They're attracted to your magic!'

Cinder subdued his power immediately.

'No, wait!' Juniper said – the passengers were completely baffled as they watched her apparently talking to herself. 'You can distract them! Lead the Shades away from us, and let me get these people to safety!'

'I have a better idea. Why don't *you* act as bait and *I'll* pole the rest of us back to safety?!' Cinder snapped.

The Shades were getting closer, turning the air a biting cold.

'Cinder! You can travel through shadows – you can outrun them!'

Cinder eyed the Shades. It was the first time that Juniper had seen him look worried about anything. 'Urgh, fine,' he relented, 'but you owe me!'

'Yeah, yeah, yeah – just go!'

Cinder flared his eyes, Juniper's sigils tingling at his magic, then dived from her shoulder. He merged with the shadows bobbing on the water's surface, using them like a bridge to glide across the flood like some horrible water snake. To Juniper's amazement, the Shades lurched after him, their movements awkward, and yet sometimes surging forward with frightening speed. Seems they'd forgotten all about the raft.

Juniper had never seen anything like it – but she wasted no time in poling the raft back to the other side of the square, Thea and Everard pulling on the rope as hard as they could.

'The Shades – how did you distract them?' Everard gasped as the raft made it to safety, onlookers there helping the rescued passengers off.

'It's my magic; you wouldn't get it,' Juniper said,

pushing the raft back into the flood waters. 'Everard, focus! We have people to save!'

'R-right!' He gripped the rope, as Juniper poled back the way she'd just come.

To anyone who didn't know, Cinder's eyes looked like little more than two bobbing lights in the heavy rain, but Juniper could just about make out his shadowy shape leading the Shades on a merry chase. It looked like it had worked too – until a Shade with grotesquely long arms snatched Cinder's tail as he leaped into the air. It wrenched him back, its ethereal claws somehow clasping round Cinder's intangible body like it was solid, stopping him from squirming away.

'Cinder!' Juniper cried.

'Juniper, get them off me!' he pleaded, reaching out for her.

The Shade's touch hadn't killed him, as it would a human, but some kind of other-worldly energy was stopping Cinder from shadow-jumping out of its grasp. Despite her better judgement, Juniper made her way towards them as fast as she could. The Shade raised Cinder up to its fathomless face, its eyes burning brighter than ever, inspecting him closely.

'You will rue this day!' Cinder growled. 'I will destroy you! I will wipe out your very essence!'

Then the Shade did something incredible. It released

him, dropping Cinder into the racing waters, all interest in him lost. But why? Was he not what the Shades were looking for?

There was no time to think – Juniper's heart swooped when she saw that the Shades' attention had returned to the people still stranded on the rooftop.

'Over here! Look over here!' Juniper yelled, trying to get the Shades' attention, but it was no use.

The Shades floated on to the rooftop, the people backing up against the wall. Tash-face did his best to fend them off with a stick, for what little good it would do him.

Juniper closed her eyes tight, unable to watch.

Someone screamed. And then there was a loud crash.

Opening her eyes, Juniper watched as a Requisitions wagon skidded to a stop on the edge of the flooded square. Wardens and Candidates

from the Order of Iris leaped out, all directed by a high-ranking magister. Juniper could've cried when she spotted Elodie among them; she was so happy to see her.

The Candidates and wardens pulled out polished stones from pouches at their belts, each inscribed with magical symbols by The Watcher herself. With fast, well-practised movements, they threw the stones as one. The stones landed on the roof harbouring the stranded people, forming a loose circle round the Shades. A wall of light burst out of the stones, forcing Juniper to shield her eyes as the circle built up into a blinding flare before disappearing.

And, just like that, the Shades were gone, banished from the world. The stones throbbed red, like the cooling embers of a fire, and the square fell silent, except for the drumming rain.

'Always remember,' the magister declared from atop his wagon, 'though you cannot see her, it doesn't mean she's not there. The Watcher is always watching over you!'

As it dawned on the stranded people that the danger was over, they began to mumble and mutter with relief. Loved ones hugged each other; others laughed nervously, barely able to believe their narrow escape.

'It doesn't take a genius to see that this imposter was powerless to help you,' the magister announced, sneering at Juniper. 'Only the power of the Arcanists and their revered Orders can keep you safe.'

Juniper didn't know what to say. She could barely process what had just happened. All she knew for sure was the rage boiling up inside her like water in a kettle. Who did this magister think he was, safe behind his wardens while she'd put herself in danger?

'At least she tried to help us!' someone shouted. To Juniper's amazement, it was Tash-face. 'Where were *you* when we needed you?'

'*We* just saved you all!' the magister hissed.

'Only just!' shouted the mother Juniper had rescued. 'The Arcanist of the Dregs did all the real work, while you were hiding, afraid to get your hair wet!'

At this, Everard lowered the scrap of wood he'd been trying to use as an umbrella.

The magister looked flabbergasted at this open defiance. 'How – how *dare* you!' The wardens formed a protective wall round him, rifles clutched in their hands. 'Such disloyalty!' he screeched. 'That girl is not your Arcanist. The Watcher is – and you'd do well to remember that!'

'The Arcanist of the Dregs stood up for us when no one else would, and she ain't even the ruler of this district!' someone shouted, and a cheer rose from the onlookers.

The wardens remained still, watching Juniper as if they couldn't decide whether she was friend or foe. Past their shoulders, Juniper locked eyes with Elodie. She was staring at Juniper, but this time it wasn't with embarrassment. It was with something like surprise.

Her magister, on the other hand, was looking at Juniper as if he'd just seen a drowned rat drag itself out of the water. 'Th-the roads –' the magister stammered, searching for an explanation. 'They were – The floods blocked our – We – we –'

The crowd began booing him, and the magister blinked in disbelief. Deciding he didn't like where the situation was headed, he retreated into the wagon, the wardens pushing back against the jeering throng.

'That's it – run away! Leave us here, like you always do!'

The mother Juniper had saved pulled her into a tight embrace as the boos grew louder. 'Thank you!' she gasped . 'I – I can't thank you enough!'

'I didn't really –' Juniper started.

Tash-face placed a hand on her shoulder. 'I don't know what you did with that weird talkin' shadow-thing, but you saved us all.'

'Three cheers for the Arcanist of the Dregs!' Thea declared.

'Hip, hip, hooray!' the crowd chanted, louder each time.

It didn't seem real. Juniper felt like she should've been in the crowd cheering someone else on, someone who'd actually done something to earn it.

Then it hit Juniper. She had given the people hope. Just by standing at their side, by trying. It wasn't just her family that needed help, it was *everyone* in the Dregs. They were desperate, having been ignored for far too long, left to wallow in the floods and decay of the lower city. And, if Juniper played her cards right, she'd actually be in a position to help them. If she could complete the challenges, if she could convince the city she was an Arcanist, and help Cinder regain his powers, then she could inspire them like the Arcanists did – and be able to make a difference.

Juniper felt the warmth of her own hope rising inside her, overcoming the cold of the rain and her soaking, clinging clothes.

'Ungrateful little urchins,' Cinder's voice hissed into her ear. 'I'm the one who did all the hard work.'

'And I won't forget it,' Juniper replied. 'Promise.'

The wardens and Candidates retreated back into the wagon, as people banged its sides and made faces at the windows. Elodie paused at the door, looking back at Juniper as though she were a different person. Juniper had thought her sister would be mad that she had made a magister of her Order look like a fool. But Elodie gave her a little smile and a nod of approval.

It was a bigger compliment than all the people cheering her name. Juniper could barely contain her happiness.

Then someone grabbed hold of her wrist. She tried to pull away, but they gripped it tight. What was this guy's problem? She spun round to confront them, coming face to face with a man in a deep hood and a neckerchief pulled over his nose. 'Hey, mister, what're you –'

'Word from Bleater,' he grunted into her ear, his voice broken and husky. 'He knows where to find your Boden.'

22

HERBAL TEA

Word of Juniper's actions had spread fast. It had only been a day since the Shade attack and it was already all over the papers, being talked about in the manufactories, and had become the starting point of conversation in the tearooms of the Uppers.

She seemed to have split the city down the middle. Some were saying Juniper was a hero, a worthy friend of the Arcanists, while others were saying she was a troublemaker trying to make the Arcanists look bad. Whichever side they took, people were starting to take her seriously.

Just as well then that Juniper now knew where to find Boden. The sooner they got Cinder his powers back, the sooner she could use them.

Boden just happened to be in the last place she'd have ever thought to look.

The tower of the Crux may have been at the very centre of Arkspire, but really it was a monument marking where The Visitor had first come through the Veil and entered this world. The deepest depths of the crater it had left behind were still meant to be an unstable mess of strange magics. The city was kept safe by countless wards keeping the magic at bay, but it was considered a pretty dangerous, if not downright suicidal, place for a person to visit.

Great place to hide, though, Juniper thought, scratching at her collar. The servant costume she wore was driving her crazy.

The Misfits were no strangers to disguises. They'd dressed as rival gangers before, complete with fake tattoos drawn on with pen, and they'd dressed as Candidates too for one particularly sneaky heist. Juniper had once even put on a fake moustache and sat on Thea's shoulders, pretending to be a manufactory boss. It hadn't gone well, and really the less said about the whole affair, the better. But out of all those costumes this servant uniform was the worst. The waistcoat was too tight, the collar was scratchy, and the shoes were rubbing her toes.

'A few modifications here and there, and I think I

can make this work,' Thea said, admiring the stitching. Of course, they'd had to ditch Everard. Couldn't have him reporting *this* little adventure back to The Tempest.

'The papers are doing a story on my rise to power,' Juniper had told him that afternoon, 'and I told 'em I couldn't have done any of this without the help of my trusty ally Everard Amberflaw the Seventh.'

His face had paled at that. 'You said *what*?! I would be seen in a badly tailored suit before I *ever* helped you! How could you –? Why would you –? And I'm Everard Amberflaw the Fourth! The *Fourth*! ARGH!' He'd marched straight to the printing presses to put an end to the ridiculous rumour before it got out.

It was a shame they'd had to trick him like that. Everard had just sent a report to The Tempest detailing how shocked he was at the terrible conditions in the Dregs, and how urgent aid was needed for the lower levels. Juniper had started to think she might be able to like him. Maybe. A little bit. One day.

For now, Juniper peeked out from her hiding place behind a wall, tapping her foot impatiently as she eyed the clock mounted on the guardhouse ahead. They'd climbed over the barbed-wire fences and various checkpoints to get this far, but the guardhouse watching over the Iris District's section of the crater rim posed more of a challenge. There were no windows or hatches to sneak through, only a guarded metal door. Wardens lined the walls above, searchlights scanning the open ground between the girls and the building.

Even though Juniper had come up with the plan to break in (with the help of Thea, of course, and a very excitable Madame Adie), seeing how heavily guarded the place was she was now having second thoughts. 'Why are we doing this again? It's wild even for us.'

Cinder stirred on her shoulder. 'You're doing it because I command it! I must find Boden. I must have my answers! But if you want an incentive, consider that when I'm back to my all-powerful self I'll be sure to judge you two fairly when I come to wreak vengeance upon this world.'

'Aw, thanks, Cinder,' Juniper said.

'After all, yesterday, when those puffed-up shadows held me in their grasp, you came back for me.' Cinder paused, apparently struggling with what he wanted to say. 'You failed miserably, of course. And it was foolish, ill-conceived and frankly idiotic. But it was also . . . *considerate*.' He pulled a face, as though the word offended him. 'And for that I despise you a little less. A little.'

Juniper blinked. Had she just received a thank-you from Cinder, or at least the closest you'd ever get from him? 'Hey, you woulda done the same for me,' she said.

'No. No, I absolutely would not have.'

Juniper was snapped out of their cheerful exchange when the clock struck eight, a deep gong marking the hour. She tensed as two wardens led a group of servants past their hiding place. Time for a shift change.

Swift as cats, Juniper and Thea slunk out of the shadows and joined the back of the line, keeping their heads down like the rest of the servants. Even though a few at the front looked closer to Papa's age, most were teenagers, meaning the Misfits didn't look too out of place. The girl in front of Juniper turned her head slightly, noticing the new arrivals.

She frowned at Juniper. 'Do I know you? You look familiar.'

Juniper's pulse quickened. She couldn't afford to be recognized, not here. 'Don't think so. I used to work up in, er, Amberflaw's mansion, over in the Radiant District.'

The girl chuckled sympathetically. 'You must've been *really* bad to get transferred to this graveyard post. The crater may sound big 'n' scary, but, trust me, *nothing* exciting ever happens here.'

Juniper's pulse didn't slow as they lined up to get inside the guardhouse, waiting for the exhausted servants who'd been working the day shift to leave the building. The wardens watched over them all as they passed, gesturing for the new group to go inside.

Juniper bit her lip. What if the wardens realized they'd never seen Juniper and Thea down here before? They might have the costumes, but they didn't have any fake identification.

Juniper stepped up to the wardens, whose goggles were lifeless in the gloom. They waved her through, and Juniper let out a breath.

One of the benefits of being a nobody from the Dregs, she supposed. No one really took any notice of you.

The servants filed into the servants' quarters and got straight to it, some grabbing brooms, others donning aprons and preparing pots and pans at a large stove.

'OK, you lot, you know the drill,' said the oldest of the servants. Judging from her slightly fancier uniform, Juniper assumed she was the boss, and she did her very best to hide her face from her. 'We've got a long night ahead of us, so let's keep our valiant wardens fed and watered.'

The servant who'd nearly recognized Juniper was busy piling cups and a teapot on to a tray.

'I'll take that!' Juniper said, rushing over.

At first the servant looked surprised, protective of her tray even. 'That keen to prove yourself, huh?' Then she relented, chuckling as she handed it over. 'Knock yourself out – sounds like you need all the help you can get.'

The guardhouse was big, but there was one part in particular Juniper and Thea were aiming for. It was a small room, bleak and bare, but they were there for the metal door that led outside, not the decor. Two wardens lounged at a desk in front of a large window, maskless and bored, but the view from the window, now that was quite something indeed. A yawning, jagged pit, incredibly large, the tower of the Crux rising from its centre like a stone tongue. Juniper had to hold back a gasp. Seeing such a legendary site was kind of mind-blowing. Other guardhouses lined the rim at equal distances round its border, watchtowers and the sweeping white beams of searchlights looking for anything out of the ordinary. Metal platforms, stairwells and gangways rose from the dark depths like the skeleton of some ginormous beast.

The sight fed the doubt growing in Juniper's head. Sneaking into a heavily guarded place of wild magic, hoping to find some old friend of Cinder's? Could someone really be down there?

Juniper had no reason to doubt Bleater. He had a reputation for being trustworthy – he made a living off the fact. But still something felt off, and Juniper had learned to trust her gut.

One of the wardens turned to the girls. 'You making tea?'

Thea smiled. 'That's why we're here! Who'd like one?'

'Thank The Visitor, I'm gagging.'

The girls took the tray to a small table in the corner. While Thea poured the tea, Juniper pulled out a small vial of powder from her pocket that Madame Adie had given her. Moon Kiss, the stuff Madame Adie swore could put a grown adult to sleep for a few hours just from a whiff of its fumes. Thea lifted the teapot's lid and, as quick as a dart, Juniper slipped the powder into it.

'I'm just going to leave the pot here,' Juniper announced as Thea handed out the cups to the grateful wardens. 'Keep what's left warm for later.'

A warden made an 'OK' hand gesture without so much as glancing up from the book she was reading. Juniper placed the teapot on the metal stove that kept the shadowy chill of the crater at bay. According to Madame Adie, they wouldn't have to wait long before the Moon Kiss reacted.

But then came a sudden commotion from the corridor – raised voices, fast approaching.

Juniper and Thea shared a worried glance just as the door burst open. Panic clutched at Juniper's heart as Everard barged in, followed by the head servant and another warden, each looking flustered.

'*Aha!*' Everard declared victoriously. 'I *knew* you two were up to no good!'

One of the warden's yelped, nearly spilling his tea. 'Holy –'

'I'm so sorry, sir,' the head servant said. 'I tried to stop him, but he's a Candidate, and I –'

'Wardens, arrest these girls!' Everard demanded, sneering at Juniper. 'The newspapers are going to print a story on you *indeed*! They would never print such unfounded poppycock! I *knew* you were lying and decided to follow you in secret! And a good thing I did too, for I'm now able to expose your sinister schemes once and for all, you sinister-schemers, you!'

Juniper had to admit she was impressed, despite the fact that Everard was ruining *everything*.

'Can someone explain what on earth's going on?!' a warden demanded.

'We can do that,' Juniper said quickly. 'If you'd all just come inside, we can explain everything.' She ushered them into the room, doing her very best to show as little of her face as she could. Thea put her back to the door and locked it without anyone seeing. Juniper stood at the opposite end of the room to the teapot, hoping no one had noticed the smoke that had started puffing out of the spout.

'It's true,' Juniper said, scrambling for time. 'Our plan was as complicated as it was pointless.'

The head servant sniffed. 'Is something burning?'

Everyone in the room turned to see the teapot puffing like an engine, smoke now billowing out of it, thick and cloying. Juniper pulled the neckerchief hidden under her shirt over her nose. She recognized the smell immediately – it was the same liquorice-y scent she'd caught wafting out of Madame Adie's workshop numerous times.

The head servant swooned, then tumbled to the floor.

'What the –' a warden said, gasping. She reached for the baton at her belt and lunged forward, but she too collapsed to the floor at the end of her step. Then her comrade fell off his chair, the third falling on top of him.

'No!' Everard gasped out, holding his breath and staggering towards Juniper. But he'd already breathed in too much of the fumes. His eyelids grew heavy, his movements sluggish, and the sight of Juniper giving him a little wave was the last thing he saw before falling unconscious.

They were all sound asleep. The larger warden had even begun to snore.

'You know what?' Cinder said, apparently unaffected by the Moon Kiss. 'I'm starting to think I may have underestimated that Adie woman . . .'

23

DEEP DIVE

Having only about an hour before the effects of the Moon Kiss wore off, the girls moved fast, slipping on some warden coats that were hanging on the back of the door.

Juniper put her hands on her hips, surveying the considerably larger body count than she'd planned on. 'Well, this complicates things. How we gonna pull off a break-in while lugging Everard around? We can't just leave him.'

'Can't we?' Cinder asked.

'He'll tell everyone it was us!' Juniper said.

'Shall I kill him?' Cinder offered.

'No!'

'Well, you can't say I didn't try. Come, we have a Boden to find.'

'Nothing for it, then,' Thea said, placing Everard's arm over her shoulder and hefting him up. 'Come on, you.'

'Everard, you idiot, why couldn't you just stay away?' Juniper muttered, taking his other arm to help Thea.

'I have to say, you girls impress me,' Cinder commented.

'Oh?' said Thea.

'Indeed. It amazes me how you stumble from one terrible situation to the next, never putting any fires out, only starting others in your wake.'

'Hey, it's all going *preeeeetty* much to plan,' Juniper said, swiping a ring of keys from the desk and trying them all in the door's lock. Finally there was a click, and she used her hip to open the door. 'Besides, what's the worst that could happen?'

'If you say that one more time, I might have to call the guards on you myself,' Cinder threatened.

The gang shuffled towards the nearest lift, Everard's feet scraping along the metal gangway as the wind tore across the vast crater and snatched at their coats. Avoiding the probing searchlights wasn't made any easier by Everard's dead weight, but they pushed on, Juniper sliding the door open so that Thea could unceremoniously dump Everard in the lift cage.

There were just two buttons: up and down.

'Only good things happen when you go deep into

the dark bowels of the earth, right?' Juniper said, pressing down.

The lift made an alarming grinding sound, attracting the attention of the wardens in the nearest watchtower. Thea gave them a wave. Thankfully, at this distance, the warden clothing the girls were wearing looked convincing enough, and the wardens hesitantly waved back.

The lift rumbled down into the deepening darkness.

Sigils suddenly blazed to life along the rock walls as they passed, but Cinder held up his claws, energy radiating out of him as he deactivated their defences. Juniper felt the familiar prickling in her sigils, like Cinder's magic was magnetic.

He grimaced. 'Oof, that was a bad one. Ouch, that would've been nasty. Funny to watch, though. You're lucky I'm here!'

'What would they have done?' Thea asked, her eyes reflecting the magical light.

'Oh, you know, the usual stuff. Incinerated you to a crisp, turned you inside out, stripped you down to your most basic parts.'

'Turned us into frogs?'

'I've . . . not seen a frog sigil yet,' Cinder admitted.

Thea sighed. 'Shame.'

Juniper peered down into the depths, trying to see what awaited them, but could only make out jagged rock. Other than the sigils, there'd been no strange magics. But still she tapped the cage bars she peered through, her anxiety growing.

Surely only a Betrayer would choose to hide in a lightless, lifeless place like this. In which case were they really heading to see a real-life Betrayer out of *choice*? Had the Betrayer somehow organized this whole thing, and they were now blindly falling into his trap? It had seemed like such a good idea at the time. They needed answers, and this was where they'd find them. But it was one thing imagining it and a very different thing actually doing it.

'Uuuurgh,' came a woozy voice. Everard was stirring, the Moon Kiss appearing to have less of an effect now that he was outside.

'Wakey-wakey, sleepyhead,' Thea said.

'What's happening . . .?' He blinked, eyes focusing on the girls, then he jolted backwards, his chest heaving. 'What – where am I?! Wasn't I just valiantly dishing out some much-needed justice upon you both?'

'Hey, bud, you gotta calm down,' Juniper said, kneeling next to him, worried his voice might attract attention.

'You haven't answered my question. Where are we?'

'See, I'm worried that if I tell you, you're gonna freak out, and we're gonna have this whole big scene . . .' Juniper said.

'Why would I freak out? Where are we?'

'First, you gotta swear you'll keep your cool. We're in this together now, and –'

Everard grabbed both of her shoulders. 'As a Candidate in the Order of Radiance and heir to House Amberflaw, I demand you tell me where we are!'

'We're in the, erm, kinda, maybe, y'know, in The Visitor's crater. A little bit. Ish.'

'The – the crater?' The colour left his face. He fell to the floor, unconscious.

'Is he dead?' Cinder asked hopefully.

'No! He's just fainted,' Juniper said, checking his pulse. She tried giving him a shake. 'Moneyclumps? Everard? You in there?' She poked him gently on the cheek. Nothing. She slapped him across the face. He spluttered awake.

'He's seen too much; he can't be allowed to leave!' Cinder said, his eyes flaring bright.

'No, Cinder, wait –' Juniper began, but she was too late.

Cinder launched himself up on to Everard's chest, grabbing him by the neck with his tiny ethereal paws, and began shaking.

Everard tried to scream, but only managed a strangled gargle.

Juniper swatted at Cinder, but she might as well have been hitting smoke. 'Just leave him alone, OK?! You're not helping!'

'You're too soft!' Cinder said, ducking away from Juniper's hands. 'He'll tell the Arcanists everything!'

'What is that thing?!' Everard gasped, backing up against the lift's side. His voice was strained, like he was trying to hold back a scream.

'Shhh! Everard, take a deep breath and hear me out, OK?' Juniper pleaded. 'Don't let the guards know we're here . . .'

Everard whimpered, his eyes darting about as if he'd just remembered where they were. 'Why are you doing this? Are you a Betrayer?!'

'No!' Juniper said. 'I promise you I'm not! But my power, it's – it's different from the other Arcanists' magic!' She pointed at Cinder as if in explanation.

'That *thing* is your magic?'

'Pah!' Cinder scoffed.

'Hey, stick with me, bud.' Juniper clicked her fingers in front of Everard's face, sensing his rising panic. 'I don't really get it either. But we're here to try to understand. We're here for one thing, and one thing only: to find somebody. One cheeky little chat, and then we're outta here. It'll help me understand my powers, help me control them, help me to help others and help the Arcanists make Arkspire a better place!' She was stretching the truth a little, but she had to get this situation under control. 'I know you don't trust me, but all this is for a good cause, I promise.'

'That's exactly what an evil Betrayer would say!' Everard said.

Juniper huffed. 'Do I really look like a Betrayer to you?'

Everard's eyes flickered from her angry face to Cinder's threatening, blazing eyes. 'Yes!'

'Then I guess we've gotta part ways,' Juniper said. 'Just know that if you're caught down here, you'll go to jail just as quick as us.'

Everard went to say something, but his jaw suddenly dropped. He hadn't thought of that. He rubbed his hands down his face in despair. 'Why are you doing this to me? You won't rest until you've dragged my reputation through the mud, will you? All my hard work in the Academy! All my loyalty and dedication!'

'You can keep your reputation,' Juniper said. 'I just need you to be quiet, stay low and follow our lead, got it? So, are we all on the same team or what?'

'*If one trips up, those behind will be quick to follow*, as my grangran would say,' Thea added.

Both Cinder and Everard harrumphed.

Juniper took that as a yes.

Good thing too, as the lift had just clunked to a stop. They were at the bottom of the crater. Cautiously they slid the door open, half expecting kaleidoscopic colours, rocks turning into clouds, bolts of crackling energy and other such wild magics. But all they found were rocks. Lots and lots of rocks and a few strange stone blocks that encircled the base of the Crux, a thin mist curling over the floor.

'Coast is clear,' Thea said, creeping out of the lift. Silence hung as heavy as a storm cloud, the damp air the kind that seeps into your bones and bites with its chill.

'So much for the crazy unstable magics down here,' Juniper whispered, her voice still sounding too loud.

'Maybe there is, and it'll kill us all the moment we trigger it?' Everard squeaked.

'Or maybe it's just a rumour to keep people away?' Cinder said.

'Away from what?' Juniper asked, her doubt becoming almost unbearable.

'Wait!' Everard hissed urgently.

'What?' the girls asked.

He pulled out a pocket mirror, adjusted his hair, then clapped it closed. 'OK, ready.'

They approached one of the stone blocks. It was a little longer than a person, its front carved with symbols and letters Juniper couldn't understand. At its top was a symbol of a crescent moon.

'*The Silent*,' Everard read over her shoulder, frowning. 'It's written in Arcana script.' Of course it was. Arcana script was a language taught only to Arcanists, magisters and students of the Academies. It was deemed too secret and powerful to teach to anyone else, something Elodie seemed all too happy to mention ever since she'd started learning it.

They moved to the next one. This one had the emblem of a scorpion. '*The Unseen*,' Everard said. 'Wait . . .' He suddenly staggered back as he recognized the words, and his face twisted in fear. 'Get away from them! The Silent, The Unseen. Those are names of the Betrayers! We're looking at – at –' he swallowed – 'their sarcophagi!'

24

RECOLLECTIONS

There were loads of them. Juniper counted at least twenty, and they continued to curl round the tower and out of sight.

'They're all here,' she whispered, a chill blooming in her belly. 'All ninety-five of 'em, I bet you.' She strode from sarcophagus to sarcophagus, looking at their emblems. A hawk, a hyena, a hare.

Thea whistled. 'Who'd'a thought they'd all just be buried here right in the middle of the city?'

'I must insist that we leave; no good can come of us being here!' Everard urged.

'As soon as we speak to the guy we're looking for, we'll go, I promise!' Juniper said.

'Who on earth could you want to speak to down here?' Everard squeaked.

'Good question,' Juniper said. 'Any idea where your friend might be hiding, Cinder?' She was beginning to suspect she already knew the answer. She turned to face Cinder when he didn't respond, only to discover he wasn't there. His eyes gave him away – shimmering like stars in the distant darkness. He was standing atop a stone sarcophagus, looking down at it intensely. For once, there was no maliciousness in his eyes, no sinister glare, no wicked smile. His ears were dipped, his tail drooping. He looked almost . . . sad.

She walked respectfully behind him, looking at the sarcophagus. It showed the symbol of a phoenix.

'*The Seer*,' Everard read.

'He had the power to see the truth in someone's soul, to read the things left unsaid and unwritten,' Cinder said, his voice cracking. He reached down and touched the sarcophagus. 'His real name was Boden. At least, it was to his friends.'

Juniper's heart sank. She'd had a suspicion that the one person who could make sense of this whole mess would be long dead, but it didn't make the truth any easier.

'Help me open it,' Cinder said.

Everard gasped. 'Why would you do such a thing?'

'Just to make sure they're in there?' Thea offered.

'Firstly, the Order of Midnight teaches us to respect

the dead, lest they return from beyond the Veil in anger. Secondly, it's a Betrayer! Who knows what unimaginable evil may still cling to their body, even after all these years! There must be a reason these coffins are down here. They must be warded to the hilt. It'd be utter foolishness – no, *madness* – to even *consider* opening –'

Everard was interrupted by the sound of scraping stone. The girls heaved at the heavy lid, pushing it far enough aside to peek within.

There was a body inside, all right. A blackened skeleton, its jaw hanging open as if death had done nothing to dampen its sense of humour. Juniper reckoned it wasn't chuckling about the large hole in its skull, though – the edges of which were still glowing with embers of magical light.

The children recoiled at the horrific sight. Everard turned away, retching.

'The Arcanists weren't messing around when they beat the Betrayers, were they?' Juniper whispered. She knew the Betrayers were bad, but . . . *man*. 'We were always told the Arcanists stripped the Betrayers of their powers, not – not –'

Juniper shivered, trying not to imagine meeting the same fate in the upcoming challenges.

'So this is where Boden lies,' Cinder said. 'At least I found him. At least he was real, and not some figment of my broken memories . . .' He closed his eyes and touched a claw to the skull.

Juniper felt a tug, an attraction, like something was pulling her closer to Cinder. It was deep inside, as though someone had thrown a lasso round her soul. She tried to resist it, sensing something terrible and destructive beyond. She struggled, but it was no use. The fury inside Cinder screamed into Juniper's mind with sudden overwhelming force. She felt like she was tumbling through a firestorm, unable to escape.

'THEY DID THIS TO US!' Cinder screamed.

Despite the white-hot fury frying her mind, Juniper managed to focus, arranging Cinder's scrambled feelings together into one thought. *The Arcanists.*

'But . . . why?' Juniper asked through gritted teeth. 'What did you do, Cinder? Why did they imprison you?!'

Cinder just howled with rage. But she knew being here was jogging his memories. She could feel it. Somehow she just had to keep digging. 'What about Boden? What did he do?'

Boden's name extinguished the searing fire of Cinder's anger, replacing it instead with the warm sensation of affection. After the terror of Cinder's anger, Juniper welcomed it, as it lapped against her heart like waves. It was just as welcome to Cinder, though it was still an emotion he barely recognized. He had only ever known selfishness, chaos and loneliness. But Boden had showed him something else. Something to fight for.

Together they'd discovered a way to tether Cinder to this plane forever, to stop him from being torn back through the Veil. Their bond was strong. Stronger than anything Cinder had ever known, and yet as fragile as a thread. The Arcanists had ripped them apart in their bid to build a world neither of them wanted to be a part of.

Then, without warning, Juniper found herself in a memory. Cinder was broken, defeated, trapped behind glass. A woman stood on the other side of the mirror shard, eyes dark in her long pale face. The shadows seemed deeper around her, flickering and reaching, her headdress made from flowers and bone. It was The Shrouded, but one from long, long ago.

She hadn't seen Cinder, but she was searching for him.

'You're either very brave, or very stupid, coming to my hideout like this,' came a voice. The Shrouded turned to see the young man Juniper recognized from the first memories she'd ever seen of Cinder's. Boden.

His young, friendly face looked angry, his fists were balled and his muscles were tense as though awaiting an attack. His eyes flickered to the glass shard Cinder was trapped within but didn't linger. He didn't want to alert The Shrouded to Cinder's presence.

'Is that any way to greet an old friend?' The Shrouded asked. 'Especially one who had to search high and low to find you . . .'

Boden's eyes narrowed. 'You're no friend of mine.'

The Shrouded tutted. 'Hasn't there been enough bloodshed, dear Seer?' Her voice was hard, sharp and as cold as death.

'Not until I spill yours,' Boden growled.

'Haven't you heard? I'm in the business of making peace now. I've made a truce with four of the others.'

'And *you're* happy with that?' Boden asked.

'I'll have to be. It's a small price to end this war.'

'Five Arcanists versus the rest?' Boden forced a laugh. 'You don't stand a chance. The war will carry on, destroying everyone.'

The Shrouded smiled, though there was no warmth in it. 'On that note, I heard a vicious rumour that you may still have a shard of the mirror?'

Boden's features tightened, telling her all she needed to know.

Cinder had wanted nothing more than to help his

friend, to tear The Shrouded limb from limb, but he was trapped and broken.

'If your powers really do reveal the truth to you, I would've thought it'd show you how foolish you're being,' The Shrouded said. 'That creature is a menace, a danger. It will ruin everything, and you know it. It needs to be destroyed, for the good of us all.'

At that, sigils flared to life around her. She reached for her throat and began scratching at it as she hacked and coughed. She was choking, her eyes wide with surprise. Out of her gaping mouth floated words, the very words she'd just spoken and they looped round her neck and tightened like a noose.

Though he may not have stood a chance against the Arcanists one on one, Boden had laced his home with intricate, powerful wards, ready for just such an intrusion. The Shrouded collapsed to the floor, literally choking on her own words.

'This changes . . . nothing,' she gasped. Somehow, through her hacking coughs, her smile remained. 'The Watcher . . . has been watching . . . She knows how to do it . . . how to bond oneself to another . . .'

'No . . .' Boden whispered, his hands trembling, his face screwing up in horror.

'It's already done. We have each found . . . someone to pass . . . our powers to. You have not killed The

Shrouded. Our names . . . are now . . . *eternal* . . .'
Then, with a final wheeze, The Shrouded went
still.

Juniper became vaguely aware of being back in
the crater, her vision spinning, still half clouded by
Cinder's emotions. She stumbled back, and Thea
caught her before she fell.

'Juni, are you OK? You guys totally checked out
there for a minute!'

'The Watcher showed the other
Arcanists how to do the
Inheritance Ritual?' Juniper
asked Cinder, trying to
clear her head.

'She *stole* knowledge she should never have had,' Cinder growled.

'That's how the Arcanists defeated the Betrayers,' Juniper said, piecing it together. 'Their power lived on in others while the Betrayers had no one to pass their gifts on to . . .'

Cinder's emotions became a flood of sorrow, pulling at Juniper and threatening to drown her under their weight. She swam against the tide, trying to pull free of his thoughts. Using all her might, she snapped back to reality. She rubbed at her eyes, surprised to find tears there, and she was panting as though she'd just run a mile. Her sigils had been glowing, her eyes too, but they dimmed as her connection to Cinder lessened.

Thea and Everard watched, dumbstruck.

'They'll pay for this,' Cinder whispered to Boden's skeleton. 'They'll pay for what they did to us.'

Juniper tried to still the tremble building in her hands. Boden had killed The Shrouded. Luckily she'd been able to pass her powers on, but he'd still *murdered* her.

'So you . . . you were bound to a Betrayer?' She hoped her voice sounded less frightened than she felt.

Cinder turned slowly to face her, his eyes burning with anger. 'If such a word means anything . . .' He turned back to the sarcophagus, concentrating. 'Being here, seeing Boden . . . it's coming back to me . . . my memories . . .' He screwed his eyes shut, sigils flaring around his claws. 'We made a pact, Boden and I. Together we would end the rule of the Arcanists. We would tear away all they'd built and watch them come crashing down.'

The children backed away at his words. Even Thea looked shocked.

A chill ran up Juniper's spine, her skin turning cold and prickling with goosebumps. Had Everard been right this whole time? Had she been harbouring the evil familiar of some long-dead Betrayer?

No. There was more to it than that. She'd felt Cinder's emotions. There was goodness in Boden, more than most. So how did it make any sense that he could also be an evil Betrayer?

She had no time to think about it.

A cracking sound came from behind them. The children watched, baffled, as a line appeared in the wall at the base of the Crux. It grew longer and longer, forming a large rectangle shape. Light began seeping through the crack as the shape shifted and moved.

It was a door. A doorway had just appeared in a solid wall, and somebody was opening it.

'Hide!' Juniper hissed, diving for cover behind

Boden's sarcophagus, just as a figure strode out of the impossible door.

'Ah, the final resting place of our bitter enemies,' came a familiar voice. 'It never fails to bring a smile to my face.'

Juniper dared to take a peek. Her heart leaped into her mouth at who she saw.

The Enigma. And he wasn't alone. The Shrouded, The Tempest and The Maker were right behind him.

25

UNEXPECTED COMPANY

The moment Everard saw who it was, he made to shout out, but the girls piled on him, holding their hands over his mouth.

'Don't!' Juniper pleaded.

Everard struggled, mumbling and complaining, as Cinder stared at the Arcanists, his eyes burning with hatred.

Juniper gave him a warning look. Growling under his breath, Cinder flattened himself against the sarcophagus. Juniper peeked over the top.

Thankfully the Arcanists hadn't heard them. They each stood behind The Shrouded as if they were guiding her somewhere. The Shrouded's pale face looked just as Juniper remembered it way back when she'd saved Elodie, only now her brown hair had turned as white as bone. She had the eager look of someone who had something to prove. Nothing like the confident, stern person who'd judged Juniper at the Crux. If anything, she looked nervous.

'Why have you brought me here?' she asked.

'You mean, besides to enjoy the charming atmosphere?' The Enigma said.

'Sometimes it helps to be reminded of what the Arcanists had to overcome to get where we are today,' The Tempest said, gesturing at the sarcophagi with his glowing umbrella.

'I know the story of the Betrayers,' The Shrouded mumbled.

'Ah, but do you really?' The Tempest asked. There was something about his smile and his glimmering golden eyes. They made you feel safe, like you wanted to do what you could to please him. 'There was a time when all hundred Arcanists fought each other to become the one supreme leader. But the only thing they managed to do was destroy themselves.'

The children shared a confused glance. Even Everard stopped squirming. *All* the Arcanists fought to rule the world? They'd always been told it had been the Betrayers . . . and that only the five Arcanists had stood up for justice and peace.

'It wasn't until our five ancestors joined together in a

truce that they were able to end the war. Together we are stronger, especially now that The Watcher seems to have turned her back on us. Alone . . . well . . .' The Tempest held his umbrella over the nearest sarcophagus. Its light shone through the stone as if it wasn't there, revealing the maimed body within. The skeleton had been melded together like tar, almost as if melted by a great heat.

The Shrouded swallowed. 'I'm with you. Of course I am.'

'That so?' The Enigma asked, placing his arms behind his head and floating into the air.

'The magisters of your Order have come to us with some troubling news,' The Tempest explained. 'Apparently you're still resisting your gifts.' He gave her a sympathetic look. 'We've been through this, Nyx. We all have to be on the same page for this to work.'

The Shrouded's deathly pale face gained the tiniest hint of red. 'I – I want to let the magic in,' she said, unable to meet his gaze, 'but it – it just doesn't feel right. The more I let it in, the more I feel like I'm losing myself, like I'm becoming someone else.'

'You *are* becoming someone else,' The Tempest assured her. 'You're becoming someone more. Someone *better.*'

'But the dreams I've been having,' The Shrouded continued. 'They're happening all the time. I'm me in the dreams, and also not me at the same time . . . like a faded version of myself.'

'Hey, kiddo, *all* Inheritors experience that at first,' The Enigma said, floating casually through the air. 'We certainly did! It's simply your mortal body reacting to powers beyond human comprehension.'

'I know they're dreams, but they feel so . . . so *real*,' insisted The Shrouded.

'They will fade in time, but only if you let the magic in and master it,' The Maker said, his voice like grinding gears, his glowing eyes barely visible in the shadow of his wide-brimmed hat and high-collared coat.

The Shrouded nodded, but still looked unconvinced.

'That little upstart charlatan from the Dregs must be put in her place,' The Tempest said. Juniper flinched, hearing him talk about her like that, The Tempest's smile making his bitter words all the more shocking. 'You will be the first one to challenge her and must do everything you can to make her fail in the most spectacular fashion for all to see. Only then will the people see her for the liar she is.'

The Shrouded scowled. 'I can defeat her.'

'But can you? What if, by the very slimmest of chances, the girl is telling the truth? We don't know what she's capable of, but we certainly know what your limitations are.'

The Shrouded stared down at her feet.

'If you look weak, we all look weak. We cannot allow that – The Watcher and her pathetic Order of Iris have already done enough damage to our reputations.'

'But I've tried to make life better for my district,' The Shrouded explained. 'I've even started the new ration-sharing programme for our lower levels. I –'

'Oh yes, we've heard about that,' The Tempest interrupted. The Enigma chuckled, shaking his masked head, while The Maker made a clanging sound that sounded strangely mocking. The Shrouded looked embarrassed, as though it was silly and childish to try to help people.

'The people admire us,' The Tempest said. 'They worship us. And rightly so. But do you know why that is?' He waved his umbrella at her, illuminating her in a spotlight.

'Because we're powerful? Because . . . they want to be like us?'

'Exactly! They want to be like us. Their lives are hard. They have little, but they need a lot. But the very idea that one of their children might become an Inheritor, might raise them up to a beautiful mansion in the luxurious Uppers, such a dream keeps them going. It keeps them focused on doing all they can to be like us. But if you changed that, made life better for them, what then?'

The Shrouded struggled for words, so The Tempest answered for her. 'They stop being desperate. They stop dreaming of something better. They become lazy and less useful. Then, in order to get people to do what you want them to, you have to use force. And force is so messy.'

The Enigma snickered. 'Fun, though.'

'I don't know about you, but I much prefer it when people worship me of their own free will,' The Tempest said.

Juniper's belly turned. It was the way they were speaking that disturbed her the most – so casually, as though ruining people's lives was a little game the Arcanists played, something that they were proud of. The Dregs – and the way it had suffered – was that all because the Arcanists wanted to be worshipped? What kind of sick monsters would do that?

Everard was making a quiet whimpering sound behind the girls' hands.

The Shrouded seemed to share Juniper's shock. 'That's not why I became an Arcanist!'

The Tempest smiled. That smile – that perfect, friendly smile – Juniper wondered how she'd ever found it comforting. Looking at it now made the bile rise up in her throat. 'Of course it is!' he said.

The Maker grabbed The Shrouded, not with two hands but with four, the extra limbs slipping out from his large coat. They were made from ornate metal and segmented like the arms of a marionette.

'You wanted power,' The Tempest said to The Shrouded as she struggled, like he was talking to a child. 'Well, now you have it. But don't ever forget what it is we're up against.'

He waved a hand, extinguishing some of the warding sigils carved into the floor. A sphere of light flared in his other hand.

The chill in the crater grew sharper, and Juniper's breath clouded in front of her face.

A shape materialized before the Arcanists, a long, spindly body, a featureless face clicking round to look at them, attracted to the magic. It was a Shade.

The Maker held The Shrouded out towards it. She

291

recoiled in horror, her skin slick with sweat, her breath coming out in panicked gasps.

'All it takes is one weak link and the whole chain can break,' The Tempest said, watching the Shade stalk hungrily towards her, its long fingers reaching for her face.

'We need you strong. We need you to accept the power within you, to give yourself to it and become the Arcanist you were destined to be!'

The Shade was almost touching The Shrouded, who was desperately struggling to escape, but The Maker had her in a vice-like grip. Tears streamed down her face as she realized that the Arcanists really would let her die here and now.

'So what will it be? Will you be the weak link? Or will you help us forge a stronger one?' The Tempest asked.

'I'll help!' she cried. 'I'll help – I promise!'

The Tempest smiled, raising a hand. The wards flared back to life, engulfing the Shade in scorching light. 'I thought you might. Master your powers and kill the Bell girl. Make it look like an accident – or, better yet, her fault.'

Juniper felt like she'd been dipped in ice, like she was going numb, despite all her senses screaming out at her. But she'd been so horrified by the scene that she hadn't noticed she'd lost her grip on Everard. He'd let out an anguished cry, then placed his own hands over his mouth as he realized what he'd done.

The Arcanists spun round. 'What was that?'

'Into the sarcophagus – go, go!' Juniper whispered, her heart in her throat.

They squeezed through the small gap they'd made and slid beside the dry, lifeless skeleton of Boden, just as The Maker scuttled towards them with frightening speed. The children held their breath as his large form loomed over a nearby sarcophagus, searching for the source of the noise.

Juniper could feel Everard trembling behind her, could feel Thea's pulse racing.

The Maker let out a low rumbling sound, more mechanical than human. His eyes scanned the gloom.

Boden's neck made a sickly crunching noise, his skull dropping to the side, staring at Juniper with those empty, hollow eyes. She struggled to control her breathing, trying to push down the panic she felt at the awfulness of this whole situation.

'Anything?' came The Tempest's voice.

The Maker seethed. 'No.' He threw a lid off a nearby sarcophagus with terrifying ease, the stone crashing loudly to the ground. After peering inside, he dashed to another, tearing it open too. He moved to the next, The Tempest using his umbrella light to peer inside other sarcophagi all the while.

Juniper's nails dug into her palms. It was only a matter of seconds before they'd find them!

'I'll head up to the control tower,' The Enigma said, 'and tell 'em to lock the whole crater down. If someone was down here, we can't let 'em escape.'

There came the click of a lock being turned, another impossible doorway appearing in the stone wall. Then another sound further away.

It was the clanging of a lift beginning its ascent back up to the top. The Maker gave a roar of fury and disappeared, racing towards it.

Juniper knew the danger of getting cornered in a fight. As frightened as she was, as much as she wanted to hide away forever, she knew they had to move.

She signalled for the others to follow, then slid out of the sarcophagus, keeping as low as possible. The Arcanists were gathered below the lift, The Shrouded holding it still with strands of shadow. More importantly the new doorway The Enigma had opened was left unguarded, only a short distance away.

'Go, go, go!' Juniper whispered to her terrified friends, though they did not need to be told.

They dashed through the door to wherever it led. Juniper stole a final glance back at the Arcanists, catching sight of something slithering towards her on the ground. It was only then that she realized Cinder had gone and understood it was him snaking back towards her.

He'd sent the lift up. He'd caused the distraction.

Juniper waited for him to catch up, urgently signalling for him to hurry.

The Tempest raised a hand towards the lift. He didn't wait to see who was inside – whether it might've been a warden or a servant. Bolts of purple-white lightning arced from his palm like tentacles, engulfing the lift with scorching electricity, destroying it entirely as it burst into a raging ball of fire and melted metal.

Juniper and Cinder dived through the door.

The next moment, they found themselves in a guardhouse back up on the rim – and in a large room full of wardens staring at them in surprise. Juniper's head spun at the strangeness of travelling such a distance with a single step.

Everard and Thea hesitated, unsure what to do. The wardens were just as speechless.

'We're under attack!' Juniper yelled, desperate for an excuse. 'The Enigma sent us; he needs your help!'

There was a moment's pause, but seeing the flames of the ruined lift through the magical doorway, the wardens scrambled to grab their rifles, bundling past the children to aid the Arcanists. The kids wasted no time in running in the opposite direction.

'Order business!' Everard squealed to anyone they passed. 'I'm taking these two out of here, but the Arcanists need your help!'

The children pushed forward, escaping the guardhouse as fast as they could. Not once did they dare to look back.

26

BURNING THE MIDNIGHT OIL

The journey back had been tense, to say the least. The children's quick steps were fuelled by the fear that the Arcanists were just behind them, hunting them down, faces twisted with fury. They flinched at the merest glimpse of a warden, passers-by eyeing the children strangely as they ducked and dived between alleyways. Though they made it back without trouble, dread dragged at Juniper's insides when she found wardens outside Adie's Apothecary. Had they already figured out it was them who'd been in the crater?

'What're we gonna do?' Everard said despairingly. He'd been so ruffled by the evening's events that he'd even allowed his hair to become a mess, regularly grabbing his head as though it might explode from all the terrible things they'd just learned.

'Play it cool,' Juniper said. 'We're just coming back from a lovely evening stroll, that's all.'

'But be prepared to run if the wardens decide otherwise . . .' Thea whispered.

The wardens watched them closely as they drew near. Juniper gave a curt nod as she entered the shop, her heart pounding.

To her relief, the wardens said nothing.

Thea gave them a happy wave, as Cinder slinked in through the shadows. Everard, on the other hand, walked as stiffly as if someone had dropped a broom down the back of his trousers. To Juniper's surprise, she discovered Elodie waiting for her inside the shop, standing next to a worried-looking Papa and Madame Adie. That explained the wardens, then.

'Juni, it's late! Where've you been?' Papa demanded.

Juniper groaned inwardly. She'd just had her entire world turned upside down and shaken about – she didn't need a grilling on top of it all!

Papa's expression softened as he saw the distress Juniper and her friends were in. 'Are you OK? What happened?'

'We – we –' Juniper couldn't find the words. Seeing Papa after what had just happened was almost too much. She wanted to run into the safety of his arms, to tell him everything, to hide away while he went out and sorted it, like he'd always tried to do. But what would she tell him? That every Arcanist the city had adored for centuries was a liar? That they were scheming monsters who had everything yet still took from those who had nothing? That the heroes – the legends – that people dreamed of becoming were planning to have her killed and swept under the rug for everyone to forget?

Her family stared at her, worry creeping on to their faces. Even Madame Adie looked perturbed.

'It's nothing,' Juniper managed. Thea and Everard shot her a look, but she widened her eyes in warning. *Don't tell them.*

'We were just so busy training for the challenge, an' time got away from us, right, guys?'

'All that exercise – sure makes me look upset!' Thea confirmed.

Everard just stood there, sickly pale and gawping.

For once, Juniper wanted nothing more than to tell the truth, to come clean, but she couldn't. They'd never believe her. The whole city loved the Arcanists; they'd been raised on stories of their greatness. Their word was law.

Besides, even if they did believe her, it'd only put them in danger. The Arcanists had only tolerated

Juniper so far because they didn't see her as a threat. Sure, they planned to kill her, but in their own time, and they were going to make it look like an accident. But if they discovered that Juniper knew their secret, she didn't doubt they'd come after her and her family, witnesses be damned.

'The challenge is in two sleeps' time – gotta be prepared, right?' Juniper forced a grin, and Papa and Elodie returned the smile, happy to hear she was working hard for something worthwhile, even if they still wore their doubt as clear as day.

'I actually came to wish you luck,' Elodie said in a small voice. 'I know things have been a bit . . . weird between us, but after seeing what you did to help those people at the flood . . .' Elodie wrung her arm like it was a wet towel, looking anywhere but at Juniper. 'Well, it was very selfless of you.'

She held out her hand, which was clutching something. Juniper took it from her. It was the necklace Elodie always wore, a leather cord tied through the lucky coin Mama had given her when she'd first applied to the Academy.

Something fluttered inside Juniper. She had to swallow back a sob. Smiling, she slipped it round her own neck.

'It brought me luck, so I thought maybe it'd do the

same for you,' Elodie said. 'I – I'm sorry for being so hard on you before. I was wrong. Maybe you do have what it takes to be an Arcanist, after all.' She lunged forward and gave Juniper a hug. 'I'm proud of you, Juni.'

Juniper could feel tears stinging her eyes and threatening to roll down her cheeks into Elodie's hair. Papa was grinning widely at the two sisters acting like their old selves again, like Jelliper, the inseparable duo they'd once been. After years of feeling like a let-down, like she was nothing but trouble, Juniper could see it in their eyes, hear it in their voices. They were actually proud of her. Which was why it hurt so much.

They were proud of a lie – one that was fast getting away from her. It was snowballing down a mountainside towards the jagged rocks at the bottom with her stuck inside.

Juniper swallowed. 'El?'

Elodie beamed at her. She'd joined the Academy to try to make life better for everyone in the Dregs, but she was unwittingly working for the very people who'd deliberately made it so bad in the first place, even if the Arcanists had said The Watcher had turned her back on them. Juniper didn't know what was what any more, but she did know the Academy wasn't what Elodie thought it was.

'El, I – I think you should leave the Academy.'

Elodie kept smiling at first, like she'd misheard Juniper or thought she might've been joking. But then her brows furrowed, her smile twisting in confusion. 'Excuse me?'

'I just . . . I have a bad feeling about the whole thing.' Juniper couldn't think of an excuse fast enough; her mind was a whirling mess. 'Being as close to it as I am now – it's not all it's cracked up to be. It's hard. People treat you differently. I don't know if you have –'

'I can't *believe* you!' Elodie pushed Juniper away. 'I feel so stupid that I'm surprised. It always has to be about you, doesn't it? Now that you're becoming an

303

Arcanist, you think I should just pull out? That you're better at this than me, like *everything* else you do, so I should just give up on my dreams, is that it?'

Juniper had had no idea Elodie felt that way. 'No! It's not like that! I just –'

'I've put everything I have into being a Candidate, Juni! *Everything!*'

'I know you have!'

'Well, I hope the challenge goes well for you, Juniper. I hope you succeed and get all the attention you crave. And don't worry about me stealing any of that limelight either. Dreggers never get chosen to become Arcanists, isn't that what you said?' Then Elodie stormed out of the apothecary without saying another word.

An awkward silence hung over the room.

'You sister seemed very pleasant,' Everard said.

Papa sighed. 'Did you have to say that?' he asked Juniper. 'I know this is amazing for you, Juni, and I'm so proud. But you know this is all Elodie has.'

'Papa – I didn't –'

He turned, shaking his head with disappointment. 'Somehow it's never your fault. Well, you missed the supper Elodie helped make for you. We saved you some, but it's cold.'

Juniper watched him head upstairs, not knowing

what to say. Guilt wriggled in her belly and made her feel sick. She hadn't meant it to sound like she was bragging; she'd just wanted to keep her sister safe!

Thea dashed over to give Juniper a hug, nearly taking her off her feet.

'We have to stop the Arcanists,' Juniper said. 'We can't let them get away with this. I don't know how, but we have to try!'

'I've only been saying it since I met you,' Cinder said darkly.

'Oh, I agree,' Madame Adie said. 'Of course it would really help if someone explained what on earth was really going on here.'

They told her everything that had happened, every awful detail.

Her face went from sceptical to shocked and then downright livid. 'For what it's worth, darling, I believe you,' she said. 'Always had a feeling about them. And I will *not* let those stuck-up, self-inflated frauds bully you.'

Juniper smiled her thanks, the tears getting harder to hold back.

'And you still have me,' Cinder said. 'Only because I'm hell-bent on revenge, you understand, otherwise I would've abandoned you long ago.'

Juniper nodded, turning to face Everard. She hoped he was as shocked as they were about what they'd learned that night not to go running to the Arcanists. He just stared back, his mouth opening and closing like a fish. His eyes were wide, watery. He then shook his head and, without another word, pushed through the front door and disappeared from sight.

It wasn't like Juniper even blamed him – she knew they barely stood a chance. There were hardly any of them, and who were they really? Gutter rats, Dreggers, *nobodies*. And they planned to go up against the most powerful people in the world. At times like this, she wished doing the impossible wasn't quite so . . . well, *impossible*.

It was the day before the first challenge. And there was no doubt now that this wasn't a challenge to test Juniper; it was an excuse to kill her. The street phonographs played the grim sound of the Midnight Tower's bells once again. It sounded more like a death knell each time Juniper heard it, the same five bongs tolling the time before her certain doom.

Juniper slapped both her cheeks. 'Pull yourself together, girl! The Arcanists haven't won yet.' The Misfits made a living out of fooling people from higher stations, and they'd do the same to them.

'We still need to find a way to get my magic back,' Cinder said. 'Returning me to my full brilliance is the only way we'll stand a chance at taking those self-serving skunks down.'

'First, I've got a challenge to survive,' Juniper said. 'Unless your magic's just lying around in the shop somewhere?'

Cinder didn't answer, though his eyes did do a quick scan of Adie's private quarters.

'Well, I certainly haven't given up on you!' Madame Adie said, chuckling as she bustled about collecting various alchemical items.

Lanterns had been burning in Adie's alchemy workshop all night and day; all kinds of coloured pungent vapours poured out of her windows smelling of cinnamon, burnt toast, cat wee and rain-soaked metal. There'd been a few rare ingredients that she'd needed, but it was nothing Juniper hadn't been able to find for her that morning, especially as some merchants in the Uppers had carelessly left them lying around on their store shelves. Madame Adie had worked like a woman possessed, potions bubbling, powders smooshed and concoctions brewed. And there'd only been three fires they'd all needed to put out!

She laid out the results of her labours on a bench, looking as proud as punch. Juniper picked up the first item, a cylinder about double the size of her index finger.

'Now, we all know that The Shrouded has a thing for shadows, do we not?' Madame Adie asked. 'Well, try pulling the top off that.'

Juniper did as she was asked. A jet of near-blinding white light burst from within the cylinder, flaring out like a fountain.

'WHOA!' Juniper yelped, grinning. The thing was still going; it seemed to last for several minutes!

'It's so sparkly!' Thea said, dancing in the falling embers.

'I suspect shedding some light on the situation should even the odds a bit, don't you?' Madame Adie wiggled her eyebrows.

Next was something that looked a bit like a corkless drinks flask with an extra-long neck at the top. Pipes connected two vials to the flask, one containing a clear liquid, the other a vibrant green.

'Go on – give it a good squeeze!' Madame Adie said. 'And point it upwards if you wouldn't mind?'

The container was rubbery and flexible, squishing under her thumb. Thea leaned in for a closer look, but Madame Adie pulled her back just as a plume of emerald fire jetted out with a roar.

Juniper gasped. '*Cooooooooool!* I can't think of time it isn't useful to have a flame-spitter.'

'Pressing the pad mixes the chemicals tog useful for when you're left with no opti *everything down*,' Madame Adie explaine in her eyes.

'Good for marshmallows too,' T

Last was a small glass orb n looked like green mist was v vivid light reflecting off th

Madame Adie grinn favourite.'

'Do I throw it?'

27

UNDERDOG

die, it may as well

shrouded

... any

... ether. Very

... but to burn

..., a manic look

... hea added.

... bigger than a plum. It

... hirling about inside it, its

... e bench.

... d. 'I must admit, this one is my

... Juniper asked, pulling back her arm.

an eerie light that reflected off the still waters of the canals that ran between them. Lonely lanterns broke through the mist that clung to the water and marked the barges guided by silent ferrymen. Candles were placed at every window, the flames looking particularly menacing next to the black flowers that crept over the walls like some hungry beast.

Juniper had remembered finding the district beautiful once, back when she'd come here with Elodie and Mama all those years ago. Now she felt as though she was walking over the skeleton of some long-dead giant.

She checked over her equipment, even though she'd already done so about seventeen times. Thea had outdone herself with the outfit she'd made.

It looked *awesome*. It consisted of a long-tailed coat with a hood that Juniper could pull up to make herself look all mysterious and Arcanist-y. It was a blue so dark it looked almost black, with turquoise lining, and the back was embroidered with the symbol of a rat. She wore trousers and boots that allowed for quick movement. The flares Madame Adie had made for her hung from a bandolier strapped across Juniper's chest, the flame-spitters attached to protective armbraces on her forearms and the boom-orb had been carefully tied to her belt.

Juniper felt like an absolute action hero. She felt like an Arcanist.

The Midnight Tower loomed above them like some temple to the dead, all sharp edges and rib-shaped buttresses. Tall blood-red windows stood out starkly against the white walls, pointing up towards the bell tower at the peak. It looked impossibly high. People said the Midnight Tower was a gateway to the Beyond, and Juniper could see why.

'And you were *surprised* to discover the Arcanists were evil tyrants?' Cinder whispered, looking up at the ominous structure.

Juniper gulped. 'What, you mean you don't find the big scary tower that looks like a gateway to the underworld welcoming?'

'Don't be scared,' Papa murmured, thinking she'd been talking to him. He looked about as terrified as Juniper felt. 'You've got this.'

A large courtyard in front of the tower had been transformed into a viewing area. There was barely any space to move, forcing the carriage to pull up outside the tower walls. People from all over the city had crammed round the raised seating on which the magisters from the Order of Midnight sat (obviously protected by a small army of wardens), everyone eager to catch a glimpse of this historic moment: the trial of the first so-called Arcanist in centuries. The Tempest, Maker and Enigma were seated on luxurious thrones,

facing a large glass sphere sitting in front of the tower's main doors.

Juniper caught sight of Madame Adie at the entrance to the courtyard. She was being moved on by some wardens who were busy taking down the makeshift stall she'd set up. She'd been selling small effigies she'd made of Juniper as mementos, as well as ultra-rare health potions she claimed had been made by Juniper herself (which were just vials of iced tea). She spotted Juniper exiting the carriage and waved excitedly.

Juniper nodded back. She wished that Thea was there too, but she knew she was in position. Operation *Hey, You, Look Over Here!* was go.

The crowd parted for Juniper as she entered the courtyard, murmurs travelling like waves through the crowd. Papa took hold of her hand and Juniper was happy for it. Some people looked at her as though she were a famous villain, pointing and whispering as she passed. Angry shouts and curses were thrown her way, placards held high, expressing some pretty unpleasant opinions on Juniper's character. Some had pictures of owls on them, which she knew were The Watcher loyalists who believed she was trying to steal the Iris District from its true ruler. But she had some supporters too. A lot less, sure, and most were unwilling to show their support under the eyes of the Arcanists, but they were there. They watched Juniper with hope in their eyes, some daring to bang their fists to their chests in solidarity.

Juniper forced herself to smile as she approached the Arcanists. It was a smile to suggest they didn't intimidate her, even though they really did. It was a smile of defiance, even though the idea of going up against them filled her with dread. The Maker's face was hidden by his wide-brimmed hat. The Enigma, as always, was wearing his mask. The Tempest gave her that warm, handsome smile of his – the one that made Juniper feel sick.

'Ms Bell, how lovely it is to see you again,' he said.

Papa was almost on his hands and knees he bowed so low.

'All right, Worships?' Juniper bowed, trying to choke down the bile at the back of her throat.

'I think I speak for everyone when I say we're looking forward to seeing what you've got,' The Enigma said.

Juniper winked. 'You're in for quite a show, let me tell you.'

The light suddenly shifted. Every streetlamp and every candle flared deathly red, the shadows lengthening and growing deeper, darker.

The noise of the crowd hushed to an expectant murmur. It was quiet enough to hear unnerving music drifting on the air, which was getting louder as it drew closer. It was a choir of some kind, accompanied by the thrumming of a large drum pounding through the streets of the Midnight District like a heartbeat. A regiment of wardens from the Order of Midnight marched across the bridge towards the tower. The crowd made way for the wardens, who formed a column through the packed courtyard. They were followed by dozens of white-robed magisters, each carrying a

candle as carefully as if it was some sacred relic. A giant open-topped carriage came after them, although calling it a carriage did it no justice. The thing was like a moving altar, a tiered shrine to darkness covered in red-flamed candles and shadow-black flowers. The choir responsible for the singing stood at the front, each of them dressed in robes of white, each wearing coins in their hair.

Atop the carriage, upon a mighty throne shaped like bones, sat The Shrouded herself. She wore a ridiculously embellished black dress that curled and coiled like the shadows she controlled, with a shawl over her shoulders that was embroidered with intricate designs of flowers and moths, vines entangled round skulls and bones. Jewellery hung from her neck, ears and elaborate, spider-like headdress, which was decorated with more of those black flowers. She looked like a beautiful nightmare. Juniper didn't know whether to be scared or jealous.

Strangest of all were the shadows around her. Thousands of them flittered and twitched like moths. One rested on The Shrouded's pale, outstretched finger, its wings as black as night.

Juniper clutched at Elodie's lucky coin, hoping Mama would watch out for her too.

Her opponent stood up from her throne, the

moths taking flight in a roiling cloud of shadow. They formed a bridge of darkness for The Shrouded to walk down, her dress flowing behind her like mist. As if by some unspoken command, the audience all bowed as one.

'So, you really think we stand a chance?' Juniper whispered to Cinder, the only two still standing.

'With you leading us?' Cinder scoffed. 'I think it's more a case of how quickly The Shrouded will splatter us across her walls. Though I was certain you'd have died a horrible death a lot sooner than this, so I suppose you're full of surprises.'

Juniper smiled. That was about as close to a vote of confidence as you were likely to get from Cinder. 'Y'know, I think we've made a pretty good team, all in all.'

Cinder's shadow-wisps flickered at the words. He remained quiet, probably trying to think up a suitable insult, as ready as ever to mock any sign of kindness. 'I could've bonded with a lot worse, I guess.' He looked down, as though embarrassed.

Juniper decided to enjoy the moment, and so she said nothing else, just grinned at him.

Cinder narrowed his eyes. It was only now, staring into them, that Juniper realized how truly other-worldly they were: the colours, the gleam to them. She didn't know if they were comforting or terrifying.

'The Arcanists will pay for what they've done. I'll make sure of that.'

The way he said it, Juniper believed him.

After sharing a meaningful glance with the other Arcanists, The Shrouded stood beside Juniper, her every movement full of creepy grace, her shadow-moths fluttering around her. The crowd shuffled forward, fighting for the best view. Juniper held her hands behind her back to stop anyone from seeing how badly they trembled.

'Welcome, proud citizens of Arkspire,' an announcer standing at a podium declared into a mic, 'to this historical day!' He wore a fancy suit, had swish blonde hair and a roguish, chiselled face. Juniper recognized his voice instantly. It was the phonograph announcer himself – Everard's papa! 'Today marks a momentous occasion! This girl, Ms Juniper Bell from the Iris District, claims to be blessed by The Visitor itself!'

There was mocking laughter from the crowd.

'Can such bold claims be backed up with proof? Or is Ms Bell simply a liar, an agent of the scheming Betrayers, who some fear may still lurk beyond our fair city, just waiting for the moment we let our guard down?'

The crowd gasped at the very idea. Boos and jeers were thrown at Juniper, the atmosphere quickly turning bitter. Mr Amberflaw kept quiet and allowed the crowd to continue. The insults grew louder, the booing rolling like thunder. The noise was crushing, the insults sharp as blades. Juniper looked to her few supporters, but they were too intimidated to speak up for her. What were Dreggers like them before the eyes of the Arcanists and their Orders?

The Tempest sat back in his throne, smiling from ear to ear.

Juniper had never felt so small, so overwhelmed by the challenge before her. How would she ever win over so many people, each of them brainwashed to believe the Arcanists' lies?

But then she heard it. One voice barely audible above the angry shouts: '*Ju-ni-per! Ju-ni-per!*'

Was she imagining things? It sounded like someone was cheering her name. She searched the mocking faces of the crowd – and spotted the person responsible.

She couldn't believe it. It was Everard.

'*Ju-ni-per! Ju-ni-per! Ju-ni-per!*' He was all alone, but he threw up his fist with each shout, making a right ol' fool of himself. Then, astonishingly, someone else took up the shout, then another.

'*Ju-ni-per! Ju-ni-per! Ju-ni-per!*'

It was as if a dam had broken. Everard had given Juniper's supporters the confidence they needed to make their voices heard. The more who shouted, the more joined in. Dreggers, all of them, mostly from the Iris District, each of them yelling her name.

'JU-NI-PER! JU-NI-PER! JU-NI-PER!'

'Arcanist of the Dregs!' a particularly shrill voice screamed.

Juniper's heart swelled, feeling so full it might've burst. She shot finger guns at Everard, unable to keep her laughter back.

It's not that she found this funny. She was simply overwhelmed with gratitude towards Everard, Thea, Madame Adie, Papa and, yes, even Cinder for not leaving her to face this challenge alone.

But for the first time since Juniper had met him The Tempest wasn't smiling. He gave Amberflaw a murderous look.

'Quiet now! Quiet, please!' Amberflaw yelled into the mic quite a few times. 'Ahem. To prove herself, Ms Bell must complete five challenges to determine whether she is, indeed, what she says she is. The first challenge has been laid down by Her Worship, The Shrouded! Ms Bell must climb to the top of the Midnight Tower and play the tune we've all come to know well by now . . .'

There was more laughter. People were understandably sick of hearing the five-note tune every morning.

'But what surprises has The Shrouded got in store? There's only one way to find out! Let the challenge begin!'

The Maker threw something into the air. It was a small mechanical bird that swept above the audience on bronze wings. A moving image flickered to life within the large glass sphere in the centre of the square. It showed the crowd and the courtyard from up high. They erupted with thunderous applause, somehow sounding a million miles away to Juniper. She'd barely heard a word. She'd been entirely focused on The Shrouded, who'd simply stared back, as still as the dead she represented. It took Juniper a moment to realize that the sphere was showing what the mechanical bird was seeing.

The large doors to the tower rumbled open.

'Follow me,' The Shrouded said to Juniper.

Papa tried to speak, but his voice caught in his throat. He put a hand on Juniper's shoulder, his face pleading with her not to go.

'*When the world gives you an empty bag, it's your job to fill it,*' Juniper said, barely swallowing back her emotion. Mama's saying. 'Be right back – just got an empty bag to fill.'

Papa laughed, or had it been a sob? It was hard to tell.

They shared a meaningful smile, then Juniper gave him a mock salute. And, with that, she followed The Shrouded into the depths of the Midnight Tower.

28

THE MIDNIGHT TOWER

It took a moment for Juniper's eyes to adjust to the darkness. The cavernous circular chamber rose up so high that she had to crane her neck to see the top, and a spiral stone staircase ran round its walls. Unlike the perfumed air and lavish furniture she'd been expecting, the place smelled musty and was completely empty, except for the hundreds of candles and flowers laid out in circular sigil-like patterns.

Aside from the long red windows that dripped down like blood, there wasn't a spot on the walls that wasn't decorated with stone carvings. Wait. *Were* they carvings?

Juniper's blood froze as the shapes came into focus. They weren't carvings at all. They were bones.

Thousands upon thousands of bones, uncountable numbers, were inlaid into the walls all the way to the top. Many were complete skeletons, but more were separate bones formed into beautiful yet macabre designs. Juniper shuddered.

The Shrouded took up position in front of her – and now that they were closer together Juniper realized the Arcanist looked like she wanted to be there as much as Juniper did.

'You don't have to do this,' Juniper said quietly, trying her best to hide her voice from the mechanical bird circling above.

The Shrouded hesitated, but only for a moment. 'I'm sorry,' she whispered, then threw her hands out.

The shadows around the tower trembled. They began to flow towards her open palms like they were terrible wells of darkness.

She's letting the magic in, just like the Arcanists told her to. So they were doing this. Maybe that's what happened to all the Arcanists – they start with good intentions, then get corrupted by the others in an endless cycle. The thought of the same happening to Elodie turned Juniper's stomach.

The tower itself seemed to sigh, as a whisper echoed down the stairwell.

The Shrouded gave a sudden violent jerk and doubled over. She composed herself, straightening her back.

Juniper immediately understood that something had changed. Something in the way The Shrouded stood, the way she held herself.

'You have no idea what I've had to do to get this far,' she hissed, her voice cold, ghostly whispers echoing her words. 'You have done nothing to achieve your position. *Nothing!*' She shouted the last word and Juniper recoiled at her ferocity. 'You're a nobody. I will not let you sully The Shrouded name, a name that has lasted through the ages, which carries power and inspires fear.' The shadows circling The Shrouded exploded into a cloud of moths, thousands of them swirling around her like a storm. 'Run, little nobody, and disappear back into the nothingness from where you came.'

The moths grew steadily in number, the swarm extinguishing the candles one by one.

'Here we go . . .' Cinder said, tightening his tail round Juniper's arm.

The challenge had begun. And Juniper absolutely legged it.

She dashed through the flittering moths to the spiral staircase, her feet clacking on the hard stone.

'*Out in the open, I'm dead; out in the open, I'm dead*,' she chanted.

'Perhaps try a more motivational song?' Cinder suggested.

She took the stairs three at a time, the curve of the staircase allowing her to lean into the climb, bones whooshing past her as she ran. The mechanical bird fluttered after her, following her every move, the loud cheers of the audience coming from outside.

'Glad they're all havin' a good time,' Juniper huffed.

'Who wouldn't want to watch a person get torn to shreds by moths?' Cinder remarked.

To Juniper's surprise, The Shrouded hadn't given chase. She simply stood on the ground floor, watching Juniper run. Darkness engulfed her like a steadily rising pool of water. Maybe this would be easier than Juniper had thought . . .

She instantly regretted thinking that.

Incredibly the moth swarm seemed to be growing, engulfing any light it touched.

'I mean, this can't be good, can it?' Cinder said.

Juniper picked up her pace, the staircase going round in what felt like an endless loop. Her lungs were crying out for air, her legs burning, but still she ran.

'Faster, must go faster!' Cinder urged, the rising moths catching them up.

'Why don't you try running and I'll sit on your shoulders?' Juniper gasped, her heart pounding.

But it was no use. In a rush of wings the swarm tore up the centre of the tower like a tornado. Juniper yelped as they crashed over her, screwing her eyes shut as she tried to shield her face from the scratching, fluttering wings, the endless surge of insects. That was, until she realized she hadn't felt a thing. The moths had swept past her like a chill fog – no papery wings or searching feelers. She may as well have tried to shield herself from shadow.

Everything went still. The tower had fallen silent. She couldn't even hear the clinking of the mechanical bird's wings.

Juniper opened her eyes. At least, she thought she had. But she couldn't see *anything*.

She blinked, trying to make sure. She'd been engulfed by a darkness so pure that she couldn't see the faintest glint of light, nor her hand right in front of her face.

'Cinder . . . ?' Her voice sounded almost offensively loud in the empty blackness, the solid silence.

'I'm here,' he replied.

Juniper peeped with happiness to hear his voice, so glad not to be alone. 'Can you see anything?'

'Not through this magical darkness.'

So she hadn't just gone blind. That was something.

She tried taking a step. She heard the clack of her foot on stone. She took another. *Clack.*

She reached out for the banister, her hand waving around in nothingness until she felt the cold railing. She used it to guide her upwards. One step. Another step. Another. This was gonna take ages.

Something made a sound behind her. She spun round to face it, only to find stifling darkness. She listened carefully, all her senses alert.

Nothing. Had she imagined it?

She began to walk again when she heard another sound. A faint rustling, like dry leaves in the wind.

'You hear that?' she whispered, though it still felt like a shout.

'No,' Cinder said. 'Yes. Maybe. I think I'm going mad in here.'

Was it The Shrouded sneaking up on her? The darkness carried a weight, one that felt like it was getting heavier by the second, pushing down on Juniper. It made it feel like the walls were closing in. It made Juniper fear that she wouldn't ever see the light of day again.

Her breaths were coming fast. Could she even remember what light looked like? Wait. Adie's flares! Almost desperately she felt for one and pulled it out of the bandolier, ripping off its top like her life depended on it. Perhaps it did.

The light was almost blinding, but Juniper could've stared at it all day. The sparks gushed out into the nothingness, illuminating only the smallest area around her. Shadow-wings flittered here and there as the darkness pushed back against it.

Juniper held up the flare and gave a start as she saw countless skulls staring back at her from the walls. Their hollow eyes seemed to eat up the light, their skeletal grins amused at her attempts to keep the dark at bay. She swished the flare around but couldn't find the source of the rustling sound.

'Let's keep going,' Cinder said, just as the flare began sputtering out.

The darkness swallowed them once more.

Not wanting to use up her flares at once, Juniper continued through the black, carefully feeling for each step at a time. All she could hear was the sound of her breath, the pounding of her pulse.

She flinched as there was a rustling at her side. She felt a shift in the air, like something had moved. She froze, trying to sense what it might be.

All was quiet. Even the crowd outside seemed to have disappeared.

She took another step. There was that sound again

– like sticks breaking underfoot – that same sense of movement.

She pulled out another flare.

This time, she saw what was causing it.

The skeletons were reaching out for her, cords of shadow twisting through their bones like veins. They snatched and grasped, their jaws hanging open in silent gasps. Juniper more than made up for them, screaming at the unnatural sight.

She swung the flare like a sword and the skeletons recoiled from the light. Thankfully they appeared unable to detach themselves from the wall, but that didn't stop Juniper from running any faster, the mechanical bird following her every step. She tore up the stairs, ducking away from the snatching hands.

'Can't help but feel like we should've seen this coming,' Cinder murmured.

Bones rattled and skulls clattered as Juniper ran past them, thrashing the flare at any that got too close. The dead flinched from the light as if it hurt them. The whole tower wall seemed to be alive, writhing with bone-dry cracks and soundless voices. Juniper was so desperate to reach the top of the tower, to escape this nightmare, that she didn't realize her flare had fizzled out until it was too late.

The darkness pounced like an animal, robbing Juniper of her sight. Her foot clipped a step, her legs got in a tangle, and she hit the stone steps hard, the wind knocked out of her. She tried to get up, but the skeletal hands were already on her, dragging her towards the wall. She kicked and struggled, but it was no use. Bony fingers clawed at her, gripping her supernaturally tight.

'Release her, you overambitious xylophones!' came Cinder's voice amid the sounds of creaking bone and shifting shadow.

'*It's no ussssssse,*' voices whispered. Hundreds of them all in harmony. '*There is no usssssse in trying. It's over for you. Your challenge hassssss failed.*' The voices seemed distant, yet were all around Juniper, even inside her head and hiding in her thoughts. She realized with horror that it was the voices of the dead, that The

Shrouded was somehow bringing them through the Veil, ready to drag Juniper back with them.

'*Come with usssssssss,*' they sang together. '*Join usssssssssss.*'

Juniper resisted with all her might, but she only seemed to sink further into the wall of bones. 'No!' she bellowed. 'You can't have me!'

'Juniper, where are you?' Cinder cried. He sounded so far away.

She tried to call out to him, but bone-dry hands covered her mouth.

'*You cannot win. You are no Arcanissssssst. You have no magic.*'

Juniper felt herself sinking, tumbling deeper and deeper into the darkness.

'*You are a gutter rat. You are a nobody . . .*'

Juniper gritted her teeth, unwilling to give in. *You're right*, she thought, *I'm not an Arcanist. And thank The Visitor for that.*

A jet of livid green fire exploded from her wrist, forcing the dead to release their grip on her. She'd managed to shuffle her hand through the mass of bones to reach her flame-spitter armbrace. She burst from the wall, gasping as if she'd just risen from the ocean depths.

'There you are!' Cinder said, leaping up on to her shoulder. 'I was starting to think I'd have to do everything myself, as per usual.'

''Fraid you don't get all the glory just yet,' Juniper said, spraying another jet of fire for good measure. The skeletons danced in the flames, the lurid green glow lighting enough of the staircase for Juniper to see her reflection in a long window.

'Hate to ruin the moment,' Cinder said, 'but we'll never reach the top with all these corpses snatching at us, even with your fancy gadgets.'

He was right – there were just too many steps and skeletons. Even now, the shadow-moths were furiously working to smother the light of the flames.

Juniper looked back at the window. 'Suppose it's time to start acting like the gutter rat I am.'

'What on earth are you talking abou– Aaaaaaargh!'

Cinder was unable to finish his sentence before Juniper sprinted forward and dropped into a slide under the grasping arms. Her boot cracked into the glass at the window's base. She kicked it again and again until she'd created a hole big enough for her to slip through.

She swung herself outside, clinging to the windowsill as the wind snatched at her. She felt like she could finally breathe again, the gloom of the Midnight District feeling gloriously bright compared to the endless void inside the tower.

'What are you *doing*?!' Cinder yelled.

'Improvising!'

The Shrouded had expected her to climb the stairs of the tower, knowing it would prove impossible. But Juniper didn't intend to play by her rules.

A stream of shadow-moths burst out of the window after her, trying to surround her. Juniper unbuckled the bandolier round her chest.

'Cinder, ignite the flares!' she cried, unable to do it herself with one hand.

'Have you gone mad?!' he said, though he did as she asked, each flare spitting out a stream of bright white sparks. The moths were immediately drawn to it, trying their best to smother the light.

'Smother *this*!' Juniper shouted, throwing the bandolier down the dizzying height of the tower. The moths swarmed after it, a swirling mass of shadow soaring down to the streets far, far below.

29

OUR NAMES ARE ETERNAL

'"*Smother this*"?!' Cinder repeated. Admittedly it hadn't been Juniper's best quip.

'Look, I got a lot on right now!' she said, bracing herself to climb up the outside of the tower.

They were high. Like, *really* high.

Juniper could see the courtyard far below and hear the murmur of the crowd gathered there, watching her through the eyes of the bird that still followed her. But the courtyard was in the Uppers. The tower went much further down, all the way to the Midnight Dregs, which looked little more than a hazy smudge from this height.

Juniper pulled herself up on to a ledge beside the window, flattening herself against the sheer wall. Looking up, she was glad to see ledges, protrusions and alcoves she could use to climb, if only that mechanical bird would stop flapping around her head.

'I've had quite enough of this thing,' Cinder said. His eyes flared. The glowing sigils etched into the bird's wings went out, and, with a little tweet, the bird dropped like a stone.

'Better luck *nest* time!' Juniper said with the widest grin.

Cinder gave her a deathly glare. 'I could throw you off this tower too.'

'You've gotta admit it's a step up from "Smother this".'

'I will do no such thing.'

'You could say it was . . . im-peck-able.'

With a withering glare, Cinder turned into a shadow, slithering up the tower ahead of her. Juniper chuckled, before climbing after him.

After what must've been the hardest climb of her life, Juniper hauled herself over the edge on to solid stone tiles, and then crawled under the tall arches at the base of the bell tower.

She collapsed on to the floor, exhausted. Her fingers were on fire and her shoulders felt like they'd been pummelled with a bat.

Cinder tapped his paws impatiently. 'You can sleep when you're dead. Which might well be soon. I doubt it'll be long before our shadowy friend joins us, and we need to be ready.'

'Says the one who can surf up shadows,' Juniper groaned, forcing herself to stand. She was in a tall stairwell that led up to the belfry where she knew she'd find the bronze bells she was meant to ring.

Right on cue, the shadows in the belfry grew deeper. Juniper backed away as they began roiling like raging water on the floor of the stairwell. The Shrouded emerged from the vortex, darkness dripping off her in rivulets.

'Enough tricks,' she whispered furiously. 'I will end this myself.'

She floated forward on coiling shadows, her long dress hissing as it dragged along behind her. The air between them wobbled, growing as cold as the grave.

'Juni–' Cinder warned.

Juniper spun on her heel, dropping into a slide just as an eruption of shadow tore past her head.

The blast caught Cinder, knocking him off his feet – and over the side of the tower. It happened so fast he'd not even made a sound.

'Cinder!' Juniper cried, skidding towards the edge. She couldn't see him anywhere. But she had no time to search, as The Shrouded was right behind her.

The Arcanist slashed down with a blade of darkness, but Juniper rolled out of the way just in time. The blade cut through the stone like it was clay. Juniper scrambled to her feet and slipped round the corner, only to find The Shrouded already there, blocking the way. She raised her hand, black vapour dripping from her fingers. Juniper ducked back into the stairwell, weaved between the arches and dashed up the stairs. But everywhere she went, The Shrouded was already there, using the shadows as short cuts.

'If you like me that much, you coulda just asked to hang out!' Juniper yelled.

A tendril of darkness wrapped round her leg, wrenching her off her feet. She hit the stone floor with a flash of pain, the taste of blood in her mouth. The tendril dragged her towards The Shrouded, her shadow-blade held at the ready. Then:

BONG.

The first bell rang out across the district.

BONG.

Then the second.

'*What?!*' The Shrouded hissed in confusion.

Juniper couldn't help but smile, despite the danger she was in. Operation *Hey, You, Look Over Here!* had worked.

Thea had made it to the top, just as they'd planned. Juniper's job had been to keep everyone's attention on her and all eyes off Thea, who'd been busy climbing up the back of the tower unseen. She was up there, dressed exactly the same as Juniper, making a real show of ringing the bells for all in the crowd to see. From that height it would've looked like Juniper was completing the challenge. The only thing Juniper had needed to do was keep The Shrouded busy and Thea's path clear.

BONG.

The third chime. Two more to go and they'd won.

'NO!' The Shrouded shrieked, disappearing into a pool of darkness.

'*Thea!*' Juniper yelled.

BONG. The penultimate ring.

Juniper rushed up the stairs as fast as she could, her exhaustion forgotten.

The last bell did not chime.

Juniper reached the top and found The Shrouded beneath the huge bronze bells. She was looming over Thea, who was pinned to the floor by writhing vines of shadow.

'Get away from her!' Juniper yelled, throwing the boom-orb at her opponent.

The Shrouded didn't even flinch. The shadow-moth swarm simply swept through the belfry and snatched the orb right out of the air, then flew out of reach.

'You're nothing without your tricks and lies,' The Shrouded said.

'You can talk!' Juniper croaked, her throat drying up. 'The Arcanists built Arkspire on lies!'

There was recognition in The Shrouded's eyes, like a reluctant part of her believed Juniper's words.

'Nyx!' Juniper pleaded, using the Arcanist's real name – which made her flinch. 'You don't want to do this. You . . . you don't have to do what they tell you!'

Man, Juniper's throat was dry. She was finding it hard to speak. She tried to clear it, but that only seemed to make it worse.

'Juni?' Thea said, worried.

Juniper couldn't breathe. She clasped her hands to her throat, trying desperately to take a gulp of air, but it felt like something was there already, a tight grip that wouldn't be moved. She looked down in panic. It took a moment for her to understand what she was seeing. Her shadow, her own shadow, was moving independently of her. It had reached its unnaturally long fingers round her throat and was gripping it tight in its cold, unforgiving grasp.

Juniper fell to her knees, choking, desperately trying to prise the fingers from her throat but unable to grasp anything but shadow.

'JUNI!' Thea cried, fighting to break free from her own shadow that was pinning her to the ground.

'You're – better than them, Nyx,' Juniper struggled to say. 'You – you saved me . . . and my sister . . .'

The Shrouded's eyes softened. They darted about, unsure. The stranglehold lessened, but only a bit.

'You fight . . . for your district . . .' Juniper continued, her words little more than gasps. 'You want . . . to help people . . .'

'Just give up!' The Shrouded pleaded. 'If you don't give up, she'll make me kill you!'

'*Who will?!*' Juniper gagged.

'The . . . the one from my dreams!' The Shrouded winced, grasping at her head as though it was splitting in two. 'The one who's stealing who I am! But no one believes me! No one!' She stumbled about, her teeth bared. 'She won't leave me alone! I can't get rid of her! I – I don't want to kill you . . . I'm not a murderer!'

Her voice suddenly changed, growing harsh, now underlined by those terrible ghostly whispers. 'But I *must*! I'm making us look weak! You're making *me* look weak!'

'I – I'm not weak!' The Shrouded's frightened voice cried. 'I've done everything to make it this far! Everything the Orders asked, all that work, all those sacrifices . . .'

'And, at long last, that power is yours,' her hard voice hissed. 'You will not throw it all away.'

Juniper could only watch, aghast. What was *happening*?!

It was as though The Shrouded was battling with herself, like there were two people arguing in the same body.

'Stop struggling. Stop fighting,' the cruel voice insisted.

The Shrouded's eyes widened, hopeless, before they turned black, her pupils disappearing into the nothingness.

'I am The Shrouded. You are The Shrouded. *Our name is eternal!*'

Our names are now eternal.

Juniper had heard that phrase before. In Cinder's memories The Shrouded who'd been killed by Boden had said it when she'd been talking about Inheritance.

Juniper's belly turned as a terrible realization dawned on her. Since this whole mess had started, The Shrouded, or Nyx Neverbright as she used to be called, had seemed like two different people to Juniper: one young and hopeful but nervous and eager to prove herself, the other cold and confident, as though she knew exactly what she was doing. Nyx had complained to the Arcanists about having strange dreams, about feeling less herself, as though she was being pushed out of her own body. The Arcanists had told her it was a side effect of Inheriting magic, that all Inheritors go through the same thing. But they were only telling half the truth.

'You're . . . you're in there too, aren't you?' Juniper choked. 'The first Shrouded?'

The Shrouded grinned, her smile cruel. 'Nyx is putting up a good fight, but she will fade. They always do in the end; it's as inevitable as death itself.'

That was the real reason the Arcanists had been able to defeat the ninety-five others who'd been gifted powers by The Visitor. They'd discovered a way to live forever.

Juniper gasped. 'The Inheritance ritual . . .'

The Shrouded's grin grew wider. 'Despite our unimaginable powers, in a terrible act of cruelty The Visitor still allowed our bodies to age and wither like any other pathetic mortal. But we are not mortal. We are above death. The children of Arkspire provide the perfect vessels for our life force, like life rafts on the sea of time.'

'But – but what happens to the children?'

The cold, lifeless glare of Nyx told Juniper all she needed to know. Bile burned the back of Juniper's throat. Her belly had turned to water. Her hands were trembling, out of shock, out of disgust.

The souls of the children were extinguished, their bodies stolen by an ancient, despicable soul. Nyx hadn't just Inherited The Shrouded's powers – she'd Inherited The Shrouded too. The original Shrouded, the one who'd been gifted magic by The Visitor, the one who'd helped kill all her brethren in the terrible world-wrecking war of the Arcanists. They were both in there fighting for control, and Nyx was losing, just like every Inheritor before her.

'*M-monsters* . . .' Juniper croaked, her vision going dark, as the grip round her throat tightened.

'Monsters?' The Shrouded chuckled. 'Do you know what I've learned after centuries of living? That there's no such thing as good and evil. The only difference is between those with power and those without.'

'In which case I'll be taking yours,' snarled a voice.

Out of the writhing darkness that surrounded The Shrouded rose a single shadow behaving differently from the rest. It pounced at her. The Shrouded shrieked as it scrabbled at her shoulders, leaping up for her neck.

It was Cinder. And he'd come to take his revenge.

30

HOUSE OF CARDS

The Shrouded clawed at Cinder, desperately trying to pull him off, but he slithered out of her grasp like a serpent. His jaws opened, and there was a light glowing brightly behind his fangs. It leaped out like a streak of lightning, winding its way down The Shrouded's throat. She let out a piercing shriek.

It was almost too much to watch, yet Juniper couldn't look away.

Her shadow-moths shrivelled into nothing, and the darkness around the belfry receded. The choking hands released Juniper, and she was able to gulp down precious air into her lungs, her shadow now back where it belonged. Thea had been released too. They both watched in horrified amazement as Cinder's magic pulled a strand of shadow from The Shrouded's mouth that flittered about like a trapped moth. Cinder began to absorb it into himself, black-purple lightning crackling around his body, as his own shadow-flesh started to take on solid form. But, just as things were getting interesting, an explosion interrupted everything.

The blast was deafening. The bell tower rocked violently, throwing everyone off their feet, and green flames roared up and over the side of the tower. There was an almighty groan, like rock grinding against rock. Masonry crumbled and cracked. Juniper tried to scramble to safety, but the floor beneath her was listing, turning upwards into a steep incline. The tower was leaning!

The scaffolding supporting the bells cracked and splintered. With an ear-splitting cacophony, three of the bells plummeted through the belfry floor in an eruption of stone, and Cinder and The Shrouded tumbled down after them. Juniper and Thea perched precariously on the edge of the broken wall, the floor now suddenly a ruined pile at the foot of the tower.

'The boom-orb!' Juniper cried, seeing the green flames licking the ruins below. The shadow-moths must've dropped it over the edge when Cinder had extinguished them, and the orb had detonated at the bell tower's base. 'Remind me *never* to get on Adie's bad side . . .'

Incredibly one bell remained, somehow still hanging from a broken beam. It was the largest – the one that would make the lowest note. The last note Juniper had to ring to complete the challenge.

'I can't reach it!' she said, stretching out her arm as far as she dared without losing her balance.

'You'd think there'd be a stone to throw among all this wreckage,' Thea said, but they were squatting on a wall the width of a brick. 'I guess we live up here now.'

The bells' scaffolding made an ominous cracking sound, and the bell slid ever so slightly, almost desperate to fall.

The girls shared a glance.

Without having to say a word, they dropped off their perch and caught the wall edge with their hands, steadying their feet against the brickwork. Thea leaned back, holding her hand out for Juniper, who readied herself to jump. She took a deep breath.

'Wait!' Thea said, eyeing the precarious heavy bell. 'Are you sure this is a good idea?'

'Thirty per cent sure,' Juniper confirmed.

Thea considered the answer for a beat. 'Good enough for me.'

Juniper sprang into the air and kicked the bell with both feet, using it as a springboard to bounce back and catch Thea's outstretched hand. The bell let out a low dong, but it was pretty unimpressive, all things considered.

'You reckon they heard that down there?' Thea asked, straining to hold Juniper up.

It was then that the scaffolding snapped. The bell dropped down, the hefty hunk of bronze crashing into the wall with an almighty clang. It was the note Juniper had needed. But it had also been the wall the girls were hanging from, and the heavy thud threw them down the ruined shaft of the belfry. They slammed against the slanted wall, past the bell that was smashing through what little was left of the tower around them, and slid down to the debris-covered floor. They both broke their fall with a roll, but pain shot through Juniper's body. She fell on to her side, just in time to see the large bell plummeting towards her.

She closed her eyes, clutching her mama's coin. *Least I completed the challenge, Mama*, she thought, before the world quaked around her.

Her eyes fluttered open. Her ears were ringing, the world a muffled mess.

The noise had been earth-shaking. And yet, somehow, Juniper was still alive. At least, she thought she was.

She may not have known much, but she knew that a person doesn't just walk away from being squished by a giant bell. Dust was everywhere. Broken stone, splintered wood, shards of glass. Green flames were raging all around. And yet none of it was touching her. The floor she lay on was almost clear of rubble, and there was a small circle drawn round her and Thea. Some kind of force field hummed around them, and the bell that would've surely killed them was trembling just above, kept at bay by a shield of shadow-tendrils.

'I know . . . it's incredible and all,' came Cinder's voice, 'but would you mind . . . getting clear . . . before I just let it crush you?' His arms were held out, strain wracking his face as he concentrated on the shadows he'd raised to save them. Instead of shadow-flesh, Cinder was now as solid as Juniper and Thea. He was covered in black-and-white fur, his long tail striped, his ears large and pointy. He looked a bit like a possum mixed with a bat. Or was it a cat? His eyes still glowed turquoise, still had that wicked look to them.

Juniper gasped. 'Cinder! You're – you're –'

'Saving the day, as per usual. Now if you'd be so kind . . . *move your butts!*'

The girls crawled to where they'd be safe from the falling bell. Cinder let the shadow-shield go and the bell crashed harmlessly beside them with one last clang.

Then came a groan. It was The Shrouded, emerging from the dust like some wretched ghoul. It looked like she'd only just saved herself with her own arcane shield. She tried to pick herself up, but fell to her knees, hacking and coughing. Lines had been drawn through the dust on her face. She was crying. Or were they just tears of fury? She gazed at Cinder with a mixture of horror and hatred.

'What – what *are* you?' she hissed.

Before she could get an answer, she slumped, unconscious.

Juniper allowed herself to breathe. She couldn't be sure, but through the intense ringing in her ears she thought she could hear another sound. The sound of cheering.

She staggered to her feet and managed to stumble past the smouldering ruins to the edge of the tower. She hadn't been imagining it. The crowd really were cheering.

Thea beamed, keeping out of sight. 'They're cheering for you.'

'For us,' Juniper said.

Thea shook her head. 'It has to be you.'

Juniper made a sound, half laugh, half sob. She almost couldn't believe it.

The cheers were a nice sound. The *best* sound. And it sure beat the usual boos and jeers.

31

NEW ORDER

'I can barely breathe with you all crowding me!' The Shrouded snapped, shoving the wardens away from her as if she hadn't just needed them to help her back down the tower. Flustered, they bowed low apologetically. The Shrouded limped forward, and with a flick of her hands the large tower doors rumbled open.

Juniper, who'd been following silently behind, was hit by a storm of cheering.

'Enjoy it while it lasts,' The Shrouded hissed under her breath. 'I'll find that friend of yours and prove to everyone you cheated.'

'Friend?' Juniper asked, confident Thea wouldn't need any help dodging the wardens on her way down the tower to safety. 'Those bells musta rung your head harder than mine, Your Worship. It was only me up there. Well, me and my little pet here . . .'

Juniper returned The Shrouded's scowl with a bright smile, then stepped out into the courtyard. Cinder followed, giving The Shrouded a wink as he passed.

Juniper's supporters were overjoyed. Even some of her critics were getting caught up in the excitement, though most simply clapped politely or did nothing at all. Some eyed Cinder curiously, even fearfully. He didn't seem to mind. After so long hiding as a shadow, he appeared to be relishing the attention his new solid form attracted. Everard was there, standing with his father, whose lips were pressed into a thin line. Though Everard kept his distance, he managed to give Juniper a secret smile.

Papa pushed his way through the throng, his relief at

seeing Juniper safe and sound clear. Elodie emerged a moment later, more reserved, though even she blew air out of her cheeks, glad to see her sister unharmed.

'Juni!' Papa gasped out, opening his arms as he dashed towards her, but stopping before he reached her, remembering how many eyes were on them.

Juniper closed the gap with a single bound, leaping into his arms. 'Papa!'

'Well *done*, Juni,' he said, squeezing her tight. 'If only your mama could've seen you today. She woulda been so proud, just like I am.'

'Reckon she was there, Papa,' Juniper whispered. She touched the lucky coin hanging from her neck.

She could see Elodie over Papa's shoulder, who drew closer, her expression unreadable.

'Well done, Juni,' Elodie said, her usually

curt voice wavering. She fell forward, joining the hug. 'I'm so glad you're OK!'

After a wonderful moment, Elodie pulled away as if shocked by her own actions. She straightened her uniform, making the Order of Iris emblems on her epaulettes as clear as possible, reminding those watching that her loyalties were to another Arcanist.

Juniper smiled. 'Just doing my bit for the Dregs, like you said.'

Elodie nodded, turning her eyes to the ground.

'As if there was any doubt you'd show The Shrouded how it was done,' came another voice. Madame Adie shuffled from the throng towards Juniper, who was entirely unsurprised to discover the old lady had sneaked back into the courtyard. 'Stop hogging her, you big softie!' She prised Juniper out of Papa's arms and embraced her warmly. 'Watching you use my little concoctions was like watching poetry in motion,' she whispered into Juniper's ear. 'Just wait until you see what else I've got cooking up.'

The babble in the courtyard suddenly fell silent. The Arcanists had stood up from their thrones, The Shrouded joining them. Giving Juniper a mischievous wink, Madame Adie melted back into the crowd.

'Congratulations, Ms Bell,' The Tempest said, his winning smile plastered across his face. 'We were so enjoying the spectacle; it seems all the more tragic the mechanical bird was destroyed in the action.'

The Maker growled in displeasure. 'We'll have to take your word for what happened up there.'

'But what a great inspiration to the youngsters of our great city,' The Enigma added. 'There are always new tricks to learn, new ways to grow and improve ourselves to better serve Arkspire.' Though he addressed Juniper, his eyes were directed towards The Shrouded.

She shrank back, shamed by her failure. Judging from the timid way she held herself, Juniper could tell that Nyx had retaken control, and her heart went out to her. What a horrible nightmare she had been forced to live, having her body slowly stolen from her like that.

'Sometimes all it takes is smashing through what's expected of you and doing things your own way,' Juniper replied. She managed a smile, even though her hands were balled into trembling fists; it was the only thing stopping her from being overcome with hatred for the smug Arcanists looking down at her.

The Tempest chuckled. 'A charming opinion, though it would be wise to remind ourselves that tradition has kept us safe and prosperous for the last thousand years.'

'Apparently so,' Juniper said. At that, Cinder leaped

up on to her shoulders, curling his now ragged tail round her protectively.

The Tempest's smile twitched. While The Maker and Enigma both started at the sight of Cinder, they hid their surprise well. The Shrouded, on the other hand, looked positively repulsed. Cinder's eyes flashed as he served them all a wicked fang-filled grin. He hadn't needed to say anything to make his point clear. *I'm coming for you.*

'Make sure you don't get too caught up in your victory, Ms Bell,' The Enigma said, his eyes glinting red behind his mask. 'There are still four trials to complete, and were I a betting man, I'd wager that each will be harder than the last. Wouldn't want you getting careless now, would we?'

'That's how people end up getting hurt,' The Maker growled.

'I'm not worried about that,' Juniper said confidently, even though it was another lie.

'Oh?'

'Not with my Order behind me,' she added, refusing to break eye contact, even though the open malice in the Arcanists' gaze made her want to run far, far away.

'Your Order?' The Tempest asked, his smile growing wider.

The crowd murmured with excited surprise.

'That's right.' Juniper nodded and inclined her head at the rat emblem on the back of her outfit. 'We're the Order of Misfits and, with us around, Arkspire will never be the same again.'

EPILOGUE

Today was the day of The Watcher's choosing ceremony – the occasion when the Arcanist chose her next Inheritor. The current one, a rather meek-looking kid called Clemens, had come of age, and could no longer Inherit The Watcher's gift, and so it was time to pick his replacement.

'Look, I'm up for adventure,' Everard said, 'but do we really have to be on the rooftops after all the prestige you gained from your victory?'

The roof offered the gang a great view of the glass Iris Academy. Some of the windows were open too, just enough to hear what was happening inside. Juniper had spotted Papa down there, standing awkwardly among the other Candidate parents in the audience. He tugged at the collar of the smart shirt Elodie had managed to find for him. The crowds The Watcher drew had grown smaller and smaller since she'd gone into hiding. Now that Juniper had won her

366

first challenge, more and more people in the Iris District were turning to her for leadership.

The Arcanist of the Dregs had come out on top. The title turned Juniper's stomach, but if it helped bring people to her side and away from the other Arcanists, she'd happily play the part. At least she knew she wouldn't be stealing anyone's body from them.

'You know we *can* walk on the ground like normal people now and then?' Everard said. He was doing his best to look as though he was leaning casually on a weathervane, playing it cool, no big deal. But from where Juniper was sitting she could see his hands behind his back, gripping the vane as if his life depended on it.

'After leading that chant right in front of the Arcanists, I thought you'd got a taste for danger, Everard?' Juniper said.

He allowed himself a smile, proud his name had been used in the same sentence as 'danger'.

'Well, I – What I mean to say is . . . this is obviously the cooler place to watch from. I am a bit of a rebel, after all.'

'More than a rebel – you're a Misfit!' Thea cheered.

Everard blinked, not sure if he was being mocked.

'Easier to stay outta trouble up here anyway,' Juniper said. 'Don't think I'm particularly welcome by the other Orders at the moment . . .'

'You not wanting trouble? I can barely imagine,' Cinder scoffed, scratching at his big ears with his hind paw. 'This accursed fur – how do you deal with so much of it on your heads? Is it always this itchy?'

'Sometimes, but, goodness, you look *soooooo* cute!' Thea said, grabbing his cheeks and giving them a good scritch, as she'd been doing every few minutes since Cinder had transformed.

'Unhand me, soppy mortal!' Cinder demanded, though he didn't try too hard to escape.

Within the Academy, the twenty new Inheritor hopefuls lined up on a stage. Some creaky old magister was droning on and on about what an honour it was to have even made it this far, how proud and esteemed the Candidates should feel to be at the next stage of such a proud legacy, yada yada yada. Each of the Candidates stood to attention, straight-backed, prim and proper, though Juniper could tell they were nervous by the way they fidgeted.

Elodie, in particular, looked like she was struggling to keep from puking her guts up. Juniper felt the same, though perhaps for different reasons. At least, after everything Juniper had put the Arcanists through, there was no way The Watcher would pick Elodie.

Elodie would be upset, for sure. Devastated

probably. She'd poured her heart and soul into being a Candidate, and she was going to lose it all, thanks to her twin sister.

Guilt clawed at Juniper's insides. *At least her life won't be in danger,* she told herself. *At least she wouldn't be snuffed out, her body stolen.*

Seeing Elodie down there on the stage, her large eyes glistening with nerves and her small frame looking so ridiculously fragile, Juniper felt a surge of protectiveness for her sister. She'd imagined Elodie with her new Candidate friends so many times. How they must all be laughing at Juniper. At how sad it must feel to be such a nobody, destined for nothing better. But being here now, and seeing the Academy for herself, Juniper was surprised.

The Candidates were now giving each other reassuring looks, wishing each other luck, giggling quietly at private jokes behind the magister's back. But they all stood apart from Elodie, not even sparing her a glance.

Elodie stared down at her shoes, which had been polished to perfection, holding her arm nervously across her immaculately ironed uniform. She was on her own, even down there, as Papa was forced to stand behind the line of wardens guarding the stage. It took everything Juniper had not to call out to her and show

Elodie she wasn't alone, that she was there for her too.

'Poor kids. If only they knew what they were really getting into . . .' Thea said.

'And parents gladly offer their children up as Candidates every few years like lambs to the slaughter,' Cinder said. 'A constant supply of new vessels for the Arcanists to hop into forever and ever. If I didn't hate them with every part of my being, I'd be impressed by their deviousness.'

Juniper rubbed at the bandages on her arms. Her wounds from the challenge were nothing compared to the hurt of seeing Elodie down there. Nothing Juniper could ever say to her would convince Elodie that the Arcanists weren't a force for good. She'd have to prove it. 'The Arcanists have the city wrapped round their fingers. We might've won the first challenge, but we'll never be able to convince people to turn their backs on the Arcanists they've worshipped since forever . . . Not without some pretty serious proof.'

The atmosphere in the Academy suddenly changed, and the audience, what few there were, became excited.

'And now the moment you've all been waiting for,' declared the old magister. 'Your most sacred of leaders, The Watcher!'

Even Juniper found herself leaning forward. The Watcher was going to show herself after all this time?

Juniper supposed she had to. She'd surely want to pick the next vessel herself, selecting the most promising child the Academy had trained for her?

Something stirred above the building. A small shape was silhouetted against the dusky sky. It flapped its large wings and dived through a large circular opening among the windows, sweeping over the enchanted crowd.

It was an owl, but its eyes shone bright purple as it stared down at its subjects. The Watcher was gazing through its eyes. It landed on an ornate perch placed at the centre of the stage, its gleaming eyes considering the children carefully.

Everyone in the Academy bowed down low and whispers of excitement rippled through the hall. The magister quietened them all down before launching into another long-winded speech.

'The Arcanists will see you as a real threat, after your victory,' Cinder said. 'If only they knew how truly useless you are. But they'll be coming for you with everything they've got now – make no mistake.'

'Not if we come for them first,' Juniper said, thumping a fist into her palm. 'And it just so happens we have a magic-sapping cutie patootie on our side . . .' She raised her eyebrows at Cinder.

'Not to mention all the crazy potions Madame Adie

can make,' Thea said, looking out towards the Midnight Tower in the far distance. The very top of the tower still lay in ruins. 'Imagine what else we could blow up!'

'To be sure I follow: we need to discover a way to get you your magic back?' Everard asked Cinder, whose eyes gleamed as he grinned a fang-filled smile. Everard grimaced, still wary of the strange creature.

'Apparently I may not need to rediscover my own magic,' Cinder said, a tendril of shadow curling round his claws, eerily similar to The Shrouded. 'The Arcanists' seems to work well enough. The challenges will prove the Arcanists' undoing, allowing us to get close to them. Our job is to figure out how to weaken them enough for me to steal their powers. The Shrouded was inexperienced, but I imagine the others won't be so easy.'

Juniper gave a small, uneasy smile. There was still something about Cinder that unnerved her. What he'd done to The Shrouded had been disturbing to watch, even if it was to a villain. But he had saved her life twice now, and that was not something she'd soon forget. And, based on what Madame Adie had said, she might one day be able to channel his magic herself. She could already feel the stirrings of something since Cinder had got some of his magic back. She just had to work out how to use it.

Everard groaned. 'So we're really doing this, then? One near-death experience wasn't enough for us?'

Juniper laughed, though she had to force it. 'Not nearly!' In truth, the idea of going up against another Arcanist, one who was even more powerful than The Shrouded, terrified her. 'We're not gonna convince the people of the truth. So we've gotta do the next best thing . . . We've gotta strip the Arcanists of their power one by one – and show the world what they've done.'

'Oh, just that?' Everard said sarcastically. 'Visitor help me, we're all gonna die . . .'

Thea grinned. 'I'm in! I'm going to make evil-tyrant-toppling gloves especially!'

'Candidates, step forward!' the magister called, having finished his speech. The twenty children onstage obeyed his command, moving in perfect unison like a military regiment. They held out their arms at a slight angle – the perfect landing perch for an owl. 'The Watcher will now choose her next Inheritor. Good luck to you all!'

The owl took flight, swooping along the line of Candidates. To their credit, the children held themselves well, despite the absolute somersaults their bellies must've been doing. Juniper's heart felt like it was trying to crawl up her throat. *'Please not Elodie, please not Elodie,'* she whispered to herself.

The owl eyed each Candidate one last time. It approached Elodie. Her eyes widened, and her trembling limbs were visible from even up on the roof.

Juniper's heart clawed even further up her throat. .

Then the owl flew past.

Elodie looked devastated, but Juniper felt like punching her fist into the sky.

'It's not Elodie,' Thea said, relieved.

'Then who?' Everard asked eagerly, the Candidate in him coming out as he momentarily forgot that he knew the terrible truth about the Arcanists.

'It doesn't matter,' Juniper said, turning to her friends. 'Whoever it is, we'll stop the Arcanists before they take anyone else. Together I know we can do it.'

And you know what? Juniper actually believed it. They'd already done the impossible. What was to stop them doing it again?

'Oh . . .' Thea said, covering her mouth with her hands. 'Oh dear . . .'

'Oh dear, indeed,' Cinder commented, raising a brow.

Confused, Juniper looked back at the stage, and what she saw down there might as well have been a punch to the face.

The owl had landed on one of the Candidate's arms. It had chosen its next Inheritor, the child who would be gifted her powers should her time come to an end.

The hall was filled with gasps and surprised murmurs. Elodie looked as amazed as the others at who had been chosen. Almost like she couldn't believe it.

The owl had circled back. And it had chosen her.

Elodie Bell was next in line to become The Watcher.

CRIKEY, WHAT AN ENDING!
But don't worry – Juniper Bell's
next adventure will land in
SUMMER 2024.

Join her for her next ARKSPIRE escapade,
with more **MAGIC**,
more **MAYHEM**
and more **MISCHIEF**
from the **ORDER OF MISFITS** . . .